A CELEBRATION
on
⌈·CORONATION ST.·⌉

Maggie Sullivan writes Northern family dramas, including the bestselling Coronation Street series, that have taken her into the bestseller lists and have garnered her legions of fans and readers around the globe.

Maggie was born and brought up in Manchester where the award-winning soap was compulsory family viewing, and she acquired a lifelong passion for its legendary characters. She won't admit to having a favourite but can't deny a soft spot for feisty, strong-willed Elsie Tanner who, despite hard times, always managed to have some fun.

Maggie has a love of travelling, is a freelance lecturer, and an active member of the Romantic Novelists' Association. Maggie lived in Canada for several years, but she now lives in London.

MAGGIE SULLIVAN

A CELEBRATION
on
·CORONATION ST.·

HarperCollins*Publishers*

HarperCollins*Publishers* Ltd
1 London Bridge Street,
London SE1 9GF

www.harpercollins.co.uk

HarperCollins*Publishers*
Macken House, 39/40 Mayor Street Upper,
Dublin 1, D01 C9W8, Ireland

First published by HarperCollins*Publishers* 2023
This edition published 2024
1

Maggie Sullivan asserts the moral right to
be identified as the author of this work

A catalogue record for this book is available from the British Library

ISBN: 978-0-00-852605-4
ISBN CANADA: 978-0-00-861842-1

This novel is entirely a work of fiction.
The names, characters and incidents portrayed in it are
the work of the author's imagination. Any resemblance to
actual persons, living or dead, events or localities is
entirely coincidental.

Typeset in Sabon LT Std by
Palimpsest Book Production Ltd, Falkirk, Stirlingshire

Printed and Bound in the UK using 100% Renewable Electricity
at CPI Group (UK) Ltd

MIX
Paper | Supporting
responsible forestry
FSC™ C007454

This book contains FSC™ certified paper and other controlled
sources to ensure responsible forest management.

For more information visit: www.harpercollins.co.uk/green

Her Majesty Queen Elizabeth II

21ST APRIL 1926 – 8TH SEPTEMBER 2022

I was excited by the prospect of writing about Queen Elizabeth's post-war coronation and the effects it had on the residents of Weatherfield, as I was writing the story not long after the whole nation had celebrated Her Majesty's platinum jubilee in 2022. However, when this book was in the initial stages of planning no one would have guessed that by the time the manuscript was complete Her Majesty's epic reign would have come to a record-breaking end and we would be in the throes of preparing for the crowning of our new king, Charles III, in what would be only the second coronation to be celebrated in more than seventy years. It is strange now to think that we were living through the final days of Queen Elizabeth's reign even as I was writing about how the country celebrated the beginning, and I feel privileged to have been able to write a story set in the earliest days of the remarkable era of Britain's longest reigning monarch.

It seems fitting therefore to dedicate this book to the memory of our late queen, who devoted herself to a life of service for her people.

Chapter 1

Early spring 1953

Josie Bradshaw clamped her jaw and punched a fist into her open hand the way her father used to when his temper got the better of him. She didn't care what anyone else on the bus might think of her, she was angry. She felt the hot tears scalding behind her eyes although she knew there was no danger of them spilling onto her already flaming cheeks because she never cried and she trusted now that she was as firmly in control as ever. But that didn't mean she wasn't upset. She was furious that she had been dismissed from her job at Pauldens, one of the large department stores in Manchester's city centre

– unjustly in her opinion – and she needed to express her disapproval somehow; so, as the single-decker Weatherfield bus pulled away from its stand in the bus station, she kicked out at the seat in front, boldly meeting the gaze of the white-haired woman sitting there who turned round to indicate her displeasure. The woman glared but Josie held her gaze defiantly and the woman looked away first.

Josie then turned her attention to the raindrops that were plopping onto the grubby windows and dripping onto the pavement, turning yesterday's thin covering of clean white snow into muddy brown slush. She soon forgot about the woman, thinking back over the events of the morning and how quickly they had escalated into what the manager had insisted on calling 'a situation'.

It shouldn't have happened that way at all, as she had told the department supervisor who was responsible for overseeing the sales of all the perfumes and eau de colognes.

'I didn't mean to overcharge the lady. It was an accident,' Josie said and she had apologized immediately in her own mumbling fashion. But that hadn't been good enough it seemed, and what she resented most was being humiliated by the floor manager who had then been summoned – far too quickly in Josie's opinion – to sort out the problem. There was no problem as far as Josie was concerned: it had all been resolved. The woman had been given the extra change that she was owed and everyone should have been happy, but the manager had not been able to let it rest and had continued to chastise Josie until the young girl had snapped and spoken out in her usual forthright way without thinking.

'It wasn't my fault! I think you're just being mean to carry on making such a fuss about something that has already been sorted out,' she'd told the manager angrily. 'I've apologized and that should be enough. Or is it because I come from Weatherfield that you don't think I'm good enough to be serving in Pauldens?' She'd said the name in a hoity-toity voice and she saw, too late, that the manager had taken immediate offence. Josie should have remembered that her sassy tongue had got her into trouble in the past and she shouldn't have been surprised when she had been given her marching orders on the spot.

She hadn't been at Pauldens very long, which she knew wouldn't look good when she tried to get another job, but it was too late to think about that now, the damage had been done. She had been hired at the beginning of December in anticipation of the increase in trade at Christmas and although she hadn't particularly enjoyed being a sales assistant she had hoped to work there a little longer than a few short months.

'Just because I'm the least experienced I suppose I'm expendable now,' she muttered in defiance, as she was shepherded upstairs to retrieve her coat and handbag from the staff room. 'It's not that I wanted a job like this in the first place. I *told* my mother that I didn't want to work in a shop.' She didn't care if she did sound disparaging, but she didn't add that there hadn't been time to organize much else after her widowed mother, Marjorie Bradshaw, had announced her engagement to Paddy O'Riordan, a comedian she had met while touring on the music hall circuit. Marjorie was coming to the end of her long and successful show business career and was looking forward to a change of pace in her life. She had starred in countless variety shows, singing and dancing all over the northwest, but now she was ready to retire and had agreed to go with Paddy to Ireland, almost immediately, to take over the running of a pub he had an interest in.

The wedding had quickly followed the engagement announcement and there had been little time for Josie to reappraise her own position. As a young girl she had enjoyed the family's nomadic existence, and had had a lot of fun helping out behind the scenes, touring the region while her mother was singing and dancing on the stage. But since reaching the age of twenty-one she had realized that she wanted more from life than trailing in her mother's wake. She needed more independence, needed the time and space to fulfil her own dreams and to strike out in her own direction. The problem was that she wasn't sure what she wanted to do, although she had found out the hard way that working as a sales assistant in a large department store shop was not it.

Josie sat on the bus, frowning as she thought about her situation. She had turned down the opportunity to join Paddy and Marjorie in their new life in Ireland, and had moved into lodgings in Weatherfield, but she needed money to pay the rent even though her landlady, Elsie Lappin, was an old friend of her mother's from their travelling days. Josie knew she would have to find another job as quickly as possible if she was to pay her own way and she began to wish she had accepted her mother's invitation to go to Ireland.

Josie rubbed the condensation that had gathered on the bus window with her sleeve, determined not to let the murky greyness of a typical Manchester day dampen her spirits. The traffic was heavier than she had seen for a while and she wondered how long it would take to get to Weatherfield. It was not a journey that she usually undertook at this time of day. With that sobering thought she settled back into the almost threadbare upholstery of her seat, wondering what she should tell Elsie about the circumstances that had led to her sacking.

Chapter 2

Elsie Lappin had run the corner shop at number 15 Coronation Street more or less single-handed for several years now after she had stepped away from a fruitful stage career but she had never lost touch with Marjorie Bradshaw who, for a while, had been her stage partner, the other half of a singing duo. When her old friend had contacted her to explain her change of circumstances and her concern about her daughter's well-being, alone in Weatherfield, Elsie immediately offered to help in any way she could.

'It's a roof over her head, that's what the lass needs right now,' Marjorie had explained. 'She's adamant she doesn't want to come with us, so once me and

Paddy's hitched and we set sail for Ireland she'll be on her own.'

'How old is she now?' Elsie wanted to know. 'It's years since I've seen her.'

'She's twenty-one, not far off your girls as I recall.'

'Of course!' Elsie said, remembering.

'And she's just got herself a good job at Pauldens in Manchester. I'm ever so pleased about it, but she needs somewhere decent to stay.'

'That sounds good.' Elsie was impressed that Josie had taken such an initiative. 'At least it sounds like she's not just sitting on her backside like some girls of her age do. As you say, she's about the same age as my girls. I'm not sure they'd show so much gumption. She's obviously got her head screwed on the right way.'

'She has that,' Marjorie agreed. 'Well, most times,' she added after a moment's hesitation and she laughed.

'Though I'm sorry to hear she won't be following her mother's footsteps onto the stage.' Elsie sighed. 'Neither one of my lasses was interested in a stage career either.' She thought for a moment, then she said, 'It might be a bit of a squeeze but if it will put your mind at rest, I could offer your Josie board and lodgings.'

'Could you? Would you?' Marjorie sounded delighted. 'Just until she finds her feet in Weatherfield.

That would be fabulous. She'd be able to pay her own way, of course, I'd even pay for her myself to help her get settled as it would be such a weight off my mind – you've no idea.'

Elsie was gratified to hear the relief in her friend's voice. She was pleased that she was in a position to be able to help. She liked to think that she was doing a good deed for an old mate and she happily ignored the nagging thought at the back of her mind that maybe she ought to have checked out her offer of hospitality with her daughters first.

'You mean I've got to move out of the box room that Shelagh and I worked so hard to clear?' Elsie was surprised by the vehemence of the attack in Hilda's voice when she made the announcement. 'But I've only just moved into it! And it's mine. You promised!'

'Be your age, Hilda. Stop acting like a spoilt kid. How old are you?' Elsie couldn't help snapping back.

'I'm practically twenty as you well know and that's old enough in my book to have a room of my own and not to have to share a bed with my kid sister who needs the bigger room because it's got a fireplace in it and she needs warmth when she's bronchial. If she didn't, then she'd be having the box room, no question!'

Elsie shook her head. 'Maybe you should take a leaf out of Josie Bradshaw's book and move out! Go and find your own rooms and see what you get.'

Hilda looked so shocked it was a few moments before she rallied. 'I thought you said she was being forced out as her mother's leaving town?' she began to argue.

'Well, yes, she is, but she could have taken the easy route and gone with her mum to her new home in Ireland.' Elsie wasn't sure why she was bothering when she knew there was really no point in arguing with Hilda when she was in this sort of mood. Besides, she would get over it, particularly if Elsie showed Hilda how they would all benefit financially from the move. Anyway, the deed was done, though she did now pause to wonder exactly what she might be taking on.

Elsie unlocked the front door, pulled back the bolts and rolled up the blinds on the shop windows in preparation for the start of another day. She sighed heavily and shook her head. The lodger had arrived but it was taking longer than she'd expected for them all to settle into a peaceful new routine. *At least a peace of sorts will reign here for the next few hours*, she thought. The girls had gone off to their respective jobs at the canteen in Elliston's rainwear factory and wouldn't be back until the late afternoon shift ended, and Josie had caught the early bus into Manchester where she would remain until the store closed in the early evening. She seemed happy enough serving behind one of the smart perfume counters in Pauldens. Elsie checked the time on the large wall clock and waited as long as she could before she flicked the shop sign from Closed to Open and she held the door to allow entry to the first customer of the day.

'Good morning, Mrs Sharples!' Elsie called as chirpily as she could. It was at times like these that she embraced the benefit of her stage training. The shop bell tinkled when she pulled back the door and stood aside to let a formidable-looking woman edge between her and the counter, clasping her capacious handbag to her chest as she always did. Her hat, perched as it was on top of a coarse-looking hairnet, looked as if it had been rammed down on her head as an afterthought and her dark coat was buttoned up to the chin.

'I don't know as I'd still call it morning,' Ena Sharples said, glancing up at the clock which showed ten minutes past nine. Elsie tried not to show her irritation, although from the brusque tone of Mrs Sharples' voice she could never be certain if the caretaker at the Mission of Glad Tidings was being jokingly sarcastic or just her normal dour self.

'What can I do for you today?' Elsie replied, her manner as perky as she could muster 'You can get

11

me this lot.' Mrs Sharples slapped down a piece of paper that looked as if it had been torn from a pocket notebook. Elsie squinted at the items that had been listed in pencil and seemed to be fading fast.

'Certainly,' Elsie said brightly, though she wasn't sure she could supply all of the items on the list and she dreaded Mrs Sharples' reaction when she told her. Sharples by name, sharp-tongued by nature she'd always thought.

'Why don't you take the weight off your feet while I see what I can put together for you.' Elsie indicated the chair on the customers' side of the counter as she began to scurry round gathering the items off the shelves as she went. She carefully packed them into the two shopping bags that Mrs Sharples had brought with her and was ringing the prices into the till when the doorbell tinkled once more.

'My goodness, there's no fire is there?' Mrs Sharples said.

The newcomer gasped and automatically looked behind her. 'Why should there be a fire?' she asked, her brow furrowed.

'I was wondering what's got you out of bed so early that's all, Minnie Caldwell,' Mrs Sharples said.

'If you must know it was my new little kitten. I hadn't realized that I had no food for her in the flat apart from a few scraps but she kept insisting on reminding me.'

'And how long have you had this new kitten that she's ruling the roost already?' Mrs Sharples said. 'You need to put your foot down there, Mrs Caldwell. Show her who's boss right from the start.'

'I've only had her for a few weeks and I wouldn't say she's ruling the roost exactly.' Mrs Caldwell sounded defensive. 'She's still settling in. In fact, I haven't even given her a name yet. But I've put butter on her paws so she knows where to come back to when I let her out.'

'Butter?' Ena Sharples was scornful. 'You don't believe in those old wives' tales do you?'

Minnie Caldwell sniffed. 'Old wives' tales or not, I believe them to be true. I've never had a cat yet that's wandered off.'

Elsie put a tin down on the counter in front of Mrs Caldwell. 'I do believe this might be what you're after,' she said.

'Never mind her cat, how's about finishing my order as I was here first?' Mrs Sharples snapped.

'Don't worry, Mrs Sharples, I'm not neglecting you, yours is done now,' Elsie said hastily. 'Will that be all?'

'How's about a bagful of them broken biscuits?' Mrs Sharples said. 'I take it you still stock them?'

'Oh yes, I do indeed,' Elsie said.

'I don't want any broken biscuits.' Minnie Caldwell looked puzzled. 'The cat won't eat anything like that. She might choke on the crumbs.'

'I'm not saying they're for you, they're for me,' Mrs Sharples said testily.

'Shall I add some to your order? I've just finished . . .' Elsie said.

'Yes, please. I almost forgot that we're having a meeting at the mission this afternoon and no doubt they'll all be expecting a bite or two of a sweet biscuit as we'll be discussing serious business,' she said, reaching out to sample one before Elsie had time to close the bag.

'What meeting's that?' Elsie liked to keep abreast of any local events.

'The one for talking about the Coronation party. We're to officially decide today what we're doing. Cos if we're doing owt we've got to inform the authorities and officially appoint a committee who can get on with the planning. There's lots to sort out and June will be here before you know it.'

'I look forward to hearing what's decided,' Elsie said. 'I must admit that the thought of the Coronation and the street party are the only things that have been keeping me going lately. I mean, we had such a miserable time during the war and that seemed to go on forever. All those years of bombing raids and blackouts, the never-ending rationing, and the things that are still in short supply, not to mention the freezing fogs and smogs of the last bitterly cold winter. They've been more than enough to get anyone down.' She shuddered as she spoke. Then she gave a huge sigh as she thought of the gloom that had descended on her entire household because of the tensions that had arisen between her fractious daughters when their new lodger had arrived, but she didn't add them out loud to her list.

'There's nothing wrong, is there?' Minnie Caldwell enquired, looking from Elsie to Mrs Sharples. She seemed to be alarmed by the awkward moment of silence.

Elsie shook her head and tried to smile. 'No, no, there's nothing wrong, Mrs Caldwell,' Elsie said. 'Not really. I was just thinking of that old saying about being grateful for what you've got – only there are some days when I find that a very difficult thing to do.'

Chapter 3

Elsie had no sooner turned the key in the lock and switched the sign she'd had specially made to read Closed for Lunch than there was a loud knocking on the shop door. Not stopping to look who it was, she pointed to the sign and was about to shoo the woman away, but when she realized that it was a distraught looking Mrs Caldwell, one hand hooked possessively around her handbag, the other holding on to her hat against what looked like a fearsome wind as she peered through the window. Elsie took pity on her and opened the door again.

'I can't believe the wind that's got up since I were here earlier,' Minnie panted, 'but after all that talk about my new little moggie, would you believe I forgot to buy her some milk?'

'You'd best come in then, chuck,' Elsie said, 'before that wind blows us all over; it is a bit wild.' She inched the door back while keeping a firm hold on the handle and then closed it on the latch while she went into the cool room at the back to fetch a pint of milk from the small stock she kept for such emergencies.

'The milkman must have forgot to leave me a pint this morning – I don't usually run out,' Mrs Caldwell said apologetically.

'Never mind, I've got a spare one here,' Elsie said.

'Thanks ever so much. I'm so sorry to disturb you when I know it's your dinner hour.'

Elsie rang up the pennies and put the coins in the till then turned to show Mrs Caldwell out, trying to prevent the door from slamming with the wind when she felt pressure of someone on the outside trying to force it open again. The bell jangled and Elsie jumped back as a woman's head, her hair firmly tied back with a headscarf, peered from behind the door.

'Hello, it's only me, Ida Barlow from number three,' the woman called out, immediately identifying herself. 'Are you still open? Not shut up for dinner yet I hope?' She didn't wait for a reply. 'I saw Mrs Caldwell come in and I thought I'd take a chance, only I've forgotten to get some baps for us tea and some corned beef. But I can come back later on my way home from work if you'd rather.'

'No, you're all right, Ida,' Elsie said as Minnie Caldwell, still muttering effusive thanks, slipped out between them. 'I don't mind serving you so long as no one else comes in with you,' she said, standing aside to let Ida in so that she could quickly close the door and flip the sign. 'In fact, now you're here, why don't you stop and have a cuppa with me? I wouldn't say no to a bit of company, truth be told.'

Ida's face lit up with a conspiratorial smile. 'It'll have to be quick, though, I'm on my dinner break and the boss always shouts if we're late back.'

Elsie put her hand on Ida's arm, not giving her a chance to refuse as she guided her into the shop and indicated that she should go through to the kitchen at the back. 'It might sound a bit daft as there's folk coming and going in the shop all day long, but I can get a bit lonely sometimes,' Elsie said as she followed her through, 'though I know folk don't always believe it. But I never seem to get a chance to stop and have a proper chat with anyone these days when I'm rushed off my feet like I have been this morning.'

'I can imagine that,' Ida said.

'We're still short of lots of things from the shelves,' Elsie said, 'but that doesn't stop the neighbours from constantly popping in and asking about them.' Aware of the look on Ida's face Elsie quickly added, 'Though I suppose I should be grateful for small mercies that, apart from sugar, rationing is off most foodstuff now.' She filled the kettle and put it on the back burner of the gas stove.

'I bumped into Mrs Sharples just before,' Ida said, 'and she reminded me that there's to be a meeting at the Mission Hall later today about the Coronation party. I told her I'm happy to be involved with it so, I thought I'd drop in there after work and see what was happening.'

'Yes, she and Mrs Caldwell were talking about it earlier. I would love to be involved and I suppose I will be, one way or another, when the time comes but the meetings are too early for me to shut the shop.' Elsie reached up for two white cups and saucers from the shelf then changed her mind and took two prettily decorated fine-china cups from the dresser instead.

'I think they've got big plans,' Ida said. 'They seem determined to have a do that's even bigger and better than the VE day street parties that we had to celebrate the end of the war, and I thought that they were grand enough.'

'It certainly sounds exciting. I'm looking forward to it already, particularly as I didn't make it to the VE parties,' Elsie said. 'But for the time being I'm happy to leave them to it regarding the actual organizing and I'll join in when they need to actually start buying the food and things. I should be able to get stuff for them much cheaper wholesale.' She was about to add that it was likely that she would also be able to get items they wouldn't be able to get elsewhere but thought better of it. She remembered too clearly the incident during the war when she had tried to do a favour for some of her better customers who she'd thought of as friends. She offered to get them things they'd found difficult to buy and she'd kept them on one side for her 'special' customers. Unfortunately, that had resulted in one of her neighbours telling tales to the police and they had taken rather a different view of her gestures to help. She had been fined and reprimanded for selling goods on the black market and it had left a nasty taste in her mouth, so it was an incident she had no intention of repeating.

Ida merely nodded. If she remembered the incident she made no reference to it. 'I'm not sure what I can offer by way of organization, what with me working full-time,' she said. 'But I told Mrs Sharples, tell me what you want me to do and I'll do it. I'm sure they'll need practical help with all sorts of things nearer the time. But what about you? And I'm not just talking food here. Isn't there going to be some entertainment later on? They were talking about taking the piano from the Rovers out into the street like they did on VE day, so long as it isn't raining. Haven't they asked you to sing?'

Elsie laughed. 'Not so far and I don't think they will. That part of my life has long gone, really. I don't do much singing anymore.' A pensive look crossed Elsie's face.

'Then I think you should come out of retirement for the day and give us a few old favourites,' Ida said. 'I hope you'll consider it. I remember when you used to be on at the working men's club down by the mill for nights on end,' she said. 'You were one of my old dad's favourites. "A class act" he used to call you. He'd go a long way to hear you sing.'

Elsie giggled then allowed herself a wistful sigh. 'Blonde hair always went down well at the working men's clubs.' She flicked back her curls and gestured with her head the way she used to do when she was on stage. 'Those were the days, eh?'

'They were an' all. You were right famous, Elsie. Everyone knew who you were. All the locals used to jostle to be served by you when you first came to work in the shop and I know they felt right proud to be able to say they knew you.'

'Go on with you!' Elsie's cheeks had reddened. 'I was never that good, or that well-known,' she said modestly. Then she giggled. 'I only got into it by accident, you know.'

'Really? How was that then?' Ida was genuinely interested.

'I won a talent competition. I was only thirteen. Elsie Castleway as I was then.'

'But that wasn't your stage name as I recall?' Ida looked puzzled.

'No, it weren't. They changed my name almost immediately to Melody Mae. Said it had a better ring to it. Then one of the dancers in the troupe that was on the same bill taught me how to do high leg kicks without falling over and a few fancy dance moves in the tap shoes she lent me. Gosh, that made me feel like Ginger Rogers and before I knew it I was on the bill at all the local variety clubs and music halls in the area, starting off as a supporting act and gradually working my way up the bill. Some of the men on the circuit used to tease me, told me I was known as the high-kicking glamour puss of Weatherfield, although no one actually called me that to my face. But it's true I was flying high. I even had an agent.'

Ida looked incredulous.

'Yes, I did,' Elsie assured her, 'and he was desperate to introduce me to an agent down south. They really wanted me to travel. They kept promising me if I spread my wings I could make a fortune.' Elsie was interrupted by the piercing whistle of the kettle boiling and she jumped up to mash the tea.

Ida was sitting forward eagerly, her elbows planted firmly on the table. 'And did you?' she asked.

'Did I what?'

'Make your fortune.'

Elsie laughed. 'No such luck. But I never really put it to the test, cos I never moved. I couldn't bring myself to leave home. It wouldn't have felt right.' She shrugged. 'The family made a lot of sacrifices for me. And in the end it was probably just as well I didn't go anywhere because soon after that things began to go right badly and I needed my family's help.'

'I must admit I never did understand what happened to you,' Ida said. 'You just seemed to disappear from the scene overnight and then you popped up behind the counter here.'

Thinking back, Elsie suddenly felt choked. She couldn't speak and she wasn't sure she could continue.

But Ida didn't seem to notice her distress and persisted. 'Why *did* you give it all up, Elsie? You had such a lovely voice,' she said.

'Had,' Elsie finally managed to say. 'That's the key word. I *had* a good voice.' She had to take a deep breath before she could go on. 'I damaged my vocal cords somehow. I never was quite sure what happened or how I did it and no one seemed able to tell me, but I kept getting sore throats and tonsillitis and all sorts of infections, and every other week I was losing my voice and had to cancel a concert. Eventually I was told that I had two options: give up and never sing again or face at least one serious operation that might not even be successful. I was warned I could lose my voice completely and that I might never be able to speak again let alone sing, if things went wrong, so it wasn't much of a choice really.'

Ida gasped and covered her own mouth with her hands in a startled reflex action. 'I had no idea,' she whispered.

'I was only twenty-three – a bit young to have to give up on your dreams.' She got up, and taking a handful of biscuits from a tin in the cupboard, laid them out on a plate that she offered to her guest. 'Help yourself,' she said absently, picking one up as she sat down again at the table. She didn't take care of her figure so assiduously now that she was no longer a celebrity.

'I've got some bread we could have, if you'd rather,' she suggested when Ida made no attempt to touch the biscuits. 'And there's a bit of marge left over from last night. We can toast the bread if it doesn't feel fresh enough because the girls won't eat it.' Ida looked surprised and Elsie said, 'I don't know where they get their fancy ideas from after what we've been through during the war but they've gone all uppity about eating what they call any kind of left-overs.'

'Well, I think that's very generous of you to offer,' Ida said. 'Thank you, it sounds very nice. I certainly don't mind a bit of toast and marge. I must confess I ate my lunch sandwich at tea break this morning. Not something I normally do but I came over all hungry, like.'

It took several minutes for Elsie to come back to the table with their toast already spread with marga-rine, by which time she had been able to collect herself and not be overwhelmed by the memories.

'When my voice first began to go,' she said as she sat down, 'it sounded rough all the time, as though I had a permanent cold or flu or something but no one realized that it might be something more serious. The doctor thought it might be helpful if I wasn't having to work so hard, and to try to lay off singing for a bit. I never told him that I was being asked more and more to fill in any empty slots on the playbill as well as my own slot. But then my agent introduced me to Marjorie Bradshaw and suggested that maybe we could perform a double act. We pretended she was my younger sister Suzy, though of course it wasn't true. But we did begin to be billed together and at least I wasn't doing all the singing.' Elsie had a dreamy look in her eyes as she thought back to those days. 'We soon became good friends, Marj and I, and we worked together very successfully for quite some time.'

'What happened to her?' Ida asked. 'Did she have to give up at the same time?'

'Not at all. She changed her name and actually did very well on her own although she also refused to get an agent down south. Funnily enough I heard from her recently as she's about to retire. She's just got married again after she was widowed and they were moving to Ireland, but her daughter Josie wasn't going with them and she was looking for digs here in Weatherfield; she wondered if I knew of anywhere.'

'That's nice that you kept in touch,' Ida said.

'We've done more than that, Josie's come to lodge with us.' Elsie grinned. 'You may have seen her about. I know she's come back from the Rovers with tales about Annie Walker getting all wound up about the coronation.'

Ida giggled. 'I can imagine.'

'But what brought you to Coronation Street and the shop in particular after being on the stage?' Ida wanted to know. 'You wasn't born round here, was you?'

'Not far away,' Elsie said. 'But it was really on account of my first husband, Tommy Foyle; you remember he owned the shop. The funny thing was that when we first met he had no idea who I was. He'd never heard of Melody Mae and I found that quite refreshing. It wasn't that I didn't enjoy being a bit of a celebrity in the neighbourhood, but at the same time it was nice to find someone who didn't know anything about me and liked me for being me. As you know, after we got wed we worked together in the shop. Then we had the girls and it all worked out rather well, really. At least it did until poor Tommy got ill. Though the girls were marvellous. They really helped look after their dad.' She sighed deeply. 'Sadly he died on VE day of all days, which is why I never got to the party we had then and he never got to see "peace break out" as he used to say. He so wanted us to be able to have good times together again. That's why I'm looking forward to enjoying the party for Queen Elizabeth's coronation. I'll be thinking of him and I know that he'll be with us in spirit at least. He was always fond of a good knees-up was my Tommy.' A dreamy look crossed Elsie's face.

'I remember what a doting dad he was to those girls,' Ida said after a momentary hesitation, 'he always acted as if he were their real father.'

'He did that, and in so many ways he *was* their dad,' Elsie said. 'He were a good man, was Les. He was a family friend originally and when Tommy was almost at the end he more or less made me promise I would marry Les when he'd gone, or that I would at least think about it. "Then I know I won't have to worry about you," Tommy always said. He didn't want me to be left moping about on my own. Left to me I might not have bothered, I wasn't really looking to get married again. I had the girls, we were a family, but what with Tommy trying to persuade me and then Les keeping on pestering me, I thought what the heck.' Elsie paused. She couldn't stop a smile at the memory. 'It's a good job that none of us knows what's ahead. I mean, we did get married Les and me, but who'd have thought that we would only have five years together?'

'It's not very long, is it?' Ida said. Elsie had told this story so many times and none of it was new, but Ida knew that what Elsie really needed was a sympathetic ear.

'Aye, last January it was when he had his heart attack and then I was left on my own. I'm only grateful that my Tommy at least had had the good sense to make sure I were left with the shop. After all the years of insecurity when I was on the stage it's been a great comfort to have the shop behind me, I can tell you. Even if I do have to work all hours. But Les was a great help when he was here. He gave up his sales job and came to help run the shop and he was always good to us. He looked after my girls as if they was his own, I can't deny that.' Elsie paused, caught up in her memories. 'That's why we were all knocked for six when he went so sudden.' She snapped her fingers together. 'Like that! In an instant. If you'd have asked me I'd have said Les was the last person to pop off, sudden like.'

'I'll never forget that day as long as I live. I remember saying so to Frank at the time. I happened to be in the shop at the time, don't you remember? He was serving me. You certainly have had your share of ups and downs,' Ida sympathized, and there was a moment of silence as they were each wrapped up in their own thoughts.

Elsie nodded, thinking back to that tragic day. 'You've always been a good friend to me.'

Ida glanced at the clock on the mantelpiece over the hearth. 'Oh my goodness! Is that the time?' She gulped down the last of her tea and stood up abruptly. 'Much as I've enjoyed our little chat I really must be getting back to work before I get the sack.' She made a noise at the back of her throat that made her sound like a naughty schoolgirl. 'I'm afraid that next to yours my life sounds very boring. What do your girls make of it? Are they proud you were so well-known, or would they rather not know? Kids can be funny sometimes, about things like that, can't they?'

Elsie stood up too. 'I don't know about proud,'

she said modestly, 'but they've never said anything rude, at least not to my face!' and they both cackled out loud. 'Though to tell the truth we never really talk about it. Don't forget it all happened long before they were born and if ever the subject does come up they do tend to roll their eyes and look a bit dubious, as if they don't really believe it. And I must admit – sometimes I don't believe it myself.'

'Don't believe what?' The clunking sound of a bolt turning in the lock followed by the prolonged sound of a buzzer being pressed announced a new arrival at the back door and when Elsie looked up she was startled to see her elder daughter coming into the kitchen.

'Hilda?' Elsie sounded astonished. 'What are you doing here?' But Hilda took no notice of her as she made a beeline for the stairs as if she had hoped to make it without being spotted.

'Hilda!' Elsie called again. This time Hilda paused with one hand on the banister. She looked embarrassed at being caught out and she hesitated, seeming unsure which way she should turn.

'Don't mind me,' she said at last. 'I've just nipped home in my lunch hour to fetch summat. Sorry to interrupt. You looked well wrapped up in whatever it was you were talking about. I didn't mean to disturb you. I won't be long,' and with that she carried on up the stairs without saying anything more but when she came back down, Elsie was waiting for her at the bottom of the steps.

'I've just come to get my new lipstick,' Hilda said, waving a make-up case in Elsie's face before Elsie had time to say anything. 'I meant to take it with me this morning but I forgot.' Hilda smiled and Elsie could see that her normally pale pink cheeks had been highlighted by a fresh application of foundation pancake and a light dusting of face powder that was a tone darker than her natural complexion. A slash of deep vermilion marked out her lips. Elsie had noticed that now that it was in plentiful supply, both of her daughters had taken to wearing the occasional splash of make-up if they were going somewhere special but she seldom saw Hilda wearing it for work.

'Why was it so important to find it now?' Elsie asked, puzzled.' Are you going to meet someone after work?'

Hilda lifted her shoulders in a noncommittal way. 'No reason,' she said, although as Elsie watched her cheeks were suffused with a pink glow.

'Before you rush off you can come in and say a proper hello to Mrs Barlow. She popped in for a cup of tea and she's about ready to go back to work.'

'Nice to see you, Mrs Barlow,' Hilda said politely although without enthusiasm as she stepped up towards the table. 'Not seen you for a while.'

'No,' Ida said, 'likewise. Your mum and I have just been catching up and having a lovely chat.' Ida stood up and grabbed her coat from the back of the chair. 'But I must be getting back to work now too.'

'Don't go on my account,' Hilda said.

'Oh no, don't worry, dear, I'm going because I value my job and it's high time I was getting back to it.'

'Time for me to open the shop again too, or folk will be thinking I've died in here,' Elsie giggled as she cleared away the teacups.

'How are you getting on with your new lodger, Hilda?' Ida said. She had got as far as the front door when she turned back. 'It must be nice for you and your sister to have another companion. Someone of your own age.'

Elsie was preparing to reopen the shop door but she felt her shoulders stiffen. Knowing how the girls felt about Josie Bradshaw she hoped Hilda wouldn't say anything out of turn. Hilda could be extremely kind, generous even, like the time she had helped Shelagh to find a job when she left school, working alongside her in the canteen in Elliston's raincoat factory. But Elsie also knew that when the mood took her Hilda could also be very mean, especially if she'd already taken a dislike to someone. Elsie took a deep breath and was relieved when Hilda seemed to ignore the question.

'I bet you're looking forward to the coronation, Mrs Barlow?' Hilda enquired instead.

'Isn't everybody?' Ida's face lit up.

'I know I am,' Elsie said, 'I missed out on VE day, but I can't wait to have a bit of fun this time around. After all the years of rationing and privation it's about time we had something to celebrate and I'm really looking forward to it.'

'It's only a shame the king had to die in order for the coronation to happen, if you know what I mean.' Elsie said with a laugh.

'Imagine being told news about your father like that when you're stuck out in Africa and haven't seen him for several weeks.' Ida added a sombre note. 'Poor King George, he was hardly an old man, was he? He seemed too young to die.'

'It's hard on the queen as well, having to give way so that her daughter becomes the queen now,' Elsie said.

'It must feel strange being called the Queen Mother; it makes her sound even older than she is,' Ida said.

Hilda giggled. 'Can you imagine if we called you that, eh, Mum, when we get married? Old Mother

Elsie. It's like being called a mother hen.' She made a loud clucking noise but Elsie ignored her. 'I think it's nice that we'll have someone who's young and pretty on the throne,' Elsie said. 'I think Prin— No! *Queen* Elizabeth is already shaping up to make a very good queen.'

'How can she go wrong with a gorgeous bloke like she's got by her side?' Hilda chipped in. 'Give me a fella like that and I'd be a great queen too. With everyone dead jealous, fighting to get at him.'

'What I'm looking forward to most is having a day off work on coronation day,' though it's a shame it's not a long weekend,' Ida said. 'Still, it's so good to have something to celebrate at last and I think it could turn out to be something very special.'

'We shall all be able to let our hair down and have lots of fun on the day, no doubt,' Elsie said 'and I, for one, think we deserve it.' She turned to Hilda for approval but it was Ida who spoke up first.

'And what's more, wouldn't it be lovely for Coronation Street to have its own star turn at the party,' she said. 'I'm sure a spot of nostalgia will be called for and who best to do that and to pull it together with all the old favourites than our very own Jenny Wren?' Ida said. She beamed in Elsie's direction then looked towards Hilda. 'I've been

35

trying to persuade yer mam that she should offer her services to sing at the street party,' Ida said. 'What do you think, Hilda? I hope you'll encourage her.'

Elsie was surprised to see Hilda smile at that. 'Sounds like a good idea to me,' Hilda said.

'You could lead us in the rallying songs we used to sing during the war, Elsie,' Ida said enthusiastically. 'Your mam's been telling me all about her stage career,' she said to Hilda. 'You must be right proud of her.' But Hilda was already heading through to the shop, towards the front door with Elsie in her wake.

'See you at teatime, then luv,' Elsie called after her daughter, and although she thought Hilda said something in response as she unlocked the front door, she wasn't sure what it was. Elsie stopped to check that the Closed/Open sign was facing the right way for the afternoon's business and she thought she could still hear Hilda's voice as she stepped out into the street. It was then that she noticed a set of stepladders propped up against the shopfront and, glancing up, she realized that Hilda was conducting a conversation with young Charlie Wright the window cleaner, who was clinging precariously to the top of his ladders. He was a good-looking boy, Elsie noted; Hilda always insisted that he looked like the Duke of Edinburgh and he had taken over the family's weekly window-cleaning round in Coronation Street since his father had become ill several months previously.

Chapter 4

As the bus began weaving its way through the cobbled streets towards Weatherfield, Josie went over and over the incident of the morning in her head. She wondered if there was anything she might have done differently in order to avoid getting sacked, but she could think of nothing. It wasn't her fault – things had conspired against her the way they always did . . . although just what those 'things' were was a secret she was not yet ready to share, maybe never would be.

When she had landed the job at Pauldens, the large department store that was on a par with Lewis's although not quite as high-class as Kendal Milne, she had had such high hopes that everything would be different and that things would work out well. And yet here she was, only a few weeks into the job and already furious at the way things were turning out. Josie was angry that the floor manager had been too short-sighted to appreciate her true worth, and had sacked her without investigation into what she might be capable of if given the chance.

Further concerns arose, not unnaturally, when she contemplated how she should explain to Elsie why she had been sent home so early and what excuse she could give for her sacking. If she was lucky Elsie might be busy in the shop and she would be able to sneak indoors without having to say anything immediately. That would buy Josie some time so that she could at least wait until the shop closed at the end of the day before she had to talk to Elsie at any length. Then the easiest thing would be to tell Elsie the full sequence of events as they had occurred so that she could see for herself the abrupt nature of the manager's reaction and how disproportionately harsh the punishment had been.

But the matter was taken out of Josie's hands because when she turned the corner into Coronation Street she could see Elsie on the doorstep, holding the shop door open and waving goodbye to a woman who had come bustling out of the shop. Josie recognized her as one of the neighbours, and she was calling apologies over her shoulder. 'I'm really sorry, I didn't mean to stay so long but I lost track of the time!' she shouted as she went hurrying off down the pavement.

It wasn't until she had disappeared from view that Josie realized Hilda was also in the entrance way, standing beside her mother. Josie felt her muscles stiffen and was relieved to see that Hilda hadn't seen her at first as she was too busy talking to a blond-haired young lad who was halfway up a ladder that was leaning against the upstairs windows. She seemed to be very animated but she stopped talking as soon as she saw Josie.

'What are *you* doing here at this hour? Gone on strike already or have they thrown you out?' The tone of Hilda's voice changed immediately as she addressed Josie.

'Don't be so unkind!' Elsie jumped to Josie's defence. 'The girl might be poorly.' She turned to Josie, her brow furrowed. 'What's wrong, love? Are you not feeling too good?' she asked solicitously.

'I'm telling you, it's more likely she's got the sack,' Hilda sneered.

'Now that's just cruel,' Elsie gasped. 'What's got into you, Hilda, to say a thing like that?'

Josie scowled and looked away, determined not to allow her surprise at the accuracy of Hilda's guesswork show on her face.

'I think you should apologize at once. You know that can't possibly be true.' Elsie frowned as she turned to face Josie. 'Can it?' A note of doubt crept into her voice.

Josie clamped her jaw tightly shut, not knowing what to say. But then she shot daggers in Hilda's direction as she realized she was trapped. Unless she wanted to embark on a string of lies, which didn't seem like a good idea, she had no choice but to admit that Hilda was right. She took a deep breath before plunging in.

'It's true, I'm afraid, Mrs Lappin.' Josie spoke up as boldly as she dared, all the while concentrating on keeping her expression neutral, and she was gratified when an astonished-looking Elsie shook her head in disbelief and stood aside without further comment to let her into the shop. Josie walked past as quickly as possible, bearing all the dignity she could muster and doing her best not to look in Hilda's direction.

'What did I tell you, Mum?' Josie could still hear Hilda ranting and realized that she and Elsie had both followed her into the shop. 'Didn't I tell you from the first? She'll be up to mischief in no time that one, I said.' Hilda's voice was relentless. 'As soon as you told us she was coming, didn't I say, "she'll be nothing but trouble that one, you mark my words"?'

'You never said anything of the kind, Hilda,' Elsie said sharply. 'At least, not to me. And now Josie's our lodger and if there is something that's gone wrong at work the least we can do is to listen to her and to give her our support.' She flapped her hands at her daughter. 'Now will you get back to work and stop mixing it!' Elsie turned and practically pushed Hilda back out of the shop, allowing the door to slam firmly shut behind her.

Elsie put her hand on Josie's arm. 'Her nasty temper's got nothing to do with you getting the sack.' She lowered her voice almost to a whisper. 'She's upset because she's had to move out of the single room to share a bed with her sister. She can get very jealous at times, but it's nothing for you to have to fret about; believe me she'll get over it.'

'I'm sorry if it's my fault,' Josie said. 'P'raps I shouldn't have come in the first place?'

'Not at all,' Elsie dismissed her apology. 'I invited you to stay and, what's more, I made a promise to your mum. I told both Hilda and Shelagh at the time: they're not the only two people in the world and they've got to be prepared to share and share alike. They slept together in the same bed before and they'll do it again now. It won't do them any harm.'

Elsie went to all the windows in the shop as she spoke and rolled up the blinds to show that she was ready for the afternoon's business, and finally she flung open the shop door, setting off the bell into a violent jangle. Josie was surprised that she could still hear Hilda's voice; she was talking once more to the young window cleaner. Not that he seemed to be listening. He was concentrating on using his chamois leather to soak up the water that was trickling down the upper windowpanes and didn't seem to be taking much notice.

'Hilda!' Elsie shouted, her tone now angry. 'I thought I told you to be getting back to work and leave Charlie to get on with his, before you both get the sack,' and she once again closed the door firmly on her daughter.

Fortunately for Josie there was a steady stream of customers in the shop for most of the afternoon so that she was able to stay in her own room with plenty of time to gather her thoughts before having to explain herself to Elsie. It was soon after closing time that Elsie called up to her to come down and join her in the kitchen for a cup of tea.

'I managed to find a couple of cubes of sugar so I've made it strong and sweet,' Elsie said in the most motherly of tones as she handed Josie a cup across the table. 'They say that's the best thing for dealing with shock and I reckon you've had a bit of a shock today, eh? Getting sacked from your job when you've not been there more than five minutes!'

Josie silently nodded agreement as she stared down at the table.

'The girls won't be home for a while yet,' Elsie said, 'so why don't you tell me exactly what happened this morning?'

Josie lifted her head and looked Elsie straight in the eye as she began to speak. She frowned as she told her story, feeling aggrieved afresh by the incident, not able to believe how fast it had all happened, but she was relieved to see Elsie's face wore a sympathetic smile.

'I don't know if that seems fair to you?' Josie said when she had finished, her tone belligerent, 'I know it certainly doesn't to me. I could hardly believe it when she said I was to go immediately to fetch my cards before I left the building.'

Elsie made a tutting sound, in agreement, when Josie said this, for it did indeed appear as if the punishment had been unnecessarily severe. They had hardly given her a chance, but Elsie hesitated before actually speaking, wary of saying the wrong thing. She had promised her friend Marjorie that she would look after Josie like a daughter and she couldn't help feeling partly responsible for what the young girl had suffered today. Marjorie had been delighted that Josie had been offered the position at the department store, but Elsie now worried that her friend might have ill-advisedly encouraged her daughter and pushed Josie peremptorily into accepting the position without checking whether she was really suited to it. But Josie herself had been so keen and she knew how badly she needed the job; she couldn't afford to be out of work for very long and Elsie tried to imagine what her reaction might have been if the same thing had happened to one of her girls. Would she have wanted to march down to the store, calling for justice and demanding that they reinstate her immediately? How had things gone so badly wrong so quickly? Was there something Josie hadn't told her?

'I must admit instant dismissal does sound a bit unreasonable to me,' Elsie ventured when Josie had finished her story. 'There's a famous Gilbert and Sullivan song about making the punishment fit the crime, and it seems to me that this one doesn't.' She sat back in her chair. 'They offered you no second chance?'

Josie shook her head. 'I apologized straight away and said I was sorry but it had been an accident and at first I thought it was all going to be straightened out. But then when the manager turned up she just said I had to go.'

Elsie raised her brows at what seemed to have been such an extreme reaction. She was about to ask if perhaps Josie's attitude might have come across as cocky, or even a bit cheeky, and that might be why they had acted so severely but then she caught a flash of defiance in the young girl's gaze and decided to keep her counsel.

'Would it make any sense for you to go down to Pauldens and ask them to give you another chance?' Elsie felt she was clutching at straws but she didn't know what else to suggest. 'If you went back and tried to reason with them . . .?' She was not really surprised when Josie interrupted with a sneer.

'No thank you. If they got down on their knees and begged me to go back, I'd refuse,' she said haughtily. 'Though I doubt they'd do that,' she added with a laugh.

'I feel we need to be practical here.' Elsie felt as if she was floundering as she tried to refocus the direction of the conversation. 'The thing is, on a practical level you know that you need work,' Elsie said. 'Unfortunately, as you say, no one from Pauldens is going to come chasing after you with a job offer, I'm sure you're right there, but I've been thinking that a more sensible solution would be for you to look for something that is much nearer to home. There really should be no need for you to have to travel so far every day. I imagine it's working out expensive as well as costing you a great deal of time.'

'More than I'd budgeted for originally, I must

admit,' Josie said. 'Did you have something or some-where more local in mind?' Elsie used the moments of silence that followed to think carefully about what she was about to propose.

'Well . . .' Elsie said eventually, 'I was wondering how you would feel about coming to work in the shop with me?'

Elsie was trying to interpret the look that flashed across Josie's face as she made her offer when there was the sound of a buzzer ringing followed by a door slamming and two voices shouting simultane-ously from the direction of the back door, 'We're home!'

'Gosh, you two look very serious. Has it been confession time?' Hilda said as she bounded into the room, more like a young schoolgirl than a responsible twenty-plus-year-old.

'Yes, do tell us everything, we're dying to know,' Shelagh joined in as she followed Hilda into the kitchen.

Elsie looked up; this was what she had been hoping to avoid but it was too late now. She would leave it up to Josie to decide how much she wanted them to know about what had happened at Pauldens, but she felt she owed it to them to tell them about the job offer she had just made.

'Actually, we were discussing Josie's future,' Elsie began and both girls raised their brows at this. 'I have just asked Josie if she would like to come and work in the shop. With me.'

'What, our shop?' Elsie was surprised to see Hilda look so shocked.

'Of course, our shop. I can't speak for anyone else, now can I?'

'And what did she say?' Hilda asked, speaking as if Josie wasn't there.

'She hasn't said anything yet,' Elsie said, looking across at Josie. 'No doubt she needs time to think it over. You'll have to ask her.' She made a sweeping hand gesture intended to include Josie.

'You don't really mean that, do you, Mum? Why would she want to work in *our* shop?' Hilda said, and Elsie couldn't help but notice her emphasis.

'Why not?' Elsie asked. 'It shouldn't affect you in any way. Neither of you two have ever shown any interest in working with me . . . except to fill in when there's been an emergency,' she hastily added.

'No, I know that, but—' Hilda began.

'But nothing!' Elsie interrupted. 'I'm just waiting on Josie's reply; it's really nothing to do with either of you.'

Josie was aware that all eyes had turned to her. She devoutly wished she was back in her bedroom upstairs and she began to squirm and fidget in her chair.

'So, what do you think?' Elsie asked Josie. 'Are you at all interested?'

'I'm certainly very touched by the offer,' Josie said 'and I'm sure you understand why I don't want to say or do anything in haste.' She was aware that the sisters were leaning forward, their elbows on the table, almost thrusting themselves in her face, and her only thought was how much she would have liked at that moment to bang their heads together, but she managed to camouflage the laugh that rose to her throat at the thought of that image and resisted the temptation. 'As I say, I think it's a very generous offer, Mrs Lappin,' Josie said, eventually looking only at Elsie, 'and I really thank you. Y-you are most kind,' she stammered. 'But before I decide I'd like to know a bit more about what kind of things you would expect me to do.'

At that Hilda guffawed loudly. ''ark at her,' she cried, pointing her index finger at Josie. 'It's the corner shop in Weatherfield we're talking about, you daftie! You'll not be selling the bloomin' crown jewels. What do you think you'd be expected to do? Fill up the shelves and serve the customers, stupid!'

Elsie glared at her, horrified, while Shelagh giggled but at least the younger girl had the grace to cover her mouth with her hand and pretend to look disapprovingly at her sister.

Josie was so shocked at being called the kind of names she thought she had left behind in the school playground that it was all she could do not to punch Hilda in the mouth. She was actually preparing to do so and she was making a firm fist of her right hand when a sudden movement by Elsie reminded her where she was, just in time for her to unclench her fist and hold back on the strike.

'I'd like to be able to think about it a bit more, Mrs Lappin, if I may?' Josie said as politely as she could, focussing again on Elsie. 'This business at Pauldens has knocked my confidence and I'm not sure I'm really ready to take on a great deal of responsibility.

'That's a good way of saying she's lazy without having to use the word,' Hilda said disparagingly. 'I don't know why you're bothering, Mum.'

Josie felt a flash of anger and could feel a blush rising from her neck to her cheeks and into her hair but she felt unable to defend herself in any way that would be satisfying and she knew that, for the time being, she would have to let it go. She was definitely not prepared to share her secret even with Elsie, so there was nothing more she could say and for the moment she didn't know what else she could do.

'You know you don't have to plunge in and do everything all at once.' To Josie's relief Elsie spoke up. It was like being thrown a lifeline and Josie looked at her with gratitude.

'I wouldn't expect you to be able to take on everything at once, and certainly not at the beginning,' Elsie said. 'I mean, you could spend time initially getting to know your way around the shop and all the different things we sell. You'll need to get used to the place so you could start by taking in new stock as it arrives and filling the shelves. Then, maybe you could put together any orders for delivery or that are to be picked up. You certainly don't need to start serving customers or getting involved with the paperwork until you feel more confident and are feeling more familiar with our systems. They're bound to be very different from Pauldens or anyone else's systems for that matter.'

Josie noticed that Hilda looked to be seething during this discussion while Josie herself smiled for the first time since she had come home earlier. Her heart rate finally felt as if it had begun to revert to normal and her breathing was also calming down.

'Thanks, Mrs Lappin, that sounds extremely helpful. If I can take my time getting to know my way around the shop like that, then I would be willing to give it a try. Thank you very much for the offer.'

'You realize that I won't be able to pay you huge wages?' Elsie said. 'But I could reduce the rent.'

There was a loud noise like an exploding sneeze that came from Hilda's end of the table and Josie jumped but when she looked in that direction she was in time to see Hilda looking straight at her and making a childish face.

Chapter 5

'How long do you reckon it takes to plan a good party?'

Annie Walker looked up from the final glass she was drying on the linen tea towel and smiled at Dot Atkins who was helping out behind the bar. Annie's husband Jack was leaning on the counter and he grunted in response and rolled his eyes heavenwards.

'I don't know, Dot, but I'll play along,' Annie said good-naturedly. 'How long does it take?' She nudged Jack with her elbow. 'This is not the time for being curmudgeonly, Jack,' she teased. 'Didn't we agree that we were never going to be maudlin again?' She turned back to Dot. 'Or is Jack right and it's just a trick question?'

'It sounds more like something our Billy might come out with when he wants to make fun of us,' Jack said, shaking his head, and he reached up over the bar to hang away the last of the freshly washed glasses that Annie had lined up on the counter.

'No, I'm serious, I'd really like to know what you think,' Dot said. 'I understand it's something they've been talking about down at the Mission for the last little while. There's been lots of debate but they can't agree on an answer. Mrs Sharples feels very strongly that you can't start planning early enough and she's pushing to get things moving for the coronation party. She says that with so many different streets being involved we might have already left it a bit late to properly coordinate the arrangements and pull everything together. But there's others equally convinced that with the coronation still being six months away they've got plenty of time yet.'

'I didn't realize you were on the organizing committee,' Annie said, somewhat haughtily.

'Oh no, I'm not,' Dot said. 'But I drop in at the Mission occasionally to see what's going on. I like to keep up with things, you know.'

You mean you go to pick up all the local gossip, more like, Annie thought, though she said nothing and her face continued to maintain a broad smile. She was careful not to hurt Dot's feelings; she relied on her too much. Dot was always ready to lend a hand behind the bar whenever she was needed, at those times when the regular barmaid was unavailable or when Annie was caught out by one of what she called her 'little emergencies' and she was summoned unexpectedly to Billy's school.

'All I can tell you,' Annie said, 'is that the committee in charge of all the official aspects of the coronation started meeting and planning it well over a year ago, so Mrs Sharples has a point.' Annie stood back as if to appraise Jack's handiwork in arranging the glasses that were all once more hanging in rows over the bar.

'Ready for the dinnertime onslaught then, are we?' Jack asked.

'We most certainly are,' Annie said and there was no more time to discuss the coronation or street parties as she stepped forward to serve the first customer of the day.

'Well, if the idea behind making such a big fuss over the coronation was to involve the whole country and to put a smile on everyone's faces after all our years of suffering then I would say that it's a very clever ploy that is certainly succeeding,' Annie said to her customer. It wasn't far off three o'clock and she would soon be calling time to ring the bell for last orders. It was also the first moment Annie had had to pause after serving a steady stream of thirsty customers, the last of whom seized the opportunity to step up to the bar.

'I believe the whole of the coronation service as well as the procession is going to be broadcast on the television, so that should make some people smile even more,' the woman said as she drummed her fingers on the counter, waiting to be served. Elsie Tanner, one of the Rovers' regulars lived in the Street with her two young children and was not known for her patience. She indicated to Annie that she'd like three more refills of the port and lemon glasses she had already set down.

Annie's face stiffened somewhat but she nodded acknowledgement of the comment and the order. 'I understand they've agreed to let the cameras into Westminster Abbey for the first time ever,' Annie said as she measured out the renewed drinks, 'and it's going to be shown all around the world.'

'How will that help *us*?' Dot had snatched a couple of moments to sit on one of the bar stools but she got up without complaint when another customer, antici-pating the bell, requested a final pint. 'That won't make much difference round here,' she went on. 'I don't see too many aerials going up in Weatherfield. How many folk do you know have got a television set?'

She had addressed Elsie Tanner but it was Annie Walker who answered. 'I would imagine they are trying to encourage people to go out and get one for the first time,' Annie said. 'After all, it will be for a very special occasion.'

'Who'll be able to afford that?' Elsie Tanner sounded scornful.

'Don't ask me,' Dot said. 'How much do you think one would cost?'

Annie laughed at that. 'I think the idea is to rent them, not to buy one,' she said. 'But I really couldn't say how much they are.'

'Well, it won't affect me and I don't see many folk around here being able to think of getting one either,' Dot said, dismissively.

'I believe it's the Duke of Edinburgh who's keen on having the event televised,' Annie said.

'Yes, I imagine it would be,' Mrs Tanner said disparagingly. 'It's all right for some. He's probably got a set in every room of the palace,' she added, not without sarcasm, and everybody who was at the counter laughed. 'But there's lots of women I know will be nagging their husbands to get one because they adore Prince Philip. They'll love the idea of being able to see him up close in their own living rooms.'

'Do you really think it could have that effect?' Dot sounded sceptical, but Elsie Tanner was positive. 'I know so,' she said.

'But most folk that I've talked to don't seem to be that interested in getting one,' Dot said as if that proved something.

'Not yet.' It was Jack Walker who joined in this time. 'But you just wait and see. I wouldn't be surprised if there wasn't a mad rush on them closer to the time.'

'I'd like to take bets on who'll be the first on this street to get one,' Dot said.

'You can count me in to put a tanner into the kitty on that one,' Elsie Tanner said with a broad grin, 'though sadly it won't be me getting a set. But I reckon whoever it is should invite the rest of the street in to watch with them and I'll be the first in the queue for one of those invitations.' She glared at Annie Walker, then carefully placing the three refilled glasses on a tray, she carried them over to the table in the corner where her friends were waiting for her.

When the last pint had been served after Annie had called time, Dot wiped her brow and kicked off her shoes. She didn't bother to replace them with slippers as she sometimes did but she watched with satisfaction as Annie Walker slipped the catch and slotted the chain across the double doors. 'From the crowds we've had in here today you'd have thought it was Christmas,' Dot said.

'People are still reacting to their new-found freedom,' Annie Walker said. 'They're making the most of being able to go out to enjoy themselves whenever they want.'

'And I reckon the excitement about the coronation is beginning to bite as well,' her husband added.

'I agree with you, Jack,' Annie said, 'and for once I agree with Mrs Sharples. The sooner we start planning the parties the longer we've got to look forward to them. It's been so long since we've had something to smile about or to get excited about that we need to make the most of it. I only hope their smiles last through till June.'

'I'm sure they will and beyond,' Dot said reassuringly. 'Once folk get involved and feel they are part of the event, then the excitement will be able to build and that will put everyone in a good mood.'

'People have had enough of moping about,' Annie said. 'They're only too glad to be able to get their lives going again. You just think back to how many years we've had of travel restrictions when there wasn't enough fuel to go anywhere, of blackouts and curfews that forced us to stay indoors, not to mention all the rationing that was in place for so many years,' Annie continued, 'and all the shortages.'

'Some of which still exist,' Jack added.

'I know,' Annie sighed. 'Not everything is smoothly back on tap yet, if you'll pardon the pun. Though we do have a lot to be thankful for.' She smiled as she patted the baton-like black handles of the beer taps. 'I still can't get all the cuts of meat I want, or a decent piece of liver.'

'I know I'll be pleased when sugar finally comes off ration,' Dot said. 'They say it should be before the end of the year and I can tell you that for me it won't be a day too soon. I'm dying to make some decent biscuits and cakes after all the rubbish substitutes we've had to put up with.'

'I'm glad to say that things are really beginning to shift on the roads again.' Jack came to join them as they washed up the remaining dirty glasses. 'At least cars are moving about freely now that petrol is no longer rationed, although it doesn't help that no one in the countryside at least has a clue about which direction they're going.' He chuckled. 'I think it's high time whoever's responsible for them should put the signposts back up, particularly in places like up on the moors. I know we can use headlights once again but that really doesn't help if you don't know which direction you're going.'

'I know which direction I'm going right now,' Dot said with a chuckle. 'If it's all the same to you, Mrs Walker, I could kill for a cup of tea.'

'Good idea, Dot! Why don't you make us a brew as I'm sure we could all do with one?' Annie hung the small hand towel over the taps and, with a satisfied smile, followed Dot into the small living room in the Walkers' private quarters.

'I can't stop thinking about the coronation now, after all our discussions, and I must say it really does cheer me up,' Annie said. 'I only hope the weather is good on the day, for if it isn't then it won't matter how long in advance you've been planning, it could all be washed out.'

'I reckon we have to be optimistic,' Dot said sitting down with a pleased sigh as she rested her feet on the footstool. 'But I'd like to think that after all the smog and the rain and the miserable below-freezing temperatures we've had this past winter that we can safely put all that behind us come June the second. I do think it will be fine,' she said. 'I have a feeling . . . well, I mean how bad could it be at that time of year? It will be practically full summer.'

'I suppose the worst I'm imagining is having to eat soggy sandwiches and over-moist cake,' Annie said and Dot chuckled.

'I'd have thought that was another reason to start planning early. Then you can give yourself plenty of time to build in contingency plans such as in the event of rain.' Jack came to join them having been in the cellar to change the beer barrels. Annie handed him a cup of tea.

'You do have a point,' Annie conceded, 'but then I've also been thinking beyond the level of sandwiches,' she said. 'More on the stage of entertainment that might follow on from the food. I know, for instance, there has been some talk of taking the Rovers' piano outside like we did for the VE day party,' Annie said.

'Yes,' Dot agreed. 'They were talking at the Mission about maybe persuading Elsie Lappin to give us a number or two,' Dot said.

'Were they indeed!' Annie responded immediately. 'I wouldn't have thought Elsie Lappin's repertoire was Mrs Sharples' cup of tea,' she said peering down her nose.

'All I can say is that I'm glad I'm not on one of the official organizing committees,' Dot said. 'Can you imagine the headaches they must have trying to put everything together. It must be a nightmare.'

'Well, it will all be worth it. I think Prin— *Queen* Elizabeth – my goodness, it's still hard to remember her new title – is going to make a wonderful queen and I'm glad she won't be changing her name,' Annie said. 'Long may she reign. Particularly as it's taken me a long time to remember to say Long Live the Queen, instead of King. I hope she will reign a lot longer than her poor father, or her Uncle David come to that. Albert changing his name to George and David changing his to Edward didn't help to keep either of them on the throne for long, did it?'

'No, and it was sad about George but it was Edward's choice to abdicate,' Dot said. 'He didn't give it much of a chance.'

'I wonder how Princess Margaret is feeling right now,' Annie said. 'She doesn't really get a look in, does she? And she has no choice in the matter.'

'Do you think she might be jealous?' Annie said.

'I don't know,' Dot said. 'I suppose she must be on one level, although the two sisters do seem to be very close.' Dot looked thoughtful as she added, 'I'm sure I would be jealous if our Carol had hogged all the limelight and I got nothing.'

'She'll no doubt have at least some beautiful new dresses to wear at the various parties and ceremonies and things.' Now Annie looked wistful.

'I'm sure she gets those all the time, together with glorious real jewellery to match, but it somehow doesn't quite compensate for not being able to wear a priceless crown covered in jewels, and her ermine-trimmed cloak won't have anything like the train her sister's will,' Dot said.

'At least she won't have to drag around the weight of a crown and train all day.' Annie was determined to see the bright side.

'But all eyes will be on Elizabeth for that whole day, let's face it, while poor Margaret won't even have a boyfriend on her arm,' Dot persisted.

The two lapsed into a thoughtful silence until Dot said innocently, 'Wouldn't you love to be able to see it live on the television, Mrs Walker? The procession, all those people inside the Abbey?' she added dreamily.

'Hmm,' was all Annie Walker said.

'Rather than having to wait till you can get to the pictures to see it on the Pathé newsreel?'

'Hmm,' Annie said again. 'We'll have to see.'

'Whoever is the first to get a TV set, do you think they'll invite the neighbours in as Mrs Tanner suggested?'

'No reason why not,' Annie said. 'People in this neighbourhood are usually very hospitable, but it will depend . . .'

'It would be very special to be the first ones with a TV,' Dot said, looking thoughtful.

'I think I might even have a new dress for the occasion,' Annie mused. 'It seems like a good excuse after all the years of make-do and mend. I'm delighted to have a good reason to dress up.'

'And what about decorations? Will you be putting those up in the bar?' Dot wanted to know.

'I certainly hope so. I believe some people have taken out their bunting already. Just thinking about it makes me feel very patriotic again and I will have to look up in the loft to see what might be reusable from our last street parties.'

'It does make you feel full of hope again, doesn't it?' Dot said.

'Yes, we've had enough years of pain and misery – this is a real new beginning.' Annie was beaming now.

'Perhaps we'd all look forward to a bright future if we had husbands as handsome as Prince Philip,' Dot said without thinking.

Annie bristled but Jack Walker seemed to take it in good spirit. 'Sorry to disappoint you, Dot,' he said, 'but we can't all be pin-up boys,' and Dot was relieved when they all laughed.

Chapter 6

Christine Hardman sat on the couch in the front room of number 13 Coronation Street and gazed out of the window that looked out onto the street without really seeing anything, as she often did now on rainy afternoons. She didn't bother attending school regularly any more because she would soon be celebrating her fifteenth birthday and she would be able to leave officially. She couldn't wait. But to please everyone, she attended intermittently and convinced herself that no one cared.

'I'm not learning anything so it's really not worth my while bothering to go any more,' she argued whenever either of her parents tackled her on the subject, and then she would attend for a few days.

'I doubt another few weeks will make any difference, especially when all they seem to be talking about is the coronation,' she would argue with her father.

'What's wrong with that?' her father said. 'It should be a real spectacle and a very exciting day.'

Christine shrugged. 'That's as maybe, but what we seem to be learning is about all these people who live in palaces and who have more money than they know what to do with.' She tried to sound more knowledgeable than she really was, but she did feel anger sometimes about the privilege of the royal family getting money for doing nothing as far as she was concerned. And she didn't know what all the fuss was about with regard to the queen's handsome husband who everyone was swooning about.

'Well, if you're not going to school any more then you'd best start looking for a job,' her mother said but Christine had responded immediately.

'No, I won't,' she said defiantly. 'You know very well that I'm not doing that yet.'

'She's saving herself so that she can come and work in my shop when I get it,' her father had said.

'And when's that likely to be?' May said scornfully, but Christine jumped in quickly and said, 'I've told you before that I want to go to secretarial college to become a shorthand typist,' she said. 'And you said I could.' She was disappointed that neither her mother nor father seemed to have remembered their earlier promise to let her go.

May Hardman made no further comment but Christine felt she would have more luck with her father and she took every opportunity to work on him, to remind him of his promise and to bring him round to her way of thinking that school was no longer necessary. That was why she had taken to waiting for him to come home from the bank where he had been offered his old job as a teller on his demobilization from the forces after the war. He was making a desperate attempt to save enough money so that one day he would be able to buy his own shop and, mindful of the need to be thrifty, he walked to and from work every day in all weathers. On miserable days like this Christine would rush to hang up his well-worn, though still stylish, mackintosh that she knew would be soaking wet when he arrived home.

'Is your father not home yet?' a voice called down from upstairs. 'I bet he didn't take an umbrella. He doesn't seem to care that he'll catch his death in this weather.'

'No, Mum, he's not here yet!' Christine shouted back.

'You'd best put the kettle on; we'll all need a cuppa by the time he does arrive,' May Hardman said, surprising Christine as she came into the parlour. 'And you shouldn't be sitting in here on such a day. Why don't you shift yourself into the living room, it's much warmer in there.' She stood for a moment staring at the rain that dripped down the windowpanes and pooled on the once-whitened sills as people outside hid under their umbrellas and splashed through the puddles on the pavement. She sighed. 'What a miserable-looking street this is,' she said. 'What your father sees in it I do not know. Did I ever tell you that when I was your age my bedroom at home looked out onto a beautiful rose garden?'

Christine rolled her eyes. 'Only about a million times,' she said under her breath and she quickly drew her legs out from under her and stretched. She went into the kitchen without another word where the embers of a small fire glowed in the grate. She was surprised her mother had bothered to get dressed at this hour; she didn't always, preferring to stop in bed for the rest of the day once it got close to teatime, saying, 'There's no need to get up now, who's going to call in at this hour?' She had never encouraged neighbouring. But today she had put on a pink Gor-Ray skirt topped by a cream twinset before she had come down the stairs. Christine thought her mother looked very pretty without her hairnet and curlers in and wished she would take the trouble to get up and to dress every day.

May followed Christine into the kitchen at the end of the hall, running her fingers along the banisters and hall table as she passed. 'Hm,' she said, inspecting her fingertips, 'At least the charwoman seems to have done a reasonable job for her money this morning. I thought I heard her sweeping down the stairs after your father had gone off to work and I'm glad I was right. I trust she left a shepherd's pie like I asked her to?'

'Yes, it's ready to go in the oven,' Christine said, 'but I'll not put it on to heat yet?'

'No, of course not.' May was disparaging. 'How many years have you been in charge of the tea and you still haven't learned how to do it properly?'

Christine shrugged. She was no more interested in cooking than her mother and had retained scant knowledge about anything connected to what had been called 'domestic science' at school.

'Maybe one day we might actually move from this dreadful place to somewhere with a proper modern electric cooker,' May said, 'and hot and cold running water in summer and winter. Your father's been promising for long enough.'

'He's doing his best to save up.' Christine immediately jumped to her father's defence. 'I'm sure we will move to a better part of Weatherfield one day.'

'Go on, stick up for him,' her mother scoffed, 'though I don't know why you do.' She raised her eyebrows. 'I don't know what he's done to deserve such loyalty from you.' She picked up a packet of

Park Drive filters from the mantelpiece and lit one, puffing out the smoke almost as soon as she took a breath in.

'Is that you smoking, May?' a man's voice broke the silence from the hallway.

'Daddy!' Christine rushed forward to put her arms round his neck as he entered the room and gave him a quick peck on his cheek.

George Hardman laughed when she insisted on giving him a hug as well. 'You'll get all wet,' George said, trying unsuccessfully to hold her at arm's length.

'I'll soon dry,' Christine said.

'Yes, but your father won't unless he gets out of that sodden coat immediately,' May said crossly. 'George! Why on earth didn't you take an umbrella? Look at all the rotten drips on the floor. Who's going to clean those up? Will you never learn?'

'What's it to you if I get pneumonia?' True to form George turned the tables on May as he glared at her accusingly and Christine felt her chest stiffen. This bitter squabbling was what she hated most and yet it was what her parents seemed to do most of the time. 'I'm sure you'll be able to find someone you can pay to come in and look after me.'

'And why would I want to pay out good money to get someone to look after you if you've not been careful enough to look after yourself?' she retorted.

'Then maybe *you* should do it, or how's about

getting your charlady in? She does just about every other job in this house.'

'Only when I'm available to supervise,' May snapped back. 'You know very well I don't trust you to—' She didn't complete the sentence. 'And with good reason.'

George shook his head, a sad expression on his face. 'That was a long time ago, woman. But you can't let it go, can you?'

'I don't care how long ago it was. Are you seriously trying to tell me that I should forgive and forget? After what you did?' May started to come back at him but she didn't elaborate. Nothing ever seemed to get finished in this house.

Christine closed her eyes. It was always the same; May provoking her husband with innuendo and half-completed sentences and him rising to the bait until they were both in full flow with Christine caught in the crossfire. It was as though her mother was holding on to some old grudge, some resentment from the past about which only she and her father knew the details. Christine had no idea what it was about and they never offered any kind of explanation.

Instead, the arguments went around and around until, fond as she was of her father, Christine would have done anything to escape; anything to get out of the house. She put her head in her hands. She felt trapped, lonely and miserable without any real friends to turn to, and caught in an endless miserable purgatory of her parents' making.

Chapter 7

Josie knew from the day that she started working in the corner shop that she had made a mistake. Much as she needed the money she should never have accepted the job and she was afraid that it was becoming increasingly obvious, even to Elsie, that her heart wasn't in it. She was sorry she had ever agreed to what had seemed at the time to be a generous offer and the perfect solution to her situation, but it was too late now to do anything about it. She had done her best to stall over making the decision, but the more she prevaricated, the more Elsie had been determined to keep her promise to Josie's mother, even if it meant pressurizing Josie into accepting, and overriding the wishes of her own daughters.

'I don't know why you think you need anyone to work with you in the shop when business is still so slow,' Hilda sniped and grumbled at every available opportunity.

'I don't agree. Things have really started to pick up again recently,' Elsie said, defending her actions. 'We're busier now than we have been at any time since the end of the war and I know neither of you are interested in helping out.'

'But it's not as though you're run off your feet.' Hilda refused to let go.

'No, but—' Elsie began until Shelagh cut across her.

'The problem is that I don't think Josie really likes working in the shop,' Shelagh said, and Josie was astonished. They had been speaking about her as though she wasn't there but now Shelagh turned and looked directly at her and Josie stared back. She could speak for herself but for once thought it best not to rise to the bait and so she said nothing.

'It's not just our shop, though, is it? I don't think you like working in *any* shop. Am I right?' Hilda stared at Josie as if challenging her to disagree. 'Goodness only knows what made you think you wanted to work in a place like Pauldens,' she said. 'It's no wonder you didn't last there more than five minutes,' Hilda sneered.

'I'm amazed that you said yes when Mum offered you the job.' Shelagh's tone was gentler and not unsympathetic as Josie looked from one sister to the other.

'Or did you accept just to spite us?' Hilda had to have the last word.

Josie could only stare at her angrily as she watched Hilda put a protective arm across her sister's shoulders. She didn't really see the point in trying to discuss the matter.

Josie was not normally one to sink into a depression or to let pessimistic thoughts crowd her thinking and she was determined that that wouldn't happen now, but she didn't know how best to respond to Hilda and Shelagh's onslaught without appearing to give in. She would not let them see how much their jibes niggled her. Her natural reaction to their taunts would have been to give as good as she got, but she didn't want to do that. Besides, there was something about the distressed look on Elsie's face that made her hold back. When she considered the possible consequences of losing her job at the corner shop, regardless of disliking it so much, she knew she had to hold her fiery temper in check and keep up a solid front against the sisters no matter how often they goaded or provoked her.

As she had promised, Elsie introduced Josie slowly to the daily tasks required to run the shop. Josie worked hard as she gradually became familiar with the merchandise and Elsie praised the way she made sure the shop was kept well-stocked from the ample supplies of the most popular lines that filled the storeroom at the back. The problem was that Shelagh was right. After her unfortunate experience at Pauldens, Josie was wary about serving the customers directly and she deliberately hung back whenever Elsie tried to show her other aspects of shopkeeping. However, as rationing gradually eased – to everyone's delight sweets and chocolates wouldn't be rationed from February – and a wider variety of goods became available, the shop became even busier. Business was reviving and it became more difficult for Josie to avoid such things as using the till.

'If we play our cards right things could get even better as we get closer to the coronation,' Elsie told Josie, rubbing her hands together at the thought. 'We're bound to get some big orders from the street party organizers.'

'Yes, I suppose you're right,' Josie agreed, trying not to let her face show how sick she felt at the thought of long queues of customers waiting to be served.

She was thinking about this one afternoon when she was on her own in the shop, Elsie having taken the opportunity of a quiet moment to go upstairs. The doorbell tinkled and a young man strode in. He had tousled blond hair and was wearing an oversized jacket with enormous pockets that seemed to be stuffed full. He glanced about the shop as if looking for someone, then he grinned at Josie in a familiar way. Josie frowned back at him.

'Can I help you?' she asked in the polite manner Elsie always insisted on, though her tone was abrupt.

He thrust a dull metal pail towards her. 'How's about a bucketful of water for starters?' he said. His manner was cheeky and his look bold, though when she didn't immediately take the bucket from him he dropped his hands back to his sides and was apologetic. 'Beg pardon, but I thought you lived here,' he said, looking contrite. 'I was sure I'd seen you here before.'

'Yes, I do live here,' Josie said.

He brightened. 'Then hello again! We must have met before.'

'Have we? Josie looked puzzled.

The young man extended his hand. 'Charlie Wright,' he said. 'Last time I saw you I was probably halfway up a ladder.'

Josie raised her brows.

'I've taken over my dad's window-cleaning round,' Charlie said. 'Well, for the time being at least as his chest has been playing up. Ring a bell now?'

'Oh, yes. Just about.'

Josie nodded slowly as she remembered when she'd seen him before. He was the lad Hilda had painted her lips for and then made sheep's eyes at while he was balancing precariously and stretching across to clean the upstairs windows.

Charlie laughed. 'It seems I didn't make much of an impression the first time around. But let me tell you, you made an impression on me. You were new here that time, though I didn't catch your name.'

Josie felt the heat rise from her neck to her face. 'That's probably because I didn't give it to you,' she said.

He nudged his elbow towards her across the counter then proffered the bucket once more. 'Are you going to tell me now? And I really would appreciate a bucket of water.'

She shrugged and told him. 'My name's Josie.'

'Pleased to meet you officially, Josie,' he said. 'As I say, my name's Charlie.' And he shook her hand more formally this time.

Josie took the pail and disappeared into the kitchen, wondering about Hilda's attraction to him. He didn't look to be anything special as far as she could see. She returned, slopping water onto the tiled floor. Charlie stepped forward and, taking a mop that had been propped up in the corner behind the counter, wiped up the spillage. Josie was aware that he was smiling at her as he handed it back but she refused to engage. 'Will there be anything else?' was all she said.

'Have you got any McVitie's digestives?' he said. 'It's a long time till teatime. Not sure I'll last out.'

She plucked a package from one of the shelves and handed it to him. He put some pennies into her palm and she deposited them in the till without checking while he tucked the biscuits into one of his capacious pockets.

As he grabbed hold of the full pail there was a sound on the stairs and Josie turned to see Elsie was coming down.

'Hello, Charlie,' she said with a smile. 'I'm surprised to see you again so soon. We can't keep you away. How's your dad?'

Charlie blushed to the roots of his hair and cleared his throat. And Josie was amused to see him look so uncomfortable. 'Oh, he's still too poorly to be able to come out working and he certainly doesn't want to be exposed to all weathers, Mrs L. Anyhow, I'm not actually here to do your windows. It's next door and across the street who are down for this week.'

'And they aren't in?' Elsie asked.

'I don't know, I haven't actually tried, yet.' He looked down at his feet. Then looking up again he gave her a dazzling smile. 'I could see that someone was in here so thought I'd stop and get a fill up here before I started on my round. Thanks for the water, Josie, I'll no doubt be seeing you again before long.' And he hoisted the pail off the counter and disappeared outside.

Chapter 8

Annie Walker allowed herself a smile when she heard the animated speculation continue to rage in the Rovers about who would be the first to hire a television set in time for the coronation, and she couldn't prevent a pinkness rising to her cheeks when she heard Mrs Sharples announce that she 'couldn't be mithered with such new-fangled things' so they wouldn't be getting one at the Mission. Annie, too, had already made her own decisions but she was not yet prepared to discuss them so that even Elsie Tanner from number 11, who was always happy to get a rise out of her Coronation Street neighbours, and had been doing her best to stir things in the bar, was for once unable to provoke a reaction from the landlady at the Rovers.

Annie, however, confident that no one would be able to scupper her plans, had decided that it would be fitting for the honour to fall to the Rovers and she determined that she and Jack would spring a last-minute surprise on their friends and neighbours. She was already picturing the local residents clustering about the first television set on the street that would be newly installed in the Rovers' back room that they would do up specially. She had also decided that the occasion would definitely merit the purchase of a new fashionable outfit that she would have made specially, and one for her daughter Joanie, too, luxury she hadn't indulged in since before the war. She intended to present her plans to her husband as a *fait accompli* and she smiled to herself just thinking about it. Her only misgivings about allowing something as decadent as a television set into the house concerned the more pressing matter that had been occupying her thoughts recently. It was regarding the wayward behaviour of their son Billy that she and Jack had been trying to pass off as merely high spirits, and she did stop to wonder if they would be doing the right thing.

Annie actually raised the matter of the television that afternoon when she and Jack were shutting up the pub after what had been a comparatively quiet dinnertime session. Annie had been distracted, mostly thinking about the amount of space that would be required in order to accommodate the particular model she had already marked out in Radio Rentals' window. The television itself was set inside a large wooden cabinet that made it look like a cocktail cabinet once the screen was covered by two rollaway doors. She had been trying to work out how they might position it so that everyone could have an unrestricted view but felt she might let Jack worry about that later, once it was in position.

When she finally broached the subject, suggesting that they might be the first in the street to own such a piece of advanced technology, Annie was taken aback when Jack laughed. 'I'm not daft,' he chuckled. 'How many years have we been married? I know what's been going on in that pretty little head of yours and I know you're dying for us to be the first in the street to get a television.'

'And what's wrong with that?' Annie demanded indignantly. 'There's nothing wrong with being forward-thinking is there?'

'Nothing at all, my love. Truth be told, I've been thinking along the same lines myself,' Jack said.

Annie's face was wreathed in smiles as she pictured herself graciously receiving everyone who came to watch, as if she were the Queen herself, and was personally responsible for producing the whole show. 'Just imagine,' she said, 'if we attracted lots of new customers? Then it would be to our advantage to have an aerial fixed permanently onto the roof for I'm sure such BBC broadcasts won't be restricted to coronations.'

Jack agreed, and he smiled too as his vision stretched far into the future. 'I think television is here to stay and there'll be no harm in us being ahead of the game,' he said as he led the way through to their living quarters.

'I'm going to make us a quick sandwich for lunch,' Annie said as she dipped into the bread bin to retrieve a small Hovis, 'and then maybe we'll have time to slip out to the shopping parade. We can check in the Radio Rentals electricals shop.' As she produced several slices of cheddar cheese that she'd bought at the corner shop that morning, she smiled with satisfaction.

Jack took a bite of his sandwich at the same moment as the back-door bell rang and Annie looked up, irritated. 'Who could that be at this hour?' She frowned.

Jack looked at his watch. 'It's most likely the postman,' he suggested. 'We haven't had the second post yet, have we?'

Annie shook her head. 'Only an electricity bill first thing this morning.' She half rose but Jack got there first.

'You sit down, love. I'll go and see who wants us,' and he came back with a long white envelope, frowning as he scratched his head.

'I had to sign for it,' he said. Annie stared at him and when he turned the envelope over the colour drained from her face. She struggled to maintain a neutral expression but she couldn't help feeling as though her stomach had flipped through a series of double somersaults when she instantly recognized the school crest on the other side as Jack adjusted his glasses then slit open the envelope and pulled out a single sheet of expensive-looking vellum. 'It's from our Billy's school,' he said unnecessarily, 'from the headmaster.' His voice was sober and serious as he sat down at the kitchen table and pushed his plate aside. Annie put down her sandwich, no longer feeling hungry. She didn't need to read the name on the flap of the envelope. She knew without seeing them that the words: Mr Donald Henderson, Mrs Dudley Henderson Private Academy were printed in dark blue embossed lettering on the other side.

Billy's boarding school was a subject Annie and Jack had managed to avoid referring to since the end of the Christmas holidays when they had spoken severely to Billy before he had, much to their relief, gone back to school. There had been warning phone calls the previous term when the headmaster had made it quite clear that he would be carefully monitoring their son's behaviour as he was not prepared to tolerate any further high jinks and Annie had been relieved that things seemed to have settled down. But now she looked at the letter with dread. Was this the end of the road for their Billy? Annie watched with great trepidation as, to her horror, Jack's face paled and he seemed to be reading and rereading the short lines of the note. Her stomach tightened. 'What does it say?' Her voice was almost a whisper as she did her best not to show her fear. 'What does he say Billy's done this time?'

'Well, that's it, he doesn't exactly say,' Jack said uncertainly. 'He just says that he'd be obliged if we could come to the school at our earliest convenience to fetch our Billy home.'

Chapter 9

Charlie had thought about Josie all the way home after his last visit to the corner shop and he'd smiled each time he'd closed his hand around the packet of chocolate biscuits in his pocket. If they melted he had no one to blame but himself, but wouldn't that provide him with a wonderful excuse to go back to the shop at least one more time? It was proving to be quite a challenge to have to think up a different excuse each time. It's a pity I'm not drawn to Hilda, he thought, for she seems more than willing to make herself available. But he was only interested in Josie, and she was proving to be frustratingly elusive.

He closed his eyes for a moment and had to pause as he almost slipped off the edge of the kerb.

It's a funny thing about women, he thought, how one with easy access, like Hilda Foyle, who tries so hard to please is not the one I'm drawn to. Whereas it was Josie Bradshaw he couldn't stop thinking about, the one who had made a huge impression without really trying. He was fed up with Hilda's constant flirting and she wore too much make-up and always seemed to be batting her eyelashes at him, or trying to engage him in meaningless conversation. Josie, on the other hand, had a natural beauty and just the hint of a smile that could engage him instantly.

In fact, he realized, Josie filled his thoughts in a way no one ever had before and it was a constant challenge for him to invent possible, meaningful excuses so that he might be able to see her again. Sometimes he felt desperate, like the time when he'd found himself standing outside the corner shop hoping he might catch a glimpse of her and knowing that in order to do that he would eventually have to go inside. He could see that she was already serving a customer and if he had hoped to get a positive reaction from her then he was to be disappointed. When he became aware that she had caught sight of him wavering in the doorway he felt obliged to go in, even though he felt unusually unsure of himself as he entered the shop.

'I can see you're busy, and I'm happy to wait,' he said quickly, before she could say anything. 'And there's no water needed today, thanks. I was in the neighbourhood and I thought I'd take the opportunity to get some more of my favourite biscuits.' The excuse sounded stupid, the words stilted and lame even to him but they were out of his mouth before he could stop them.

'I'll be with you as soon as I've finished here,' Josie said, and she handed the customer a fistful of change. The woman looked at it suspiciously as she scrutinized it.

'That's not right!' the customer snapped looking again at the money in her hand. 'You've overcharged me. I might be new to this area but I wasn't born yesterday, you know.' She sounded extremely irritated and actually snatched at the extra half-crown that Josie was about to add, holding it uncertainly between her fingers.

'That is mine, young lady,' the woman said, 'and don't you try to tell me otherwise. I already told you that I don't want those and yet you're trying to make me pay for them.' The woman pushed several tins of fish back across the counter. 'I do believe you're trying to cheat me.'

Charlie was astonished by the woman's accusatory tone and was even more surprised that Josie looked so uncertain. She didn't automatically try to defend herself and she didn't dismiss the woman's charge out of hand. On the contrary, he was surprised to see that Josie didn't seem to know what to say in response to the accusation, even though it seemed totally unjustified, and he wondered if he should intervene.

'I'm sure no one was trying to cheat you.' The words fell from his mouth easily and he only hoped from the look that flashed across Josie's face that he had not misread the situation and said the wrong thing, for she had in her eyes the betrayed look of being 'found out'. He glanced from the customer back to Josie, wondering if there was something he had missed, something else he should have known before boldly taking the liberty to intervene? But nothing more was said. Josie stood there uncertainly looking as if she would happily have run from the shop at that moment, while the woman quickly piled the remaining items into her shopping bag and swept out of the shop without another word, leaving Charlie to apologize to Josie for interfering. Josie said nothing and Charlie was watching as she put away the tins of mackerel and saithe the woman had left behind when a small but brightly coloured poster caught his eye and he turned away, relieved to be distracted. The leaflet was advertising a dance that was to be held at Weatherfield's Country Barn in a few days' time and he heaved a sigh of relief at what he felt he could turn into the perfect excuse!

'Thanks for your help,' Josie said before Charlie had time to speak. 'I really wasn't sure what to do with her, she seemed determined to cause trouble before you actually arrived on the scene and I was pleased when she left without a fuss.'

'Glad to be of service,' Charlie said, with a slight bow. 'You don't need customers like that, although that wasn't the reason I came in of course. There was actually another reason . . .' He glanced about the shop but his gaze was drawn once more to the small poster until he finally succeeded in making eye contact, if only briefly. Determined to make the most of having her undivided attention he took the opportunity and ploughed on. 'I came to ask if you would like to—'

He was distracted by the tinkling of the shop bell and he could see that Josie too had looked away towards the door as Hilda came tripping in.

'Why Charlie!' Hilda cried, 'How lovely to see you. I didn't think it was our day for window cleaning today. "If I knew you were coming I'd have baked a cake," as the old song goes.' Then she giggled.

'You don't have to worry, it isn't your day,' Charlie said, 'I was just . . .' He didn't finish as he noticed Josie had put a packet of McVitie's biscuits onto the counter and he fumbled in his pocket and produced some loose change. Then he touched his fingers to his forehead in a mock salute and, with a wave to Josie, ran from the shop.

Chapter 10

Annie Walker was not often intimidated, but when she walked into the vestibule of the Mrs Dudley Henderson Private Academy, Weatherfield's prestigious boys' school, she remembered the sense of awe she had felt when she had first walked in through the high-arched portals, and she recaptured that same sensation now. She had been certain at first that this would be the best school for her son Billy, for she honestly believed that it would make him more refined and studious, not to say well-behaved. At the time she'd considered that he had wasted far too much time at Bessie Street Seniors where he had been constantly fighting and allowed to run wild, his sister Joanie was a different child entirely and seemed settled there – but when he had been asked to leave she told everyone who would listen that they had never known how to handle his unique combination of intellect and acumen that resulted in his own style of behaviour.

There was a feeling of austerity and authority about Henderson's that she had hoped might help to calm Billy down, something the teachers in his old school had never got the knack of. Annie looked across at her husband and wondered if he really was as calm as he appeared to be – after the sudden rush and flurry that followed the opening of the envelope it had taken her some time to come to herself. Then, when she had read the letter, Annie had set her face into a fixed smile, determined not to show weakness, called ahead to make an appointment with the headmaster, and they had set off to Cloister Street leaving instructions for Dot to see to things in the Rovers in the event that they were not back in time for opening.

The school entranceway was dark and forbidding as they stepped inside and Annie took several deep breaths to steady herself. She looked down the hall to where the Victorian tiled corridor gave way to a well-worn parquet floor and she was struck once more by the strong smell of lavender polish that had hit her when they had first entered the building as it clung to the banisters and stairs. A sharp bell broke the silence and hordes of young boys suddenly began rushing back and forth, their shrieks and laughter filling the corridor despite the bodyless voices that shouted over them to 'stop running, boy!'

'Mr Henderson will see you now. Please go straight in,' the young lady in the reception office said haughtily and she ushered them through the door behind her that led into the headmaster's office.

'Thank you, Miss Hillingdon,' the headmaster said. 'Please send for William Walker and have him wait out here; we shall be ready for him shortly,' he said, his voice smoothly authoritative.

Annie felt her chest tighten when he pronounced Billy's name so formally. No one ever called him William, not even Annie when she was cross with him. Miss Hillingdon nodded and left. Mr Henderson indicated they should sit on the two upright chairs that had been set out on the opposite side of his large oak desk.

'Thank you for seeing us, Mr Henderson, we wanted a chance for a chat as there seems to have been a spot of trouble with Billy, judging by your letter.' Annie was surprised to hear Jack speak up before he'd even sat down.

'Indeed, there has Mr Walker,' the headmaster said, 'and as I advised you during our previous telephone conversations, there has been plenty of warning that the situation couldn't continue.'

'What seems to be the problem?' Jack asked.

'The problem is pretty much the same as last time, and the time before that, and, indeed, the time before that. Mr and Mrs Walker, I am afraid that we must now acknowledge that your son is not really suited to this school. I feel that he would be better served completing his education elsewhere.'

Annie gasped and even Jack sat back in his chair looking as though he had been badly winded.

'We normally prefer to deal with problems in-house as it were,' Mr Henderson went on, 'and we devise the punishment and deal with each case on its own merits.' He paused, his gaze drifting to where a thick cane was hanging on the back of the door. 'But on this occasion we have been forced to make an exception and believe that there could be no further castigation as we feel we have already done everything we can.'

Jack leaned forwards as if he was about to object but the headmaster held up his hand to stop him speaking. 'Despite repeated warnings, all our admonishments have been ignored, and the offences have just been repeated many times over,' Mr Henderson said. 'Until finally we have been forced to take sterner measures. I'm sure you understand.'

'And just what are these offences?' Jack asked.

'In the first instance it was mainly fighting, boys in the same class fighting among themselves. Nasty but containable as we have discussed before.' He made a face as if he was sucking lemons. 'But then came the stealing.'

Jack's brow furrowed. 'Nicking what exactly?'

'Sweets, cakes, items from other boys' tuckboxes, at a time of rationing and short supply when all such items brought from home were of special value.'

Jack's face relaxed at that and he sat back in the uncomfortable chair as if preparing to contest the accusation. But Mr Henderson hadn't finished.

'Since we last spoke some rather more valuable items have been taken and you won't be surprised to learn that we take a dim view of any kind of theft, Mr Walker, particularly as it now seems to be escalating into something more serious.' He hesitated but not long enough for Jack to intervene, then said, 'But the final straw and what we cannot – and will not – tolerate at Henderson's is the gang that your son has been organizing and encouraging. He and some of his class-mates have been picking on boys much younger – and always smaller – than themselves, and are constantly bullying and terrorizing them. I personally have been called upon to break up several fights in the playground and, more recently, in the classroom.' He stopped and preened, running his fingers up and down his lapels as if he were boasting of this feat. 'Believe me, I have given William warning after warning on many occasions, but he has continued to ignore them.'

Annie couldn't believe what she was hearing. Her Billy? Stealing? Bullying? She felt she shouldn't be forced to listen to him being maligned in such a way when he wasn't here to defend himself. She knew the headmaster had telephoned to complain about his behaviour in the past but she had always dismissed his complaints as petty and not justified and she couldn't let him go on now; she had to speak up. 'What about the other boys in these so-called gangs?' she said.

'Rest assured they are being dealt with, but there is no question that William is the ringleader. And as it is not the first time, I'm afraid I have no choice but to let him go.'

'You're not saying that's it?' Annie was shocked. 'I feel that you have misunderstood our son; he just needs more time to settle in and I'm sure if you gave us the opportunity to talk to him . . . No, I insist you must give him another chance,' she said, trying to maintain the air of authority she had worked so hard to achieve.

'I think the time has gone for all that, Mrs Walker,' Mr Henderson cut across her. 'I'm afraid William has had second and even third and fourth chances and now he has gone past the point of no return. He's been warned on so many occasions, and each time the consequences have been clearly laid out but he has chosen to ignore them. I honestly think that he will be far better served finishing his education at another school.'

Annie sat up now and saw that Jack had done the same. She tried to give a little laugh. 'But surely boys will be boys,' she said, struggling to keep her voice steady.

'Indeed they will, but I'm afraid that is no excuse for the shocking behaviour William has been displaying recently.'

Now Jack attempted a light laugh. 'But isn't dismissal a bit harsh for what, after all, is nothing more than high spirits?'

'I regret I cannot agree with you, sir,' the headmaster said. 'That's how these things begin – and they usually end in tragedy.'

Annie could hardly believe what the headmaster was saying.

'But this is his school,' she said at last. 'Where is he supposed to go next term? He's not yet fifteen.'

'That, I'm afraid, is not my concern, Mrs Walker,' Mr Henderson said. 'Perhaps he could attend Bessie Street Seniors?' He checked the file. 'Which is where I believe he came from.'

'But surely—' Annie was not ready to give in yet.

'Is there some arrangement we can come to?' Jack Walker suggested. 'A donation to the school funds, perhaps?'

'His punishment is not negotiable, Mr Walker,' he snapped. 'I'm sorry, but that's my final word on the matter.'

Annie's face fell into disordered chaos as she tried her best to hold on to her feelings.

At that moment there was a knock on the door and Miss Hillingdon looked into the office. 'William is here, Mr Henderson.'

'Thank you, we are ready for him,' he said. 'I have nothing more to say.' He turned to face Jack, then he came round to the front from the other side of his desk as Billy entered the room. Annie could see her son's mouth was twitching in a manner she recognized, as if he was uncertain whether to bluff it out or to laugh.

'I believe you're to come home with us,' was all Annie said and Billy shrugged, a defiant look on his face.

'Aye,' Jack agreed. 'As I believe there's nothing more to talk about here, we can say what needs to be said at home,' he added sternly, though his shoulders slumped as he stood up.

'I hope your father can drill more sense into you than I've been able to do, lad, but I sincerely wish you every success in your future life,' Mr Henderson said, sounding anything but sincere, and Jack Walker pushed his son forward and out through the door.

By the time they arrived back at the Rovers Jack had recovered sufficiently to speak sharply to his recalcitrant son and before Billy could say anything Jack said, 'You will spend the rest of the day in your room, young man. You have a lot to talk about with your mother and me but not immediately. We all need time to calm down.'

As Annie watched her son slouch off to his room above the pub, she wrung a handkerchief in her hands. 'Our poor Billy. Why has he always been so dreadfully misunderstood?'

Jack looked as if he was about to say something, before setting his mouth in a hard line and instead went towards the cellar to begin the bottling up for the evening's trade, all the while muttering something that Annie couldn't quite hear.

Chapter 11

Elsie Lappin didn't often have a great deal of time for socializing but on the odd occasion that she did go out for the evening she usually enjoyed going to the Rovers.

'It's not far to walk and as I know so many people there it gives me a chance to catch up with the local gossip,' she confided to Josie. 'People in a pub are happy to open up to their neighbours in a way that they never are when they meet in a shop.' And when she walked into the Rovers she was gratified to be greeted by a chorus of, 'Hello!' 'Where have you been hiding?' and, 'Not seen you in here for a long time!' from most of the regulars.

'Well, Elsie Lappin, you've chosen a right good night to pitch up,' was Ena Sharples' welcoming comment.

'Why's that then?' Elsie asked innocently. 'Has something exciting happened?'

'You could say that, though not everyone will agree with you about how exciting it is,' Mrs Sharples said. 'Let's just say that there could well be some fireworks before the end of the evening.'

'How do you mean?' Elsie asked but Ena had already turned away.

'There's been all sorts of rumours flying about.' It was Minnie Caldwell who whispered a reply. 'I'm surprised you haven't heard about them in the shop,' and Elsie watched with interest as everyone seemed to move in closer to the counter when Annie Walker made her entrance and took up her usual position behind the bar. She set her fixed smile in position, although her lips were edged by a disdainful twist as if she was waiting for the inevitable gossip to begin.

Elsie had hardly had time to acknowledge her thanks to Albert Tatlock for the port and lemon he had kindly sent over with his compliments than Ena Sharples' voice could be heard rising above the buzz that was now emanating from the bar.

'Sorry to hear about your Billy,' she said, and Elsie was struck by the momentary silence that followed as everyone close to the bar seemed to lean forwards to eagerly await Mrs Walker's response. They didn't have to wait long.

'Why, thank you, Mrs Sharples,' Annie turned her smile to full beam. 'It is indeed unfortunate that, after all our careful research, even such a prestigious school as Mrs Dudley Henderson Private Academy for Boys is not able to accommodate him.'

'Not good enough for him? Is that right? Is that what you're saying?' Ena asked.

'I am indeed. Unfortunately, we find that they are not able to supply the standard of education that they promised when we first picked it out as the best place for Billy, and it had come so highly recommended.'

'I see,' Mrs Sharples said, taking a sip from her glass of milk stout. 'Then I must have got it wrong. I heard he'd been expelled.'

There was a sharp intake of breath from several of the other customers but Annie dismissed the idea with her short, affected laugh and a withering look. 'Mrs Sharples, I do wonder sometimes where you get your information from to start such nasty rumours. You really should check the facts before spreading malicious gossip.' With that, Mrs Walker turned her back and went into the kitchen area where she began to wash a rack full of glasses, leaving the barmaid Dot to deal with the customers who were clamouring at the bar.

'She can deny it all she likes,' Mrs Sharples said as soon as Annie had gone. 'That boy of hers is a menace and I'm telling you he was expelled as anyone would be if they were caught stealing.' Now there were audible gasps from the group that had gravitated towards her.

'No, that can't be true,' Martha Longhurst said, her eyes widening.

'It's as true as I'm sitting here,' Mrs Sharples said.

'I don't doubt Mrs Sharples' word.' Minnie Caldwell spoke up now. 'I hear the stories about what some of the kids at Bessie Street Seniors get up to. Seems to me it doesn't matter which school they go to, their behaviour is the same and some of it is truly shocking. Honestly, you do wonder about the kids of today.

'The only thing that saves the boys is conscription. At least they don't have too long to wait between leaving school and going into the army,' Albert Tatlock said. 'That forces them to shape up. Conscription's been a godsend for some of them.'

'But that doesn't help the girls. Too many of them are at a loose end with too much time on their hands. All they can think of to do is to get into mischief. It's no wonder so many of them are no better than they should be,' Martha Longhurst said. 'They leave school without any prospects of ever getting a decent job and if there's not enough young men to go round for them to marry . . .' She shrugged hopelessly.

'It's not like during the war when there were a lot of good jobs available. It's a shame that most women had to give up those jobs when their men came back,' Minnie said.

Elsie Lappin shook her head. 'It's true,' she agreed. I've seen many a young lass wandering the streets. Do you know, only the other day I saw Christine Hardman wandering about like the lost soul that she is. When I asked her what she was up to she said, bold as brass, that she doesn't need to go to school all the time and as she would soon be leaving anyway, she only drops in when she feels like it; but I wasn't sure I believed her.'

'I've seen her wandering about before now,' Martha Longhurst agreed, 'and I must say she does look rather sad and lost. They're a pathetic family if you ask me.'

'I believe they're going to move to the other end of Weatherfield as soon as her father can get enough money together to open his own shop,' Minnie Caldwell said.

Mrs Sharples made a grunting sound but said nothing.

'It's just a pity that her mother doesn't set her a better example,' Elsie said, 'but as far as I can see,

May Harding spends most of her days lying in bed, not looking like she wants to go anywhere.'

'It's a shame for the lass, but I believe that family has never been the same since the war,' Minnie Caldwell added.

'Who has?' Elsie said.

'No, I mean they've *really* changed,' Minnie insisted.

'Who knows what goes on behind closed doors,' Ena Sharples said, mysteriously, and when everyone looked at her she turned away to stare into space, her own eyes widening and her jaw clenching as if she hadn't spoken.

Only Martha Longhurst responded. 'Why? Did something happen that we should know about?' she asked. 'What really went on in this place? Sounds like it was more exciting than we've ever given it credit for.'

'Did something really happen there? More than we've been told before?' Minnie asked in disbelief and everyone turned to look at Ena Sharples. But for once her mouth remained firmly shut as she got up to order another bottle from the bar.

'I thought everyone knew that Madge, May Harding's sister, died on the night the viaduct was bombed and the factory wall fell on her. May never really got over it,' Minnie said.

'Aye, but some say there were more to it, only no one knows the whole story,' Mrs Caldwell said.

'Or if they do know it they're not saying,' Albert Tatlock chipped in. 'I was an air warden on air raid duty at the time and even I never got to know exactly what happened.' He shook his head, then took a deep swig from his pint. 'But as you can imagine it shook the Hardman family up.'

'That's the first I've heard of there being a big mystery,' Minnie said. 'I thought all the secrets in this street had already been told.'

'May this then be the last.' Ena Sharples spoke for the first time and everyone looked in her direction in surprise. Martha had the good grace to look uncomfortable and the conversation was brought to an abrupt halt.

Chapter 12

Christine lay in bed and tried pulling the blanket over her ears but it was too thin and had no effect. She wished that the walls in the houses on the street were not so thin for she could hear their angry voices. Christine could never block out her parents' rows entirely, but she couldn't hear enough of the details to make out their words so that she never did hear what their deep-seated resentments were about, although she was convinced that they always argued about the same things.

This morning, however, she was aware that for some reason they were quarrelling about her. They seemed to be disagreeing over her future and from the words she did catch she felt nothing but despair.

She had been hoping for independence for a long time and her parents had always promised her that when she left school she could go to college to learn shorthand and typing so that she could become a properly qualified secretary. That way she would be able to get a good job, move away, live her own life, but now it looked as if that fundamental freedom might be in jeopardy.

'You can't cheat her out of her future like you did to me. She should at least have the chances I never got,' were words Christine had heard before, even if she didn't know what they were referring to, and when she heard them again today she held her breath, hoping her father's reply might help her to understand. She couldn't make it out completely, but she heard enough to gather that now that her father's dream of opening his own shop seemed to be coming closer he had changed his mind about paying for her to go to college. It sounded as if he was prepared to break his promise and instead would expect her to work in the new shop that he was saving so hard to buy.

'Typical! I should have known I couldn't trust you to keep your word about *anything*.' Her mother's voice suddenly sounded closer and Christine assumed she had crossed the room to retrieve her candlewick dressing gown that hung on the back of the bedroom door. 'Promises obviously mean nothing to you as you've proved time and time again. So long as you get your own way and do whatever it is that you want, you don't give a damn about anyone else and their dreams.' Some of her words dropped away but it was still easy to hear that her voice was sounding tearful now. 'I suppose I've known for a long time, haven't I, that you have no feelings for me, but I did hope that you wouldn't betray your daughter.'

What did she mean? Christine wondered; she never did understand what the accusations referred to when her parents traded insults like they were doing now. She tried not to listen but she couldn't switch off the angry tones even if she covered her ears.

'I'll leave you to tell her,' she heard next as the bedroom door opened and Christine pulled the blanket tighter round her head, pretending she was asleep in case her mother should look in before she went downstairs. She heard the door being pulled open and her mother's words became clearer at last. 'You certainly don't deserve that I should do your dirty work for you.'

'Don't worry, I don't expect you to,' her father said.

'Well, I'm warning you, she'll be very disappointed and quite rightly so,' May Hardman said, and Christine was surprised. That was the first time she ever remembered hearing her mother sticking up for her.

Chapter 13

Christine wasn't used to hearing wolf whistles and when the sharp piercing sounds finally penetrated her consciousness it took a few moments for her to realize that they were directed at her. When they came again they were followed by a shout of, 'Hey you! Don't I know you?' and she looked up to see a young lad of her own age leaning out of the sash window that was above the sign for Newton and Ridley's Rovers Return. Billy Walker! Of course she knew him! Who didn't in this neighbourhood? She stopped for a minute and gazed up at him, taking in his youthful good looks. It was strange, but in a way she'd never really observed him before. He had a certain naïveté about him, a pleasant face with wide, innocent-looking eyes and a cowlick of mousey-coloured hair that covered a large section of his forehead. He seemed to be deliberately trying to make contact with her, eyes to eyes, before he took a deep draw from the cigarette that had been dangling, consciously, from his lips the way he'd seen actors do in films.

'You're Christine, aren't you?' He asked before exhaling a long thin stream of smoke.

She nodded. 'And you're Billy,' she called up, 'everyone knows you.'

'Why aren't you at school?' he said.

'I'm all but finished with school, though my mother doesn't know it yet. She thinks I still go there every day and that I'll keep going back to see it out. There's not long left but she's determined to drag out every last miserable minute of it,' she said.

'And what do you think about that?'

'I think there's nothing left that they can teach me so I'm not prepared to go every day, but I'm willing to look in occasionally to keep my name on the register if it makes them feel better.'

'Me too, except that I can't go back to the school I was at. I've just been expelled from the Mrs Dudley Henderson la-di-da, far-too-posh-for-its-own-good Private Academy for Boys.' Billy's manner was boastful as he put on a posh accent, and he pronounced the word 'expelled' as though it was a badge of honour. 'The headmaster suggested I should finish my education at Bessie Street Seniors where me little sister Joanie goes n'all, and that's what my mum and dad think I'm doing as they begged them to take me back – I was expelled from there, too!' Now he laughed. 'But you know what he can do with that suggestion?' he said, his bawdy manner covering over any hint of humiliation.

Christine laughed. 'I went this morning but thank goodness we've finished for the day.' She didn't know whether to be impressed by Billy's seeming self-confidence or horrified at his choice of language and she gave a nervous giggle.

At that Billy made a show of looking at the fancy watch he had strapped to his wrist. 'I tell you what,' he said, 'as school is finished for today, why don't you come up here and listen to my records? If you come round the alley I can let you in. The pub will be opening shortly and no one will notice. They'll all be too busy guzzling at the bar. And perhaps I could sneak us both a drink later.'

'How do I get in from the alley without being seen?' Christine asked.

'That's easy,' he said. 'Come round the back and you'll see a double gate. If you slip your hand through the bars you can open it from the inside. Come in past the pub's lavvie and I can let you in through the back door.'

'Oh, yeah? And then what?' Christine sounded doubtful. She did know Billy's reputation in the neighbourhood and she was unsure what she might be letting herself in for. But she was definitely tempted. Always willing for a dare.

'Then I'll let you listen to my Dansette record player.'

'In your bedroom?'

'What's wrong with that?' he asked indignantly. 'You're not a prude, are you? I've got some great records.'

'Who've you got?' Christine stalled for time, wondering if she dared.

'Frank Sinatra, Jonnie Ray . . .' he began.

'Nah!' she shrugged her shoulders. 'Haven't you got any Doris Day? She's great.'

'If you come up you'll find out exactly what I've got,' he said, a teasing note creeping into his voice. 'Watch out!' he suddenly warned her. 'There're people coming up the street, I'd better go. Don't want anyone telling tales to my mum, now, do I? See you in a mo.' He flicked the tail end of his cigarette down onto the pavement, narrowly missing the brim of Christine's hat, and slamming the window shut he disappeared from view.

Christine slipped down the end of the street and up the back alley as Billy had instructed. She carefully avoided stepping into an allotment-sized patch of cultivated vegetables as she entered what looked like the remains of a victory garden. As she raised her fist to knock timidly on the back door she could feel her heart pounding. She didn't know what she would say if anyone other than Billy answered it, but to her relief he was the one standing on the doormat. He put his finger to his lips and hustled her inside quickly.

She could hear the dull hubbub of conversation broken by the occasional whoop of laughter. It was coming from the bar on the other side of the thick velvet curtain that separated off the Walkers' living quarters. Billy walked on tiptoe and he beckoned for her to follow him up the stairs.

Christine felt awkward at first, worrying what her parents would say if they knew she had accepted an invitation into Billy Walker's bedroom; or worse still, what *his* parents would say if they knew she was here. Folk always said that you didn't want to cross Annie Walker. But there was something about Billy's bad-boy status in the local community that rooted her to the spot and sent a tingle down her spine.

'In case you're wondering, you can chuck your coat on the bed,' Billy said, busying himself with the record player that was on the floor surrounded by several piles of single and EP vinyl records. Christine looked uncertainly at the unmade bed until

Billy grabbed her coat and tossed it on top of the tangle of sheets and blankets. 'Don't worry, my mother knows better than to come in when I'm up here,' he said, although Christine worried that his bragging suggested false bravado and that Annie Walker might just descend at any moment.

She was still thinking about this when, without warning, Frank Sinatra's voice drifted out and she felt as if he was actually in the room with them. Billy reached across and turned down the volume.

'Don't want to give any Nosey Parkers an excuse to complain about the noise, do we? Especially me little sister, Joanie, she'll dob me in if she comes back from school and finds us here,' he said, and as he spoke he pulled a pack of Peter Stuyvesant cigarettes out of his breast pocket and offered her one.

'I don't smoke.' Christine shook her head as she pushed his hand away.

'Then it's high time you did,' Billy said with a laugh. He took two cigarettes from the pack with a practised hand while at the same time his other hand pulled a lighter from his trouser pocket. He lit both of the long, slim smokes, inhaling deeply, and handed one to her. Christine giggled. It was something she had seen film stars do in the cinema. She watched Billy take a draw and exhale Humphrey Bogart style. She did her best to match him with a

Lauren Bacall imitation, but that didn't stop it resulting in a fit of coughing.

Billy laughed. 'Don't worry,' he said, 'it happens to everyone at the beginning, you'll soon get the hang of it,' but Christine wasn't sure she wanted to get used to the dustbin-like taste that had filled her mouth.

'Who's your favourite singer?' she asked when she finally managed to stop spluttering.

'Nat King Cole. Hands down,' he said. 'Beats Doris Day any day of the week.'

Christine opened her mouth to contradict him but got caught up in another bout of coughing. Billy patted the small space that was left on the floor beside him and Christine gingerly sat down amid the piles of clothes, shoes and magazines that had slipped off the ottoman at the foot of the bed and she bent her knees up towards her face.

Billy laughed. 'What wouldn't I give to see my mum's face! She'd go mad if she could see us right now. She doesn't even like the cleaner seeing what she calls "your mess", never mind our next-door neighbour.'

'You won't tell her I've been here, will you?' For a moment Christine was genuinely scared. 'I don't want her telling my mum.'

'Don't worry, I shan't be saying a word to her, though it kills me to pass up a chance to wind up

Lady Walker!' And Billy pulled a snooty-style face that made Christine giggle.

The song seemed to have finished but Billy made no move to change the record. His eyes were closed and Christine wondered if she should say something but within seconds a record from the small stack that had been piled onto the central spindle dropped down onto the turntable of its own accord. Christine watched, fascinated, as the arm swung inwards, dropping the needle down onto the record's outer edge so that the next track began playing automatically.

'Autochange,' Billy smirked. 'I tell you, only the best for Billy Walker,' he said with a satisfied grin.

'I've never seen anything like that before!' Christine was clearly impressed.

'Why not? What kind of record player have you got?'

'We haven't, not since the old wind-up gramophone broke,' she said, her cheeks pink with embarrassment. 'My mum spends a lot of time in bed and she likes things to be quiet,' she went on, as if that explained everything. When Billy didn't say anything, she added, 'And my dad won't spend money on what he calls fripperies as he's saving up for his dream house and he wants to buy a shop so that we can move to a better part of Weatherfield.'

Christine didn't know why, but she had a sudden urge to tell Billy about what went on at home and why life at number 13 was so different from his. She'd often felt the need to talk to someone about all the arguments, the age-old resentments and disagreements that she had never really understood; the way her parents were always at each other's throats, leaving her trapped like piggy in the middle but she never could bring herself to voice how she felt. She somehow felt that Billy would understand and she wanted to share with him how miserable she'd felt after their huge row that morning. Her father had dropped his bombshell and told her in no uncertain terms that she should forget her dream of qualifying as a shorthand typist as he would need her to work full-time in his new shop once he'd bought it, and she hadn't known what to say. She could still feel the anger bubbling up in her chest even as she thought about it now, and she was bursting to tell Billy all about it, but when the moment came she couldn't bring herself to actually say the words.

'You OK?' Christine was surprised when Billy asked, a concerned frown on his face.

She raised her shoulders in a sort of exaggerated sigh. 'I'm fine thanks. Just thinking about . . . things. About my mum and dad mostly,' was all she said. 'I don't know about you but in our house I'm always made to feel as if everything that goes wrong is my fault.'

She hadn't expected Billy to laugh and she looked up sharply. 'What's so funny?' she asked crossly.

'In this house if things go wrong then it usually *is* my fault,' he said, and then even Christine couldn't help smiling.

Billy was sitting cross-legged next to Christine, their knees almost touching, when the next track began to play. He broke the tension of the moment by singing along with Frankie Laine and miming into his hair brush as if it was a microphone. He closed his eyes again, leaning forwards as he became more involved in the song, until Christine feared that he might topple over. The record came to a rousing crescendo then cut off and she watched as the next one was lowered gently onto the turntable. But this time Billy jumped up and pulled the arm away before anyone had time to sing.

'I don't know about you but I need a drink,' he said, 'and I reckon now might be a good time to sneak down and nick a couple of bottles while my dad goes down to the cellar to change the barrels.'

'Can you just take whatever you like?' Christine asked.

'Sure I can,' was Billy's automatic reply, but then he winked at her. 'So long as no one sees me.'

Christine looked across to the alarm clock on the

bedside table and gasped. 'Goodness, is that the time?' she said, 'I must be going home for my tea, or me mum will have my guts for garters.'

'Not even time for one beer? I'm sure you can . . .' Billy put on his most persuasive voice.

'Ooh no! Especially not that. I've never had a beer,' Christine admitted, 'and it might make me drunk.'

Billy laughed. 'I suppose if you're that nesh you could always have a lager and lime,' he said, looking at her with some disdain.

Christine picked up her hat and coat from the bed. 'Thanks for letting me hear your records,' she said. 'I've enjoyed myself.'

'You can come again sometime, if you like,' Billy said, eyeing her up and down as if making up his mind. 'I tell you what, why don't we meet up at school tomorrow? We could register, show our faces and then just disappear.'

'Ooh, that sounds like fun,' Christine said, thrilled at the thought of being seen together with someone with the reputation of Billy Walker.

'I'm not going in early,' Billy said.

'Why don't we meet by the gates at dinnertime,' Christine suggested.

'Twelve o'clock,' Billy said, and he got up to let her out while he went to sneak down to the cellar and find his first bottle of beer of the night.

Chapter 14

Josie hated to admit it but Shelagh was right; she didn't like working in the corner shop any more than she had liked working in Pauldens, but she didn't know what else she could do. Not until a casual comment from Elsie suddenly set her thinking.

Josie had eaten her tea with Elsie and the girls as she usually did and they were listening to Victor Sylvester's orchestra on the radio bringing live dance music into people's homes from one of the music hall theatres in London. Shelagh and Hilda had already left the table to spin around the room in a floaty waltz or a springy quickstep, one of them holding the rigid frame of the male lead while the other pretended to be flying in a floaty, net-layered cocktail gown.

'Talking about dancing makes me think about the coronation,' Shelagh said as she paused for breath at the end of the next set of music. 'Anyone heard how the party planning is going? I presume there'll be lots of dancing then?'

Hilda shrugged in a way that made it impossible to tell if she didn't know, or didn't care, but Elsie's face perked up. 'I'm so glad you mentioned that, love, cos I would have forgot. Mrs Sharples was in early this morning and she was getting right mithered about the parties.'

'Mrs Sharples is always getting into a state about summat or other,' Hilda said. 'So what is it now?'

'She's worrying there's not going to be enough decorations to go round all the local streets and she'll need a load more if she's to do up the Mission Hall as well,' Elsie said as Hilda rolled her eyes heavenward.

'There's always been enough before,' Hilda said.

'The problem is that she's checked all the old stuff and most of it's not usable. It's been quite a while since the victory parties. She reckons we need a whole new lot, and time's marching on. She was getting into such a dither that I offered to help her out.'

'Help her out how?' Hilda looked mindful. 'It'll be expensive if we have to go out and buy a whole load of ready-made stuff.'

'I know that,' Elsie said, 'that's why I was thinking that one of you might be interested in running some up on the machine? If so, you'd need to get cracking, cos there's not that long to go.'

Josie perked up instantly. She was not surprised to see the look on Hilda's face as soon as she heard what the task would be, but she didn't want to appear too eager.

'And who'll be paying for this extra lot?' Hilda asked.

'Don't worry, she's given me the money to buy enough bolts of red, white and blue,' Elsie said.

'Thank goodness! But don't look at me like that, Mum,' Hilda said, putting her hands up defensively. 'You know how I feel about sewing.'

'Me too,' Shelagh said almost at the same time. 'I can't sew in a straight line to save my life.' She laughed.

'How about you, Josie?' Hilda said. 'Cinderella to the rescue? I bet you're a dab hand with a sewing machine.'

Josie felt the warmth of the blood as it rushed to her cheeks as she realized the possible consequences that might result if she made a hasty offer. 'I don't know about a dab hand but I certainly know how to use a machine,' she said, trying to gauge Hilda's reaction. 'And I'd be happy to help,' she said, secretly delighted to have found something that neither of the sisters were good at.

'There you are then, problem solved!' Hilda said, the look on her face suggesting that she thought she had got the better of their lodger, not realizing that Josie actually loved sewing and couldn't wait to get started.

'Oh, Josie, would you really?' Elsie exclaimed, 'You are a life-saver.'

Josie glowed, thinking back to the days when she had worked with the wardrobe mistress behind the scenes at whichever theatre was featuring her mother, but she didn't want to show Hilda how happy she was. At that time she had enjoyed it so much that they had taken her with them on tour so that she could continue to help make up the costumes. Even now she had difficulty hiding her delight until Elsie held out her hand with the money in it to cover the cost of the material. She had spoken up without thinking, not realizing that she would be expected to make the purchases herself.

She refused Shelagh's offer to go with her on a trip into Manchester where they all agreed the best offers would be, for although she got on better with Shelagh than Hilda, she thought it would be better if she went on her own. 'Thanks, but there's no need for you to bother,' Josie said, trying to ignore the blush she felt rise to her cheeks. She was thinking back to another time recently when Charlie Wright had arrived unexpectedly in time to see her getting into a dither with a customer who had virtually accused her of overcharging. She had been extremely grateful for Charlie's intervention on that day, saving her from an embarrassing situation, but she knew how close he had come to discovering her closely guarded secret.

Josie took the money from Elsie without looking at it. It was too late to withdraw her offer now or to ask someone else to buy the material for her. She would have to find a way of managing the situation herself and she wasted no time in organizing a shopping trip.

On her return she couldn't help smiling at her achievement when she dipped inside the bags and caught sight of the yards of red, white and blue cottons that she had bought, ready to be cut up into triangles. She was particularly pleased to find that she had had enough money for the extra bale of pre-cut Union Jacks that she had bought on impulse, ready to be strung together. Of course, it would take time to sew all the pieces into suitable decorations but now that she had negotiated what she thought of as the worst hurdle she felt up to the sewing challenge. For her, the idea of being able to sew all day long instead of having to serve in the shop filled her with a renewed energy and she was delighted to find that another thought had flashed into her head. She suddenly knew how she might repay Elsie for her kindness and she was only surprised that she hadn't thought of it before. She would seek out some fashionable, modern patterns and make her landlady a new dress for the coming coronation celebrations! If it was a success, then she would offer to refashion Elsie's wardrobe. She would keep that aspect as a surprise but they could both benefit. Elsie could update her clothes and, if Josie could find some new sewing jobs she could be paid for, then maybe she wouldn't have to serve in the shop at all.

Chapter 15

Hilda looked on when Josie displayed her purchases on the kitchen table, pleased by the thought that their lodger would be kept well occupied for quite some time to come. 'The sewing machine is under its cover in the corner for now,' Elsie said, 'but we can leave it open in the future so that you can use it whenever you like.'

'Feel free to enjoy yourself all night if you want.' Hilda smothered a giggle. 'You did say you liked sewing.' She leaned across and whispered something in Shelagh's ear, but the two jumped apart quickly when Elsie snapped, 'Now, now girls, don't you know it's rude to whisper? Can't we share whatever it was, Hilda?'

Hilda wrinkled her nose. She hated when her mother treated them as if they were little girls and was tempted not to answer, but as the colour rushed to her cheeks she said, 'I was only asking Shelagh if she fancied coming with me to the Rovers. She's allowed in for a lemonade.'

To Hilda's annoyance Elsie turned to Josie with a smile. 'Now that sounds like a really good idea, what do you think, Josie? I'm sure they'll want to take you with them,' she said. 'I know you've been to the Rovers a couple of times but you've not had much in the way of outings since you've been here, have you, love? It would be a good opportunity for you to meet some more of the locals.'

Hilda puffed up her cheeks and exploded a loud raspberry noise to let Elsie know what she thought of the idea. 'Mum!' she said, exasperated, but Elsie ignored her.

'I'd come with you myself only I've got some ordering to do before my working day is over. But that's no reason for you three not to go and get changed and have a nice night out up at the Rovers.' Hilda glared daggers at her mother but Elsie continued to take no notice. 'How's about it, Josie?' she said. 'Do you fancy it?'

'It's hardly worth while any of us getting changed, Mum,' Hilda felt she had to cut in before Josie could answer. 'We shan't be stopping there long. There's never anyone worth bothering about so early in the week. We'd best leave it for nearer to the weekend.' Hilda made a dismissive motion with her hand, but Elsie refused to give up. Instead, she pressed some coins into Hilda's hand.

'Here, why don't you two older ones have a round on me,' she said, 'and you can get something suitably soft for Shelagh?' Hilda's jaw dropped in disbelief as Elsie then continued to shoo them out.

Annie Walker nodded a greeting to Hilda and Shelagh and made a point of welcoming Josie, introducing her to several local residents, including her husband Jack who offered Josie a first drink 'on the house' as he hadn't met her before.

'I remember going to see your mother when she played at the old Weatherfield Empire,' Annie said, a look of nostalgia briefly crossing her face. 'And I'll never forget when she topped the bill above George Formby at the Majestic. Will you be stopping long with Mrs Lappin? I hope we'll be seeing a lot more of you at the Rovers, while you're in Weatherfield,' she said, squeezing Josie's hand, and she moved away to serve Frank and Ida Barlow who had just arrived.

Josie looked about her to see if she knew anyone and she recognized Ena Sharples from the Mission. She offered a smile that was not reciprocated as the older woman disappeared into the Snug carrying a pint of what looked like Guinness. Hilda introduced Josie to Albert Tatlock, an older man who lived several doors down at number 1 Coronation Street. He was sitting in a corner of the bar, preferring his own company, it seemed, while several of the other patrons were battling it out in a noisy game of darts.

Hilda bought a round for the three of them as her mother had suggested and, drinks in hand, they stood together awkwardly at the bar. They were barely speaking, Hilda looking as if she was still silently fuming at her mother for interfering with her plans.

Josie nursed her half pint of lager and lime, marvelling at how quickly the evening's arrangements had changed, and wondering why she had agreed to come. From the look on Shelagh's face it was not difficult to see that she would also have been happier staying at home. It was really only Hilda, Josie decided, who, despite her anger, was actually enjoying being at the Rovers. She looked at the firm set of Hilda's jaw and the way the other girl eagerly scrutinized the face of each newcomer and she began to speculate who or what Hilda was on the lookout for. It didn't take long for her to understand when Hilda exclaimed, 'Why if it isn't Charlie Wright!' and Josie looked up, immediately recognizing the tall, fair young window cleaner as he came through the double doors.

Hilda hardly gave him a chance to clear the entranceway before she stepped forwards and linked her arm through his in an overly familiar way. At the same time she fixed him with an adoring gaze. Charlie looked startled and tried to free himself but Hilda was not to be put off.

'I didn't realize you drank here,' Hilda said, the well-prepared words hardly sounding credible; even Charlie raised his brows.

'I'd have to be daft not to. I've only been coming here to play darts once a week for the last two years,' Charlie said sardonically.

'Really?' Hilda feigned surprise. 'I didn't know that.'

A smile played on Josie's lips as she saw Charlie turn his back on Hilda with a look of disbelief.

'How's it going at the corner shop, then?' Josie was surprised when she realized that Charlie was addressing her.

'All right, thanks,' she said. 'How's the window cleaning?'

'Same as ever.' Charlie shrugged. 'I'll be glad when it gets warmer and my dad's fit again to work.'

'What time's your darts match due to start then?' Hilda interrupted, clearly irritated by Charlie's interest in Josie.

'It's already started by the looks of it,' he said. 'I'd better show my face.'

Josie was amused because she could see Hilda was doing her best to hold his attention and had fixed him with an animated smile which Josie presumed was meant to be alluring though it looked more like a grimace to her eyes, and when Charlie carried two drinks over to an empty table and beckoned Josie to join him, it was Hilda who actually strode across and went to sit down first, her eyelashes fluttering furiously.

Josie wanted to laugh. Hilda didn't seem to realize that she had no interest in Charlie, but then she had never told anyone that her hopes and dreams went far beyond a local window cleaner from Weatherfield and it amused her to watch Hilda's antics. Once she realized how smitten Hilda was, Josie couldn't resist the temptation to wind her up and she aimed a flirtatious smile or two in Charlie's direction, making sure that Hilda could see it. As far as Josie was concerned it had the desired effect, for the look on Hilda's face was priceless.

Chapter 16

Christine went straight to the school gates promptly at twelve while the echo of the dinner bell was still filling the dark corridors of Bessie Street Seniors. She was hungry, but in her excitement at the thought of meeting Billy she had forgotten to bring a sandwich with her as she usually did. Maybe Billy would have one that they could share. But Billy didn't appear. When he hadn't come by half past twelve she sat down on the steps, wondering what to do, and by one o clock, when the teachers blew their whistles for everyone to come in from the playground, ready for the afternoon's lessons, she left the school grounds and walked away disconsolately.

She was disappointed. She had gone into school specially for the morning's lessons so that she could meet up with Billy at dinnertime. The class teacher had shown surprise when she had answered to her name on the register and would doubtless not expect to see her again in the afternoon. That was just as well because Christine had no intention of hanging about the grounds longer than necessary. Having made a decision not to wait for him any longer, she headed for the park. She didn't expect to see anyone there and was surprised to find a gang of young lads who should also have been at school, kicking a ball about, their faces intent and serious as they aimed to shoot it between the piles of jackets that marked out the goals at either end of their pitch. She didn't see Billy at first until he scored a goal, at which point he yelled and punched the air wildly in celebration. And at least he had the good grace to look sheepish when he caught sight of her.

'I waited for you at school,' Christine began, not sure whether to let him see how upset she was.

'Did you?' Billy sounded vague as he shrugged his shoulders. 'Sorry, but my mates needed me to make up the team. I suppose I sort of forgot.' He shifted his feet awkwardly. 'Fancy a walk, do you?' Billy seemed happy enough to desert the team now and didn't seem to care when his mates began dismantling the goalposts. 'I'm off, lads.' Billy waved to them distractedly. 'See you same time tomorrow?' he called as they were dispersing and he set off across the field without looking back to see if Christine was with him.

Christine knew immediately that they were heading towards the bandstand and wasn't surprised when the rounded frame of the darkly painted structure came into view.

'Pity they haven't got a record player here, it would have been a perfect place for us to play some records,' Billy joked as he jumped up onto the stage and began conducting an imaginary orchestra with an invisible baton.

Christine giggled. 'My dad used to do that when I was a little girl, though he had a bad leg so he couldn't actually climb onto the stage.'

'Did he get injured in the war?' Billy asked, his eyes wide as he changed his pantomime actions to those of a soldier manning a machine gun and he added sound effects as if he was firing off round after round of gunfire.

Christine nodded her affirmative answer to his question. 'He got shrapnel in it, he says, one day when they got a bit too close to the enemy.'

'Did he ever kill anyone?' Billy asked eagerly.

Christine frowned. 'I don't think so. I've never asked,' she said.

'My dad fought in the war but he wasn't hurt.'

Billy sounded almost disappointed. 'And I don't think he killed anyone either.' He made a tutting noise of disapproval. 'But my mum made such a fuss when he came back you'd have thought he was a hero who'd won the whole bloody war single-handed.'

Christine sucked in her breath when Billy swore but made no comment. 'My mum always says that Dad changed after he came back from the war,' was all she said. Christine went to sit in one of the rows of seats that were still standing upright, facing the stage, and Billy jumped down and came to sit beside her. She swiped her hand across the woodwork which felt damp to the touch.

'I always reckoned that Mum must have changed quite a bit too at that time,' Christine said. 'But according to her, that was all my fault.'

Billy looked at her wide-eyed. 'How could that be right? You were only a baby.'

'I know, but a very troublesome one, apparently. Mum's always said that things have not been right for her ever since I were born. I reckoned it was something to do with Aunt Madge dying, but no one would ever tell me the truth.'

'Who's Aunt Madge?'

'She was my mother's sister. She came to help Mum look after me when I was a baby while Dad was away in the navy. But that didn't last very long.'

'Why, what happened to her?' Billy seemed curious.

'I'm not really sure of the whole story. We're not allowed to speak about her in our house. All I know is that I've always felt guilty because if it weren't for me she wouldn't have been in Weatherfield at that time and she might not have died.' Christine felt her chest tighten as she said the words, and she couldn't help wondering what she was doing talking to a stranger like this, but it was too late to stop now.

'Apparently, once the war got going a whole bunch of people from Weatherfield were sent to live in Blackpool,' Christine said, her voice dropping, '"evacuation" I think they called it. Mostly it was about getting the kids out of danger, although my mum insisted on going with me. Only my Aunt Madge didn't want to go. She stayed behind in Weatherfield after Mum and me left – I think she even carried on living in our house – and I don't think Mum was very happy about that.' Christine paused, thinking back to some of her parents' rows that she had so often overheard. She never could fathom what had caused the smouldering resentments that usually raged between her mum and dad, but was it to do with that? It was funny, she thought, it was the first time in ages since she had talked about any of this. She had certainly never told anyone the family story before and she wasn't sure why she wanted to tell Billy Walker now; except that he had seemed interested, especially about the gory bits. She was surprised how easy he was to talk to.

Christine sneaked a look at him when she thought he wasn't looking. There was something about the frank openness of Billy's face and the way his dark eyes drew her in that made him seem trustworthy. She thought back to all the recent rows at number 13 and shuddered. More trustworthy than her parents, she thought ironically. What would it be like to live with someone like Billy rather than her parents? she wondered, the thought popping into her head out of nowhere.

'Have you ever been to London?' The words were out of her mouth before she was able to stop them and Billy looked startled.

'No,' he said, 'but I'm sure I'll get there one day. How about you?'

'I definitely intend to get there!' Christine said, 'in fact, I'm thinking of going very soon.' She tried to sound offhand.

'You mean with your mum and dad? When's that?'

'No, I mean I'm planning on going there by myself. Running away!' She laughed. 'Or we could go together, if you'd like. Then they'll be sorry,' she added almost to herself. Christine looked at him out of the corner of her eye.

For a moment Billy's eyes flashed and then he laughed too. 'That sounds like fun!'

'I'll do anything to get away from my mum and dad. The further the better as far as I'm concerned,' she said with disdain. 'I've had enough of them recently to last me a lifetime.'

'Me too!' Billy agreed, 'I know just what you mean, my parents can be such a pain in the neck,' he said, although the immediate spark of excitement that had lit up his eyes had disappeared and he seemed to be more concerned following the antics of a young puppy that had escaped its leash and its owner and was chasing a couple of rabbits across the grass.

'We'd better start some serious planning then,' Christine said. 'Because all I know is that if I don't get away soon, I'll more than likely go mad.'

Billy said nothing, didn't even turn his head, and she couldn't help wondering if he had been so distracted he was no longer listening.

Chapter 17

Hilda had had enough! She had fled straight up to her bedroom as soon as she'd got into the house after work so that she didn't have to see their lodger or interact with Josie in any way and she sat fuming on the edge of the bed that 'thanks to Josie' she had been forced once more to share with Shelagh. She shook her head angrily. It seemed like everything these days was 'thanks to Josie' and she clenched and unclenched her fists until the knuckles showed white. 'Josie needs this, Josie wants that, we must all look out for Josie.' Hilda said the words out loud mockingly, in a childlike voice, upset that venting her anger didn't make her feel any better. She was tired of her mother insisting they must dance to

Josie's tune all the time. Josie could do no wrong as far as Elsie was concerned. But there was one thing Hilda would not give in to, and that was to let Josie muscle in on Charlie. And yet here she was, hiding in her bedroom while she tried to gather strength for what she feared could be a showdown. 'That man is mine!' Hilda said solemnly, staring at her own reflection in the mirror above the tiny dressing-table shelf. 'I saw him first and I want him and I intend to have him, and it's time everyone – including Charlie – realizes that.'

Hilda had never tried to cover up her infatuation with Charlie Wright and perhaps that had been a mistake, but from the moment his father had become too ill to work and Charlie had temporarily taken over the local rounds she had fallen for the young window cleaner's perky smile and cheeky manner. She may not have been particularly subtle in the way that she had set her cap at him from the start, but that had only made her all the more disappointed that Charlie had not reciprocated and shown his feelings immediately. If anything, she had been shocked to find that he had paid more attention to Josie, even though she had not initially shown any interest in him. It was infuriating for Hilda, for she felt that Josie had done nothing to deserve Charlie's favours, but Hilda had no intentions of giving him up now. Charlie's offhanded manner made her even more determined than ever to win him round and to teach Josie a lesson.

Hilda sighed because that seemed to be more easily said than done. It seemed that no matter how many times she gazed into his eyes as she laughed at his jokes, or how much she feigned an interest in almost anything he had to say, she had to admit that her strategy was not working. Charlie still persisted in pursuing Josie and if she wanted to hang on to him, Hilda knew she would have to act firmly and fast.

For some time now she had had her eye on the dance at the Weatherfield Country Barn and she was doing everything she could to bring it to Charlie's attention. She had even agreed to put up some posters about it in the shop and had left some leaflets on the countertop for customers to see, but so far her efforts had been without success and she paced about the bedroom as she tried to think about what else she might do. The dance was to be held very shortly but, despite her best efforts, no invitation had yet been forthcoming from Charlie.

It was the ping of the shop bell downstairs that made Hilda realize that she should be thinking of acting even more quickly than she had originally planned, for as she went to the bedroom window and peered outside she saw Charlie propping his bike up against the brick wall. Moments later as she stepped onto the landing at the top of the stairs she heard his deep voice as he entered the shop and so she grabbed her lipstick from the dressing table and quickly painted her pouting lips. She smiled as she hurriedly outlined her eyes in black with a make-up pencil before rushing downstairs, concerned that Charlie might have come to visit Josie, something she could not allow to happen. If Hilda was to win this particular contest then it would be better not to leave Charlie alone with Josie for too long.

Chapter 18

Josie had to admit she was flattered and she couldn't fail to respond to all the attention that Charlie Wright was paying her, even though she knew it was unwarranted and that she had never done anything to encourage him. Unlike Hilda, who as far as Josie could see tried too hard to draw attention to herself and seemed to enjoy openly flirting with Charlie at every opportunity, Josie wasn't particularly interested and risked nothing more than the odd smile in his direction. She had already dismissed him in her own mind with regard to a potential courtship, convinced that he was not her type; and if she was being honest, she didn't even consider him to be in the same class. It was only when she realized how keen Hilda was, appearing in the shop on the flimsiest of pretexts if she thought Charlie might be in the neighbourhood, that Josie became more aware of him and she began to take more of an interest. She had never been able to resist the kind of challenge that Hilda posed and so Josie allowed her natural impishness and sense of mischief to take over.

Since Josie no longer served behind the counter regularly she was gratified to learn from Elsie that Charlie was still a regular customer and that he always asked if Josie might be available to serve him although he never asked for Hilda. He would hang around the shop in an attempt to see Josie, offering different excuses for each of his visits. When she realized how much this annoyed Hilda, Josie would try to make sure she was available if she had any warning ahead of time, and go out of her way to put in an appearance in the shop. That was why, when Josie saw him arrive one evening when she was standing in for Elsie, she hurried down the stairs in order to serve him before Hilda had the time to come out into the shop from the back room. She knew he was expecting to see her and not Hilda when she saw him balancing the handle of his empty pail on his first two fingers, but as soon as she appeared he put the bucket down on the floor and held his hands up in a gesture of truce.

'I'm not after water this time,' Charlie said, his face beaming.

Josie drew in a long breath and hoped she seemed welcoming. 'Then how can I help you today?' she said. She sounded amused, wondering what his excuse might be this time.

He hesitated and she was aware that for once he looked almost embarrassed.

Charlie cleared his throat and shifted his weight awkwardly from one leg to another. 'There was something that I intended to ask you the last time I was here,' he said, 'but as you may recall, we got interrupted and I never did ask you.'

Josie looked puzzled, trying to recollect the incident.

'Well, I haven't forgotten what it was and I've made a special trip to come back now to ask you so I'm hoping I'm not too late.'

'Too late for what?' Josie frowned.

'To go to the Country Dance with me next week.' Charlie pointed to the larger of the two posters that were pinned up in front of the tins of tuna advertising the dance that was to be held at the Weatherfield Country Barn the following week.

Now Josie laughed, for that was not what she had been expecting and she wasn't sure how to respond. 'Why are you so keen to invite me?' she said. 'Who do you think I am, poor little Cinderella, who's not been asked to the ball?' Josie said sardonically without thinking, and she was surprised to see that he looked startled if not a little hurt.

He recovered quickly. 'You tell me who you are if you're not Cinderella and then tell me whether I need to take pity on you.' And he grinned, his eyes creasing in fun, as he spoke. 'But if you are Cinderella then you can relax cos I've come to rescue you. You don't have to miss out on going to the ball. I can arrange for a carriage to get you there on time and bring you home before midnight; and maybe we could squeeze in a dance or two in between.'

Josie could see Charlie was trying to make a joke, as he pointed to his bike that was propped up against the wall outside, but she just shrugged and didn't say anything. She was too busy looking at his scruffy work overalls, pockets stuffed full as usual with chamois leathers and old cloths, and thinking about how to let him down lightly and how best to refuse. Indeed, she actually shuddered slightly when he ran his calloused fingers through his tousled hair, but he was looking at her so eagerly that she found it hard to say the actual words, 'no thanks'. She was shaking her head, while she was considering how best to phrase her refusal when she heard footsteps coming from the room at the back of the shop and remembered that Hilda was at home. A mischievous thought flashed into her head. Why did she have to refuse? She was glad she hadn't yet spoken as it now gave her the opportunity to change her mind.

She paused for a moment while the footsteps came closer and she waited until she heard the back door opening and Hilda appeared before she said, 'An invitation to the ball! Now that sounds like a wonderful offer that's too good to miss and I hope I don't have to be Cinderella in order to accept and say thank you.' She spoke loudly and clearly, her exasperated expression swiftly converting into a smile. 'Thank you so much for asking me, Charlie, I'd love to go to the dance with you.' She purposely added a layer of excitement to her voice as she spoke and made no attempt not to look smug as Hilda stepped inside the shop. 'Oh, Hilda!' Josie exclaimed, as if she had only just become aware of her presence, 'What do you think? Charlie has just asked me the sweetest thing. He wants me to go with him to the dance at the Weatherfield Country Barn next week. You know, that one that's advertised on the poster,' she added unnecessarily as she pointed. 'Isn't that kind? You were only saying the other day how much you'd like to go. Well, it shows you, it's never too late to receive an invitation.'

Josie knew she was being mean but she couldn't help enjoying the satisfaction she felt when she saw the angry look of disbelief as Hilda's eyes filled and she clenched her jaw tight shut.

'I'm sure you'll both have a lovely time,' Hilda said stiffly. 'It's nice to see you Charlie, I hadn't realized you were here,' she added, nodding in his direction with an exaggerated flutter of her eyelids. 'I hope you've got everything you need for now because I'm afraid it's time for us to shut up the shop.'

Chapter 19

Charlie's promise of a carriage turned out to be a rather battered-looking Austin 7 motor car and Josie was astonished when the shop bell rang and she went to open the door. She had seen very few cars on the roads since she had been in Weatherfield and even fewer parked in Coronation Street itself and it had never occurred to her that Charlie might not only be a driver but a car owner as well. None of the older residents in the street had yet ventured into the market and there were few in the neighbourhood who could afford to run even an old jalopy like this one. But old or not, Josie was impressed to see that it had been freshly scrubbed on the outside, with the cracked leather seating inside having been highly polished too.

She was also amazed to see the change in Charlie's appearance.

'My! don't you look smart.' She blurted out the compliment even before he spoke although he wasted no time in reciprocating. The expression on his face made it quite clear that he approved of what he saw.

'Phew!' Charlie whistled appreciatively, his eyebrows lifting as he pushed her away to give him a full view, and she was glad she had chosen her favourite pink shirtwaister dress with the tightly fitted bodice and flared skirt that looked as if it was balancing on a multitude of stiffly starched petticoats. 'I don't know about Cinderella,' Charlie said, 'but you look every inch the princess to me. Now I really will have to make sure to get you home before midnight,' he added laughing, 'or you never know what could happen.'

'And will you turn back into a frog again, Prince Charming?' Josie said and she made a show of looking him up and down approvingly. He had obviously gone to a great deal of trouble to smarten up his appearance and he looked almost unrecognizable in his dark navy suit with a finely ironed white shirt underneath and a Windsor-knotted red and blue tie. The outfit could have been almost spoiled by what looked like his work boots but they were so highly polished they almost twinkled as they caught the light and even Josie felt she couldn't complain. When he smoothed back his carefully Brylcreemed hair she was delighted to see how clean his hands and finger-nails were.

Josie invited Charlie to step inside and took him through to the kitchen behind the store to say hello to Elsie who she knew was waiting on tenterhooks. Josie wondered what Elsie would make of the spruced-up Charlie, for he looked very different from Hilda's beau for the evening who had made an appearance earlier. Josie had been surprised when she had seen him, although she tried not to look too smug when Hilda had introduced him as a colleague from the raincoat factory for she knew that Hilda had been forced to ask him to take her at the last minute when no other invitations had been forthcoming. His appearance had caused Josie to smile, however, and she couldn't help wondering if Hilda regretted having asked him, for he looked as if he had made no effort to change or clean up. He had a crumpled appearance and the strong smell of the smearers' glue that was used in the factory to hold the mackintoshes together still clung to him; he looked as if he had come straight from work.

Josie was delighted to see that Charlie, on the other hand, was making a very favourable impres-sion, although she wanted to apologize as Elsie scrutinized him, making his cheeks redden until they were as pink as Josie's dress. For once, he looked lost for words and he covered his confusion by thrusting a small rectangular box into Josie's hands. 'I almost forgot. I thought you might like this,' he said, looking extremely embarrassed. Josie opened the box and was delighted to find a delicate white orchid corsage with lilac edging. 'How thoughtful. Isn't that lovely!' she exclaimed, genuinely moved. And she handed it to Elsie to pin it onto the wide belt of her dress that accentuated the narrowness of her slim waist.

By the time they reached the Country Barn the evening was in full swing. The band was in the middle of a set and everyone was dancing so that Josie was able to sashay straight onto the dance floor as soon as Charlie had handed in their coats to the cloakroom. She was surprised and relieved to find that Charlie was actually an enthusiastic dancer with a surprisingly good sense of rhythm, even if he didn't know all the steps. He didn't seem to care about showing off his dancing prowess, although he seemed to be concentrating hard, but he was focussing on Josie, treating her courteously as if she were his very special prize. Josie, on the other hand, was intent on being noticed by the two sisters and barely looked at Charlie. She wanted to make sure that Hilda, and Shelagh, who had also found someone from the factory to accompany her at the last minute, were impressed that she had managed to snag Charlie and that they were aware of her every move. She kept trying to catch their eye so that they could see how much she was enjoying dancing wildly with him, and when the tempo slowed and they began to whirl around the dance floor, she took delight in twirling past Hilda at every available opportunity, making eye contact, calling out to her and giving a little wave while she made a point of clinging to Charlie in a firm arm hold with her head resting lightly on his chest. Charlie turned out to be a skilled navigator as he picked his way carefully around the crowded dance floor and when the band took a break between sets he steered Josie to an empty table while he went off in search of some drinks.

'I'm not surprised you're sitting down, you must be exhausted.' Josie looked up to find Shelagh standing at her table. She leaned over and addressed Josie quietly.

'Oh, I am,' Josie said. 'Aren't you having fun too?'

'I'd be enjoying it more if you weren't showing off in front of our faces all the time.'

Josie sat back, doing her best not to smile and trying to look as though she had been punched. 'Me? Showing off? I'm sure I don't know what you mean.'

'Then you're more spiteful than I've ever given you credit for,' Shelagh said. 'Managing to upset me and my sister both at the same time.'

Josie frowned. As far as she was concerned, she was merely getting her own back for Hilda's nastiness.

'Please, Josie, no more waving and smiling,' Shelagh said. 'It really is beginning to upset Hilda and it's making me feel sick. I don't imagine Charlie's enjoying it much either.'

'Oh, I get it,' Josie said. 'That's what this is about, a fit of Hilda's jealousy because she couldn't have him. I'm sure he'll be flattered when I tell him, to think of women squabbling over him.'

'Oh, do tell him,' Shelagh said. 'And I think you might be shocked to hear what he's got to say about your behaviour.'

'How dare you! It's you two who should be ashamed of yourselves.' Josie could feel her anger rising, though she was sure that it was partly shame and embarrassment for she knew that Shelagh had a point, but she wasn't prepared to concede that. She would rather think of it as her moment of triumph.

Shelagh looked daggers at her walking away before Charlie came back with two bottles of beer.

'Was that Hilda's sister who was just here?'

'Yes, that was Shelagh.'

'What did she want?'

'Just to say hello,' Josie said, although as she spoke she realized she had been more shaken by Shelagh's visit than she had realized. 'I don't know about you,' Josie deftly changed the subject, 'but I'm feeling quite hot and out of breath.' She hoped he wouldn't notice the reddening of her cheeks as she smiled at him. 'I don't know where you get all that energy from.'

Charlie shrugged and Josie was pleased that she was able to steer the conversation away from Shelagh. She took a deep breath and hoped that might be the end of it.

'Running up and down ladders all day probably helps,' Charlie said with a grin, 'but then I play with the lads on the local football team and we go training a couple of times a week.' He looked up at her as he said this as if unsure if he should continue the conversation in that direction.

'Really?' It was not what Josie had expected him to say but it felt safer than pursuing any other route.

'I do try to keep fit,' he said. 'You've got to take care of yourself if you want to succeed in this life, don't you think? Otherwise, you might run out of steam when you most need it.'

There was a sudden sombre tone of his voice and Josie looked at him, surprised by his intensity. She giggled self-consciously for a moment when he leaned forward onto the table, his arms folded, and looked directly into her eyes. 'I don't intend to be a window cleaner all my life, you know. I've got other plans,' he said.

Josie was taken aback, not sure whether to take him seriously, but he continued to look at her directly.

'As soon as my dad is better, I'm off. I've got bigger fish to fry.'

'Like what?' Josie asked, surprised by his sudden fervour.

'I intend to branch out on my own. I know it won't be easy but as soon as the old man's fit again I'll be starting my own business and I'll need all the stamina I can get.'

'What kind of a business have you in mind?' Josie asked, admiring his eagerness.

'A cleaning business,' he said without hesitation, 'but I intend to have a gang of properly organized and trained cleaners working with me. I'll train them myself and then I'll see if I can pick up some long-term contracts wherever possible, so that I can have different types of jobs lined up that I can send them out to – cleaning offices, mainly, maybe a school or two, as well as ordinary people's houses. I've not thought through all the details yet and I'm still saving up to buy any special equipment that I might need.'

'Really?' Josie was impressed. 'You've got that far in your thinking already?'

'Yes, really! I shall be a proper businessman. I have no wish to *be* a window cleaner all my life, I intend to *employ* one whenever necessary to fulfil the contracts I negotiate.' He had a triumphant look on his face. 'I have ideas and I intend to make them work. I've already bought a vehicle, as you can see, and I reckon that's going to make folk round here sit up and take notice.'

'You're probably right,' she said admiringly and admitted, 'it did surprise *me*. You're the only person I know in this part of the world who has one.'

Charlie beamed as he acknowledged the compliment. 'And you're the first to ride in it, by the way,' he said.

'Gosh! I'm flattered.' Josie didn't really know what to say. 'It's very nice.'

'It was an absolute bargain and I grabbed it when the opportunity came up. I was warned there was something wrong with the gearbox but I reckoned I could always get that fixed and sell it if necessary. As it happens, a mate of mine has already looked at it for me and given me a quote so it won't be a problem. Then all it needs is a regular bit of elbow grease and, as you can see, it looks new.'

'It's certainly very smart,' Josie said, 'and it does set you apart.'

'For the type of business I have in mind I thought it would look more professional if I have my own transport because I want folk to take me seriously. I can go to see potential customers, check out the venues as they come up and show the workers where they are going if necessary.' He chuckled. 'The bike somehow doesn't seem to give quite the same image; it doesn't create the right impression.' His grin turned into a rueful smile. 'But now I'm thinking that I might have acted too hastily.'

'Why is that? It all sounds like a good idea to me,' Josie said. 'And you're certainly trying to think ahead. What makes you think you've acted too hastily?' Josie asked.

Charlie shrugged. 'I suppose it doesn't matter even if I have made a mistake,' he said. 'I'll probably make lots more before I'm finished. But I have been wondering if I might have been better off buying a van. Though I suppose I won't lose anything if I have to trade the car in as part exchange.'

'Are vans cheaper?' Josie was interested to hear the logic of his thinking.

'Very much so. Firstly, no windows so no purchase tax and, secondly, I would get free advertising because if I buy a van I can paint the name of the company on the side together with a catchy slogan. Give people a chance to get used to seeing me pottering about in it around Weatherfield.'

'What is the name of the company?' Josie asked, impressed.

Charlie laughed. 'I don't know, I haven't decided yet. Maybe you can think of something.'

'Me?' Her eyes widened

'Why not? You're the only one who has ridden in it so far. You might bring me luck. Anyway, you've got to think ahead if you want to succeed. You've got to be ready to grab every opportunity as it comes available,' Charlie said. 'I reckon the world's full of opportunities so long as you've got the dreams to match. All you have to do is work hard and never lose sight of your goals – and I don't care how hard I have to work!' His gaze was so intense that Josie had to look away. It was quite an impassioned speech for Charlie the window cleaner and Josie looked at him, impressed, wondering where this new Charlie had come from.

Josie stared at him and it was as though she was seeing him for the first time. Had she been under-estimating him, misguidedly thinking that he was somehow beneath her? He was obviously not the dullard she had originally taken him for and now that she was really looking, she was seeing him in a different light.

'Don't you have dreams?' Charlie cut across her thoughts.

'Yes, of course I do,' Josie said firmly, though she felt too embarrassed to say that her dreams stretched far beyond the confines of Weatherfield and window cleaning, but now she felt embarrassed by her own disparaging thoughts and she was relieved to see that the band were taking up their positions once more and were tuning up in preparation for the next set.

It began gently with the music of a slow waltz but as they glided back onto the dance floor Charlie suddenly stood still and said, 'I'm sorry, Josie, but I have to ask you something.'

Josie looked at him, puzzled, as other couples spun past them, even butting them out of the way.

'Before, when we were dancing, I couldn't help noticing that you kept waving to Hilda and her sister,' Charlie said 'It looked very odd, daft even, if you ask me. And I wondered if that was what Shelagh came over to talk to you about because she looked upset.'

Josie looked at him in surprise, managing to neatly sidestep out of the way as a couple seemed to be heading straight for them. She was shocked that he had seen through her actions and wasn't sure how to respond. She cleared her throat to play for time.

'Why do you ask?' she said eventually.

'Cos from where I was standing it looked almost as if you were pulling faces at them. I did wonder if that was what Shelagh was objecting to cos I notice that you're not doing it now,' Charlie said.

Josie hesitated. 'As a matter of fact, I did have words with Shelagh when she came over – or rather she had words with me, but I didn't say anything because . . .well, if you must know she accused me of only being here with you tonight to spite Hilda.' Josie paused, not sure whether to go on, but decided that once she had started it might be best to continue. 'She thinks I only agreed to come with you to stop you asking Hilda, because I knew Hilda fancied you and she really wanted you to ask her.' Josie dropped her voice and her face dipped to her chest. 'Shelagh knew that Hilda wasn't very nice to me when I first arrived in Weatherfield and she was concerned that I was just trying to get my own back.'

Charlie looked astonished. 'And are you? Getting your own back, I mean? Are you only here to spite Hilda?'

'No! Yes! Well, maybe I was. At first.'

Charlie stared at her, his eyes wide in disbelief. 'You mean that was the reason why you accepted my invitation? To get your revenge on Hilda?'

Josie was upset to hear it put into words like that for it didn't sound like a very nice thing to have done, and she was not surprised by the hurt look on Charlie's face. 'There was never any malice in it on my part, not against you,' Josie tried to reassure him, but the words sounded hollow, even to her, and she didn't expect him to be consoled.

'And there was me thinking you liked me,' he said, his face a mask of injured pride. 'It never occurred to me that you might have said yes because you wanted to thumb your nose at Hilda. You really were desperate to get one over on her, weren't you? And it looks like you succeeded.'

'That's not very fair. Didn't you ask me in the first place because you didn't like Hilda? You thought I was a better catch and you wanted to show me off, just a little?' Josie said defensively, but she could see from the mixed emotions that crossed his face that she was on thin ice.

'Of course I did,' Charlie said. 'But that was because I really liked you and I liked being with you. I was proud to have you on my arm and I wanted the world to know that such a pretty girl as you were my girl. I didn't expect you to treat me like just another notch on your belt.' He dropped his hold on Josie's arms as they stood together on the dance floor. 'I certainly didn't ask you because I wanted to get the better of someone else by making sure they couldn't have you.'

'Oh, but that wasn't the sole reason I accepted your invitation! I *do* like you, Charlie, I *really* like you, even if it didn't start out that way,' she conceded, dropping her voice. 'You see I—'

Josie tried to continue but Charlie turned towards her and put up his hand. 'I think you'd better stop before you say something you might regret.'

'I'd like to explain,' Josie tried to say, but Charlie had turned away and was already walking back to the cloakroom; all she could do was to follow him while trying to ignore the astonished stares their raised voices had attracted.

They made their way back to the car without saying another word, Josie determined not to lose control of the scalding tears that prickled behind her eyes, and they drove the whole way home in silence.

When they reached Coronation Street Josie felt that she must say something as she couldn't bear that the evening was ending so badly.

'I suppose I got carried away with trying to punish Hilda for the way she'd treated me,' Josie said as Charlie pulled into the kerb outside the corner shop. 'It went too far and I'm sorry. But I certainly didn't mean to hurt anyone.'

'It's too late for that,' was all that Charlie said and he leant across and opened the passenger door for her without getting out of the car.

Josie felt awful but she didn't know where to begin apologizing and as she closed the car door as quietly as possible she said, 'I . . . I'll see you sometime. Thanks for . . . thanks for asking me.'

'I'm sure you'll see me out and about, however much we both might try to avoid it, as I do have to earn my living in this neighbourhood, at least for the time being,' Charlie said, 'but I'll try not to get in your way.'

Chapter 20

Josie was upset about how things had turned out between her and Charlie but she wasn't sure she could do anything about it. Once she had begun to get to know him she had changed her mind about him but it was seemingly too late. Now, when she would have liked to have seen him, he seemed to be making sure that their paths no longer crossed. Avoiding Hilda, however, was proving to be a much more difficult task. For one thing, there appeared to be discrepancies in the till in the corner shop and this was causing no end of problems. There were differences in the amount of money that should have been left in the drawer each night and the amount that was actually there, and Hilda insisted on rounding up all those who had access to the till to discuss it.

'I'm sorry if you don't like it, Mum,' Hilda said when Elsie complained that Hilda was being high-handed, 'but we have all been using the till at one time or another and I can assure you I'm not accusing anybody in particular.' But Josie thought she saw a sly look pass across Hilda's face as she spoke. 'The fact of the matter is that almost every night now the amount of money left in the till does not match the amount that should be there according to the till roll and I think we need to look into it.'

'You mean someone is pinching money?' Elsie looked at each of them in turn and frowned, disbelieving.

'I couldn't say, Mum,' Hilda said. 'Sometimes money is missing; usually only small amounts of change, but sometimes there are extra quantities of equally small amounts left over at the end of the day and I can't make any sense of it. That's why I thought it might be sensible for us to all put our heads together to see if anyone has any suggestions as to what might be happening and what we might be able to do about it.'

'Are there any occasions when it's exactly right and there's no discrepancy?' Elsie asked but Hilda didn't answer.

'What about any regular last-minute customers? Anyone who is always in the shop when we're closing up and the till doesn't add up?' Shelagh suggested.

Elsie gasped and looked horrified. 'You can't go accusing customers!'

'I'm not accusing anyone and that's the whole point of us meeting like this, to see if we can spot any patterns or routines that might make sure that we don't shoot off our mouths making false accusations.'

'Maybe there are some routines that we could adopt that might help us decide the best way to tackle the problem,' Shelagh said.

'Like what?' Hilda sounded sceptical.

'Like cashing up early? Like someone else cashing up each night, a different person each day? I don't know.'

Hilda shrugged. Her eyes made a cursory sweep around the room then she examined each face in turn, as if to prove to them that she was including everyone in her scrutiny, but Josie was convinced that Hilda's comments had been directly aimed at her. Since the evening of the dance Hilda appeared to have given up on her chase for Charlie but Josie was not totally convinced that that would be the end of the matter. She was worried that Hilda might be plotting some kind of revenge for what had happened on the night of the dance. She was also concerned that Charlie might have told Hilda about the day he had rescued Josie when there had been some confusion over a customer's change. That might have made Hilda even more suspicious of her and Josie worried that Hilda was now trying to wheedle a confession out of her. Josie didn't know what to think, but she could feel the rush of blood to her cheeks and she refused to make eye contact with anyone.

True to his word, Charlie had kept out of Josie's way since their last meeting, although he continued to call in to the corner shop to collect his window-cleaning money at the end of each week. But Josie rarely saw him for he usually came when she was not on duty and he was no longer looking for excuses to see her. Indeed, the two hadn't met since he had dropped her at the front door on the night of the dance. Josie found to her surprise that she missed his chirpy-looking face and carefree banter and wished that she could tell him, but she knew that wasn't something she would ever be able to say. Then one Friday Josie returned home from an afternoon of shopping to find Charlie in the shop collecting his money as usual. He was standing with his back to the door while Elsie was dealing out change into his hand and Josie knew he hadn't seen her. But it was too late for her to back away and she was not surprised to see him stiffen when he realized she was there.

There was an awkward moment of silence until Elsie said with a cheerful smile, 'Charlie's just been telling me that his father has begun to develop . . . what was it the doctor called it?' she asked him.

'Significant pulmonary function, according to the hospital notes,' Charlie said with a grin. 'Don't worry Mrs L, the doctor had to explain it to me and my mam and she's been practising saying it all week, trying to get her teeth around it.'

Elsie repeated it. 'I presume it means good news?' she said.

'It does indeed,' Charlie said. 'Apparently it means he can breathe more easily now.'

'Then I'm very pleased for you all,' Josie said, trying to make her way through to the door at the back of the shop without having to engage him in further conversation. 'Maybe he'll be able to—' She stopped for at that moment there was a loud scream and Hilda came rushing into the shop, closely followed by Shelagh, almost pushing Josie out of the way.

'What on earth?' Elsie looked shocked. 'Hilda, what's happened? What are you thinking of, yelling like that?'

'Sorry, Mum, I couldn't help it; it was an automatic reaction to what I've just seen.'

'Why do you always have to be so dramatic? What could have happened that could possibly warrant a scream like that? We might have had customers in the shop,' she said crossly. 'What on earth would they have thought?'

'Oh, it's all right, I knew it was only Charlie in the shop.' Josie was surprised that Hilda was so dismissive but she held up her hands. 'I'm sorry to have frightened everyone like that but I'd just had a terrible shock myself.'

'Is that reason enough to scare us all to death?' Elsie chastised her. 'Now for goodness' sake will you calm down and tell us what's happened?'

'It's my money, my savings. It's missing, it's all gone.'

'Gone missing from where? Exactly how much are we talking about here?' Elsie frowned. 'I wasn't aware you had any money, certainly not any savings worth bothering about.'

'Well, I have – or should I say I *had* quite a few pounds. There was a ten-bob note and the rest was in half-crowns and two-bob pieces. But it's all gone from my hidey-hole. Disappeared.'

'But how did you manage to save so much money and why would you need it? You always seem to spend it as soon as you earn it.' Shelagh sounded incredulous.

'I'd been saving because I'd promised myself a new winter coat for next season and I'd seen one that I liked at Affleck and Brown. It was in the sale but even then it wasn't cheap and I was saving very hard.'

'And where was this hidey-hole?' Shelagh asked. 'It couldn't have been a very safe place.'

'If I tell you that then everyone will know and it won't be a secret hiding place any more,' Hilda said and for a moment, Josie wanted to laugh. Obviously it wasn't very secret already. Someone must have known.

'Did you tell anyone else that you had so much money? Or where you kept it?' Shelagh asked.

'Credit me with some sense! I certainly hadn't told anyone,' Hilda said. 'Why would I do that?'

Josie was aware of Charlie's eyes swivelling in her direction while Elsie was looking about the shop. 'Well, no one else has been in the shop today and I'm sure there's no one here who would be interested in stealing your money,' Elsie said.

'But you don't know that. How can you be sure?' Hilda said sharply. 'I think we need to start looking for it ourselves, first.'

'And if we don't find anything then we'll have to ring the police,' Shelagh said. 'Let them come and sort it out.'

'I don't think there'll be any need for that yet,' Hilda said quickly, and Josie thought she saw a look of fear flash across Hilda's face.

'But how can you hope to identify it even if we think we've found it?' Elsie said. 'Money is money.

How are you going to be certain who it belongs to, even if we do find some notes and coins? Can you prove that they're yours? Do they have your name on them?'

'Yes, they do, as a matter of fact.' Hilda gave what to Josie looked like a smug smile that sent a shiver down her back. 'I will recognize *my* money as you call it because I took the precaution of marking it.'

This revelation was followed by a horrified silence as it seemed to have taken them all by surprise and they turned to stare at Hilda.

'I marked the ten-bob note with a black laundry pen and I made some scratches on the silver coins,' Hilda said with a satisfied smirk as she looked from one to the other. 'I thought it might be a good idea after the discrepancies we found recently in the till.'

Josie watched Elsie's puzzled frown deepen into one of anger and frustration when Hilda insisted that they should all empty their purses and pockets.

'You can't be suggesting . . .!' was Elsie's outraged response and Josie thought she was going to refuse.

'I'm not suggesting anything,' Hilda said, 'but after all the fuss we've had regarding the till problem lately, a problem that we still haven't resolved, there's no harm in ruling people out. Surely it's better to be safe than sorry?'

Josie felt a sudden wave of fear, though she didn't know why for her conscience was clear. But if this was further evidence of Hilda seeking revenge, where would it end?

'I think that's a good idea. I certainly don't mind.' It was Charlie's voice that suddenly chimed in good-naturedly, and without further ado he laid out on the counter all the money that Elsie had just been counting out into his hand. 'And if it helps, I'm happy to turn out my pockets as well,' he said, and he pulled everything out of his loose-flowing waist-coat pockets that had been filled as usual with his cleaning rags. Then he turned his trouser pockets inside out to show that they were empty and produced his wallet containing a solitary pound note from the inside pocket of his donkey jacket.

'Thank you. That's very generous of you.' Hilda gave Charlie an ingratiating smile then turned to the others. 'See, it wasn't hard, was it?'

Nobody moved or said anything for a moment. Josie felt an icy tingle, like cold water trickling down her spine, though she didn't know why and she watched as the others turned out the contents of their pockets and their bags and felt the fear once more clutch at her chest as she emptied the contents of her own handbag out onto the counter.

'We need to see the inside of the ladies' purses as well as the contents of the handbags,' Hilda said, swiftly up-ending Shelagh's purse and scattering change across the counter. Josie didn't know why she was not surprised when her purse was pounced on by Hilda who, with a triumphant cry opened the clasp to produce a brown ten shilling note with a black mark in the corner and two cryptically scratched half-crowns, holding them up for all to see.

Chapter 21

It was still daylight, a real spring evening, when all the excitement had died down and Charlie finally finished his rounds collecting his earnings from everyone in Coronation Street. He went back to the corner shop to pick up his bike that he had left propped up against the lamppost and he was surprised to find Josie sitting on the wall outside, creating showers of cement as she kicked her heels against the rough brickwork. He hadn't been able to stay cross with her for very long and it gave him a thrill to think that she might be waiting for him, but he didn't know what to make of the relieved expression on her face.

'Waiting for me by any chance?' he said and he felt surprisingly pleased when she nodded a yes.

'I thought maybe I'd made a mistake and that you wouldn't come back for your bike tonight,' she said.

'No mistake,' he said. 'I might have a fancy car at home but that's only for special occasions. My trusty old bike is good enough for work.' He looked at her carefully, trying to read the expression on her face and hesitated, hoping he hadn't misread her signals. 'Of course, I could leave it here a bit longer and we could have a drink in the Rovers if you'd like?' he said and he was gratified to see a blush rush up her neck and embrace her cheeks.

'Thanks, that would be very nice,' she said, 'if you've forgiven me?'

He didn't answer directly; all he said was, 'I think you deserve one after the kind of afternoon you've had. I was a bit concerned about leaving you in the midst of that dreadful situation in the shop earlier. I take it you've recovered and that you're all right now?'

She nodded again, not speaking, and when she looked up at him he was surprised to see her eyes were glistening.

'Want to talk about it?' he asked.

She lifted her shoulders and quickly dropped them again. 'Mebbe, mebbe not. Let's go and have a drink while I decide,' she said.

It was busy in the Rovers as it usually was on a Friday night but they managed to find a table for two in a quieter corner. Several of the men who were Friday regulars approached Charlie, trying to persuade him to join them in a darts match, but when he indicated that he was with Josie they quickly melted away again and drifted towards the bar.

'Want to tell me what happened after I left the shop?' Charlie said after they had settled down with their drinks.

Josie sighed. 'Thanks for sticking up for me,' she said, 'but I'm afraid that despite that it all got worse after you left,' she said. 'I mean, I swear I never touched any of Hilda's money, not today, not ever. I didn't even know she *had* any money, never mind where she'd hidden it. But the evidence was there. I'm afraid marks don't lie.'

'No, on one level they don't. But it doesn't prove *you* put the money there; it could have been planted by someone else just to make you look bad.'

Josie's eyes widened. 'Who could be so mean as to do that?' Then she grimaced and looked defeated. 'No, don't say it, I already have my own suspicions.'

'Me too. If it means anything, I really don't believe that it was you who took the money. I don't think for one minute that you stole Hilda's savings and we probably agree on the real culprit.'

'Gosh, thank you for saying that. It means a lot to me,' Josie said.

Charlie put his finger under her chin in an attempt to make her look at him. 'I said it because it's true,' he said, 'and I think that Elsie believes you're innocent too.'

'Do you?' Josie said.

'I do,' Charlie said. 'And if Elsie is on your side then Hilda will not be able to have things all her own way and Elsie might be able to talk some sense into her.'

Josie nodded again. 'The only problem is that I'm afraid it might be a bit late for that now. Hilda has already had too much of her own way and once Hilda makes her mind up . . . And she has a lot of influence over her sister, so who knows what kind of a story they can concoct between them. Unfortunately the marks on the note and the coins were plain enough for everyone to see.'

'Never mind that – as I say, that doesn't prove you put them in your purse.'

'The trouble is Hilda won't go looking any further. Even if she didn't plant it, she's already made her mind up and she's insisting that I should have nothing more to do with the till, so if that isn't accusing me I don't know what is.'

'Oh dear. That's unfortunate,' Charlie said.

'In one respect, but I never wanted anything to do with the wretched till in the first place—' Josie stopped. She had caught herself in time and she didn't expand.

'Do you know, the truth is I've never, *ever* had a ten-bob note in my purse,' Josie said, 'so I know that someone else definitely planted it.' She lowered her voice. 'And I have no doubt that it was Hilda who put it there.' They both lapsed into silence then Josie said softly, 'I'm afraid she's the one who's been at the root of all the trouble ever since I arrived. She never wanted me here in the first place and I'm convinced it's her doing whenever something goes wrong.'

Charlie nodded. 'So what happens now?' he asked.

'I have to find a way to prove my innocence,' Josie said with a sigh, 'before Hilda ends up driving me away.'

'Away where?' Charlie asked quickly, alarmed to think that things could reach such a pitch so quickly.

'I've been thinking recently that maybe I made a mistake coming here and I've been wondering about upping sticks and sailing over to join my mother and her new husband in Ireland. I get on all right with him and he's always tried to be nice to me. I know my mum would like it.'

Charlie looked at her, alarmed, surprised by his own reaction. 'But if you run away like that, don't you think it's going to make it look as if you're guilty?' he tried to reason.

'I really don't know what else I can do,' Josie said, dispirited now, but she had to smile when Charlie made an exaggerated pantomime of pretending to think.

'Let me see,' he said, ponderously, 'you could stay here and drink yourself into oblivion, or you could go to the cinema and sit through film after film, and um, what else could you do?' He was relieved when Josie laughed and he saw her blushing again.

'But I must say that I'm not entirely blameless in all this,' she said. 'Not the money thing but because I do owe you an apology, and that was the main reason why I was hanging about waiting to see you.'

'Apologize about what?' Charlie said.

'About the dance, again. You were right. I was using you to get at Hilda. She had been rotten to me from the first day I arrived and I knew she liked you and I thought what better way to get back at her? In the beginning I didn't even want to go to the dance, I just wanted to spoil things for Hilda. But I wasn't really thinking about you. I admit it wasn't very nice of me to treat you like that when you had done nothing but be kind and welcoming to me and I'm sorry. I took it too far when I had no right to interfere at all.'

'Yes . . . well . . .' Charlie began, remembering how he had felt at the time, although he knew in his heart that he couldn't hold a grudge against her for long. 'I forgive you for being so rotten to me,' he said flippantly. Never one to sulk, he had made his point and was happy to let it go. 'But just think, darn it, what I've missed. I could have been stepping out with Hilda by now,' he said. 'We might even have been engaged to be married.' He gave an exaggerated sigh.

Josie looked at him quickly then realized he was joking. 'I'm afraid I spoilt things for you there,' she said, following suit and trying to make light of it.

'We should ask Hilda how *she* feels about it,' Charlie said with a laugh. 'She's the one who benefits in the end by having a lucky escape from me, and maybe she's realized that by now.'

He was aware of Josie looking at him wistfully. 'Well, I certainly don't gain anything unless I can clear my name,' she said, looking away quickly, 'and anyway, I think most girls would think themselves lucky to have a nice fella like you, not just Hilda.'

Chapter 22

Billy Walker had never been so humiliated. It wasn't like him to allow himself to be shamed in front of others but he could still feel the coldness of the old woman's fingers close to his throat as Ena Sharples grabbed hold of his collar and virtually frogmarched him up to the bar in the Rovers. His instinct was to turn around and kick the silly old cow in the ankle, but at the last moment common sense prevailed and even he realized that would have been a stupid thing to do in such a public place and would have earned him no sympathy from anyone.

'I believe this belongs to you,' Mrs Sharples had said grimly to his father, and Billy didn't know which way to look, squirming under the scrutiny.

Jack Walker was manning the bar single-handed at that moment and he'd looked up, startled, as Ena pushed Billy towards him with an air of disgust.

'Is there a problem, Mrs Sharples?' Jack asked, an alarmed look on his face.

'Not for me there isn't, but I don't know about you,' she said.

'How do you mean?' Billy hadn't seen such a look of bewilderment since the day his father had returned from the war and Billy hadn't known who he was. As his father looked from him to the old woman, Billy was desperately trying to think of what he could say, what lies he could make up in response to the accusations that he knew were bound to be coming his way. He couldn't repudiate a drinks charge as the bottle of port he'd pinched from behind the bar was half-empty and was still in his hands, and he couldn't deny he'd been smoking because Jack's sensitive nose was bound to pick up the lingering cigarette smoke on his breath and the stale tobacco on his clothes. The only thing he could refute was Christine's whereabouts because she seemed to have successfully disappeared, having slipped out of the back entry when they had snuck downstairs. They'd been listening to records as they often did whenever they decided to take the afternoon off school and thankfully she seemed to have had the presence of mind to escape so that they wouldn't both be caught red-handed when they had slipped downstairs, and with Christine on lookout Billy had been busy nicking another couple of bottles of booze.

'Hellfire, what have you been up to now, lad?' Jack Walker confronted him.

'Nothing, honest.'

'Don't you "honest" me and then come out with a pack of porkies. I know your sort, Billy Walker!'

Billy was furious when Mrs Sharples intervened before his father had a chance to say anything. And she not only dared to continue holding him by the collar but she had the temerity to give him a shake to remind him that she had not gone away.

'I caught him, large as life, with bottles of beer, this port, and packets of cigarettes, both of which are illegal at his age as you well know, landlord,' she said angrily. She pulled Billy towards her so that her face almost touched his, all the while glaring at Jack over Billy's shoulder. 'Why isn't he in school, that's what I'd like to know?'

Ena still didn't let go and Billy didn't know how he managed not to scream into her face that she should mind her own bloody business. However, he was glad that he hadn't, for out of the corner of his eye he caught sight of his mother as she came into the bar, wiping the last of the pint glasses ready for hanging up, and humming her favourite hymn. He heaved a sigh of relief for he knew he could always count on her to back him against someone like Ena Sharples; she had even stood up for him against his father on occasion. No, Billy was not a bit worried about his mother, not like he was afraid of his father. But his relief was short-lived when he saw Jack beckoning to Dot the barmaid to come back from her break immediately and take over in the bar.

'Would you mind holding the fort for a few minutes, Dot?' Jack asked politely. 'There's just something Annie and I need to sort out,' he went on, and to Billy's surprise, Jack then gave a nod of thanks to Mrs Sharples while he indicated to Billy and his mother that the family should turn about and take Dot's place in the kitchen.

Annie Walker looked puzzled though she asked no questions while they were still in public view and Billy felt a moment of panic. He had not seen such an angry look on his father's face since he had been asked to remove Billy from the boys' private school some months previously. Billy looked once more to his mother for support as he usually did but her eyes had a look of grim disappointment even though superficially she managed to hold on to the smile she had painted onto her lips earlier.

She hung on to it until the three of them were seated at the freshly scrubbed kitchen table.

'Now then, Jack.' It was Annie who spoke first, her voice struggling to sound controlled and reasonable, anxious to diffuse the situation quickly. 'Would you kindly tell me what all this is about.'

'He can tell you better than me,' Jack said roughly, pointing to Billy. 'Tell her what Mrs Sharples caught you doing.'

'Interfering old biddy!' Billy muttered while his mother moaned, 'Oh no, Billy! Not Mrs Sharples again. What was it this time?'

Billy shrugged. 'She caught me in the ginnel having a fag. That was all. So what?'

'AND?' Jack demanded.

'And she SAID she saw me take a swig of port.'

Annie's face softened. 'Oh, Billy!' she said. 'What are we going to do with you?' She didn't look like she expected an answer and Jack wasted no time before jumping in.

'I'll tell you what we're going to do with him. If that boy isn't back in Bessie Street Seniors first thing tomorrow morning, we're going to send him to Accrington to go down the mines with my cousin Jim; *that's* what we're going to do with him.'

Billy visibly relaxed with a sigh of relief at what he saw as an empty threat, though his mother didn't see it like that.

'Oh no, not that again!' Annie wailed.

'Yes, very much that again.' Jack spoke softly now but his words, pronounced so crisply and clearly, nevertheless sounded menacing, and Billy sat up, unsure whether to take them seriously.

'But this is not like before. This time I've had it up to my back teeth with him and I mean it.' Jack's voice was steadily rising now and he continued to enunciate each word distinctly. Then he leaned across the table. 'He promised to go back to school and I'd begged them to take him in again and Bessie Street Seniors was all ready for him,' Jack said, stabbing at Billy's shoulder with his finger in time with his words. 'But has he kept his promise? No, and now caught with fags and booze too. Believe me, this is his last chance. If he doesn't go to school NOW he will be going off to stay with our Jim and he'll be down that mine faster than you can say Jack Robinson.'

'Oh, Jack no,' Annie's voice was pleading now, obviously convinced that her husband had reached the end of his tether.

'Oh, Annie, yes!' Jack responded in a flash. 'He will go down that mine, Annie, and there's an end to it, until he learns his lesson.' He turned to face Billy. 'See how clever you feel when you've been stuck hundreds of feet underground carving out coal with a pickaxe for twelve hours a day, six days a week, fifty weeks of the year?'

Billy felt himself quail under the onslaught.

'That is not a threat, boy, that is a promise. I've had enough. Do you hear me? Enough!' Jack's voice had reached thunder level now and Billy gingerly sat back in his chair, finally chastened by what he had heard. He knew better than to cross his father when Jack was in this kind of a mood and to Billy's surprise Annie said nothing further either.

'So? What's it to be, eh?' Jack said after a brief pause and he leaned forward so that his forehead touched Billy's. 'Shall I send a note to your headmaster to say that you have now officially left school to earn your living down the pit?'

Billy shook his head though he didn't look up. 'I'll go back to school, Dad, I promise.' Billy did his best to avoid his father's gaze as he said this but he had miscalculated the strength of Jack's feelings.

'What's that? Can't look me in the eye?' Jack taunted him. Billy looked up, unable to duck eye contact this time. 'And you'll knuckle down so that you can get a decent kind of job when you leave school?'

Billy nodded.

'Say it so that your mother can hear as well. We

both need to know what you're actually promising to do,' Jack demanded. And Billy's cheeks burned as he repeated the words.

Billy was afraid that his mother might insist on accompanying him to school the next morning to be certain that he got there and he made sure to be up early before his alarm clock rang. But it was all he could do to persuade her not to walk with him at least part of the way.

'You don't have to worry, honest, Mum,' he said, 'I've arranged to meet up with Christine next door; she's going in tomorrow too, we'll go together,' he lied. But when he realized that Annie was watching him as she cleaned the outside windows of the Rovers bar from the street he decided it would be safer to go through the motions at least and he knocked on the front door of number 13. To his relief, Christine answered the door herself and seemed pleased to see him.

'Hang on a minute while I tell my mum I'm off,' she said, and as they emerged from the front door Billy cheekily waved when he thought he saw his mother watching him from the other end of the street. As they slowly made their way to Bessie Street Seniors, Billy filled Christine in on at least some of the story of what had happened the previous day after she had managed to escape unseen.

'Gosh, that sounds like a near miss. It was a good job I got out when I did,' Christine said, 'otherwise your dad might have been really angry at the both of us. He might have forbidden us to meet, ever again. Imagine that.'

Billy shrugged his indifference, smothering a laugh with a cough when he saw the hurt on Christine's face.

'But I must say I don't like the sound of those pits one little bit.' She shivered. 'Do you think he meant it? Would he really have carried out his threat?'

'I'm sure he would,' Billy said earnestly, puffing out his chest as if to show off the extent of his bravery. 'You should have seen his face! I could tell he was ready to throw me through the parlour window.' He always enjoyed embellishing his stories for more gullible listeners and he certainly didn't mind letting Christine believe that he had been braver in facing up to his parents than he actually had been.

'Anyway, I'd already decided that I was going back to school and concentrate a bit,' Billy said as they approached the gates.

'Really? I thought you were done with all of that?'

'Well . . .' Billy said, 'I've thought about it a lot recently and decided there's nowt wrong with getting a decent education while I've got the chance – and you should think about it too.'

'What's made you change your mind? The threat of maybe having to go down a pit?'

'Hm,' Billy was thoughtful, realizing he might have to make some adjustments to his story before he could talk about his change of heart to anyone else. 'No, I intend going up in the world,' he said, and he stuck his nose in the air and imitated the posh voice he heard his mother use whenever she talked of such matters. He was surprised when Christine laughed.

'Sorry, I don't know if it was deliberate but you sounded just like your mother when you did that.'

'Did I? Well, that's because I mean it. She might have got stuck here, but I have no more intention than you have of staying in Coronation Street for the rest of my life.'

Christine looked impressed. 'Oh, and that reminds me, I've got something to show you,' she said. Christine suddenly looked excited and began to scrabble about inside her satchel. She pulled out a tattered looking piece of paper that had been cut out of a recent issue of the *Manchester Evening News*.

'I saw this the other day and I've been meaning to show you,' she said.

'What is it?'

'It's an advertisement for a secretarial college in London where you can get all kinds of special office training. I showed it to Miss Jenkins, my commerce teacher, and she said she'd heard of it and that it was dead good so I'm going to apply.'

Billy glanced at it then passed it back.

'I thought you'd be pleased.' Christine looked disappointed at his seeming lack of interest.

'Why does it matter what *I* think? What do you want me to say? Did your teacher think you might get in?'

'Possibly, but she also said I'd probably have more chance if I got some decent qualifications when I leave school.'

'There you are then, like I told you. You need to think about your future as well, then maybe it won't matter what your parents say, or if they'll pay for you to go to college or not. You might be able to get some kind of grant, or something, so that you can do the training without their permission.'

'Do you think so?' Christine suddenly grabbed hold of his arm. 'You know I want to be a secretary, don't you?'

'Yeah, you've only told me a few hundred times.'

'Wouldn't that be great to think that we both might be able to use our education when we get to London, and that it wasn't all just a waste of time?'

Billy frowned. Here she was, talking again about London as if they were going there together. He wasn't sure where that mistaken notion had come from but then he didn't always pay close attention when Christine went off into one of her daydreams. She let go of his arm and skipped off ahead as though she was already celebrating their new life and Billy decided today wasn't the moment to spoil her fun.

Chapter 23

After the disaster regarding the disappearance of Hilda's money and the missing money from the till, there were new tensions in the Lappin household and an uncomfortable atmosphere seemed to settle over the corner shop when they were all in the same room. At times it made Josie feel utterly miserable and even though she had picked up some paid dress-making work when Elsie told everyone how skilled she was, she wasn't sure how much longer she could bear it. However, she was grateful for Elsie's continuing support and was eager to show that, even though she avoided working in the shop as much as possible.

'You know, I appreciate everything you've done for me since the day I arrived.' Josie approached

Elsie when tensions over breakfast had resulted in another squabble between the three younger women one morning. 'I appreciate how hard it must be to stick up for me when your own daughters don't believe me,' Josie said. 'And I do understand why Hilda doesn't want me using the till. Honestly, I have no wish to go anywhere near it, but it can be awkward at times as I'm sure you must know. The thing is, I've been thinking that maybe it would be easier for everyone if I just left.'

Elsie's look had been one of horror and she refused to listen to anything more on the subject. 'That is not the answer, believe me, Josie,' Elsie insisted. 'It would just be like running away. Besides, you don't need to work in the shop now that your dressmaking business is expanding.' She looked at Josie appealingly. 'You know I made a promise to your mother so I feel responsible and I won't let you even consider going to live anywhere else. This is your home and it's up to me and the girls to work out how to make it feel like that for you.'

Josie looked at her with a grateful smile. Elsie had trusted her and supported her from the first day, refusing to accept that Josie had done anything wrong. And as Charlie had said, to leave now would be tantamount to confessing to something she wasn't guilty of and it would be like giving Elsie a slap in the face which would hardly be fair.

Josie sighed. 'But if I am to stay then I can't go on living under a cloud like this. I have to find a way to put things right.' Josie hesitated as she said this, for deep down she knew what she had to do to clear her name even though she hated to admit it. There was no other way. She would finally have to share her secret. The only problem was that she wasn't sure she was ready to do that yet.

Some of the tensions did begin to ease a little, at least with regard to Shelagh whose attitude was beginning to soften, and at times it seemed as if she might be prepared to offer Josie an olive branch. It was only Hilda's behaviour that remained difficult to cope with but Josie could see no way of that ever changing. No matter how much she tried, Hilda remained obstructive. She insisted that Josie must not be allowed to be involved in any sales transactions in the shop, although she did accept Josie's offers to help to sort out the stock, and Josie took the opportunity to work closely with Elsie on such occasions for the two of them to have a private chat.

'I don't know if you saw Mrs Barlow in here the other day?' Elsie said when they were relocating some of the bottled sauces and transferring the newly arrived tins of fish onto the shelves behind the slabs of cheese.

'No, I didn't,' Josie said. 'I had a dress order to finish. Why do you ask?'

Elsie giggled and for a moment sounded like a child. 'It all seems rather silly, although Ida seemed quite serious.'

'Oh? And what's that about? I'm intrigued,' Josie said.

'It's to do with Mrs Sharples putting her oar in for a change,' Elsie said. 'Apparently, she asked Ida to see if I would consider "making a comeback" as she called it.'

'A comeback?' Josie stopped what she was doing. 'You mean to sing?' She couldn't keep the excitement out of her voice.

Elsie nodded. 'For some reason she seems to think it would be a real coup for Coronation Street to have me sing at the street party and she wanted to know if I would consider reviving Melody Mae on June the second.'

'Wow! That's exciting,' Josie said. 'I know they've been talking for some time about the possibility of taking the Rovers' piano outside,' Josie said, 'but nothing more than that.'

'Ida said they'd like me to put together a short programme of my own songs and then list a few songs where I would lead everyone in a good old-fashioned singsong.'

'And did you say yes? Would you do it?' Josie said enthusiastically.

'No!' Elsie said, too quickly Josie thought, particularly as there was an edge to her voice. 'I can't sing any more. I accepted that that part of my life was well behind me a long time ago,' Elsie went on. She hesitated, sharing a wistful look with several tins of sardines that she was stacking on the shelf in front of her. 'And even if I had the voice, I certainly wouldn't have the confidence any more,' she said with a defeated sigh.

'That's a pity,' Josie said, 'I bet your voice is still a hundred times better than most other people's.'

'What makes you say than?' Elsie asked.

'I heard you singing in the bath only the other day, and thought how beautiful your voice still was despite everything.'

Elsie paused what she was doing and stared at Josie. 'That couldn't have been me,' she protested, laughing. 'I don't sing any more, not even in the bath.'

'Then who . . .?'

'That must have been Hilda. She's the only one who sings around here these days. I'm surprised you haven't heard her before.'

'Maybe I have and not realized it was her.' She didn't like to add that she found it difficult to put

Hilda's name together with lovely singing.

'She's certainly got a sweet voice,' Elsie said. 'In fact, there was a time when she was younger when she'd have done anything to be able to sing with me. She only wanted us to do a duet. It was a pity she was a few years too late, but let me tell you she was very jealous of your mother. Partly because Marjorie and I sang so well together and partly because your mum's showbiz career went on much longer than mine.'

'Jealous? Hilda?' Josie looked at her in astonishment. She had never heard that story before.

'As jealous as any little girl can be of someone so much older than themselves,' Elsie said, 'and I think she blamed your mum for my career ending,' she finished, and Josie stopped what she was doing for an idea was already swirling around in her head. Could she pull it off?

Chapter 24

'I suppose you know that Hilda planted that money in your purse?'

Josie had been working alone in the shop, refilling and restocking, and she looked up, astonished, to find Shelagh leaning against the doorjamb.

Josie sighed. 'No, I guessed it but I didn't know for certain. How could I when she won't admit it and keeps blaming me?'

'Yes. You're right,' Shelagh said. 'She's proving to be very stubborn on the subject.'

Josie sighed. 'I know that I didn't do it and I thought she was beginning to bend when she didn't pursue it, but she's still sticking to her story about having found the money in my purse.'

'I've tried to make her see reason but so far nothing I say will shift her,' Shelagh said. 'I don't know what she's got against you. Well, I do, but she's dragging it out a bit. Even by her usual standards.'

Josie stopped what she was doing and looked thoughtfully at Shelagh.

'Funnily enough there was something I found out about Hilda that I didn't know until yesterday. Something that might explain what might be at the root of it.'

'Oh? And what was that?' Shelagh stepped down into the shop and went to perch on the high stool in front of the counter that was usually kept for customers.

'Your mother told me something that probably accounts for her hating me so much and explains why she's been doing everything she can to make my life miserable ever since I came here.'

'Really? And what's that?'

'It seems she was jealous of my mother because she wanted to sing with Melody Mae but it was too late by the time she came along. Your mother's career was over while my mum's life in show-biz still had a long way to run. She blamed my mother for ending Elsie's career prematurely and I imagine that it wasn't difficult to transfer all of that hatred and anger she felt against my mother onto me.'

'There wasn't much you could do if her opinions were already fixed before she even set eyes on you,' Shelagh said.

'I suppose not,' Josie agreed.

'And how did you find out about this?'

'It was something your mother said when we were having a chat yesterday,' Josie said. 'And rightly or wrongly I put two and two together.'

Shelagh sighed. 'Hilda has strong feelings about lots of things and it seems like she always has to have someone to hate.'

'It was just unfortunate that she picked on me,' Josie said.

'So it seems. But then you did make the mistake of bagging Charlie from under her very nose. You never should have done that.'

'No, I agree it wasn't a nice thing to have happened.' Josie had the good grace to look shame-faced. 'But in actual fact I didn't bag him so much as he chased me – in the beginning at any rate.' Josie tried to defend herself though she could see how it must have looked from their point of view.

'Either way you gave her ammunition and that was enough for Hilda,' Shelagh said. 'She felt perfectly justified in doing what she was doing.'

'I can see that now, but tell me something, how do you know for certain that it was Hilda who planted the money in my purse?' Josie wanted to know.

'Because I saw her do it,' Shelagh said, 'though I suppose I was looking out for it. I knew there would have to be some kind of retaliation for the Charlie episode.' Her head dropped and she couldn't look at Josie. 'I'm really sorry I didn't speak up before,' she said eventually, 'but she is my sister and I'm afraid my seeing it doesn't really help you because getting her to admit what she did is another matter altogether.'

'I don't know what's going to make her do that,' Josie said. 'She really doesn't give in easily, does she? I don't know what it's going to take to get her to admit that I had nothing to do with it and to confess that she was trying to get her own back.'

They sat in silence for a few moments. 'Do you think there's ever going to be a chance of us calling a truce at least?' Josie raised her eyebrows questioningly and Shelagh gave a wry smile.

'That would be fine by me,' Shelagh said eventually. 'I think this whole stupid business has gone on long enough and all I can say is that nobody, apart from Hilda, blames you.'

'But I need her to admit her part in all this if I'm to clear my name,' Josie said, 'and I'm sure you understand why that's important to me.'

'Of course. As far as I'm concerned you're not guilty and I think you know that Mum and Charlie back you too. But as to Hilda . . .?' Shelagh opened her hands, palms up in a hopeless gesture. 'You can try. But I can't see her owning up.'

Shelagh began to wander about the shop, touching things, picking items up and putting them down again as if she was expecting something to happen to one of them. She stopped when she got to the large cash register that sat proudly on the end of the counter. 'And then there's the other matter of the till discrepancies that I really don't understand,' Shelagh said. 'Not that I'm blaming you for that,' she added quickly, 'but you have to agree that is a bit of a mystery and, try as I might, I can't see how Hilda could possibly be responsible for any of that.'

Josie was grateful to Shelagh for speaking up so freely and she could feel some of the tension falling away from her shoulders as they continued to talk, but she was also aware that they were no closer to resolving anything and she wasn't sure where to go next.

The decision was made for her when the shop bell pinged, announcing that Hilda had arrived home late from work.

'Blimey, looks like a bloomin' delegation!' Hilda stopped and stepped back into the doorway. 'I'm not that late, am I? What's going on that you're both sitting here waiting for me?'

'Nothing's going on.' Josie spoke up first, though she then felt tongue-tied and wasn't able to continue.

'Some of us have got to keep the money coming in,' Hilda said, the spiteful edge still apparent in her voice as she looked around the shop. 'Where's Mum? Why isn't she in on this family pow-wow?'

'Mum's in the kitchen getting up our tea and this is not a family pow-wow although it would be nice to think we could have a peaceful solution. In any case, I'm sure tea will be ready pretty soon,' Shelagh said, 'but Josie's got something to ask you first.'

Josie was taken aback. She was grateful to Shelagh for filling what threatened to be an awkward silence but she wasn't prepared to confront Hilda now.

'Oh yes?' Hilda said, 'I'm all ears, or I will be once I've hung my coat up.' She turned to face Josie, her eyes challenging, and Josie took the opportunity to speak up before she lost her nerve.

'I'm not happy with the awful atmosphere that's been hanging over the shop recently. It's upsetting me and I'm sure it's not pleasant for your mother or Shelagh to have to live like this. I'd like us to call a truce,' Josie said bluntly to the astonished Hilda. 'I think it's time to put behind us any disagreements from the past, any bad feelings that have built up since I arrived, and start again.' Josie did her best to keep her voice steady but to her dismay, Hilda laughed.

'Why would I want to do that? *You're* the culprit here so I've got nothing to gain by surrendering, as far as I can see.'

'Then do it for your mother,' Josie said.

'Why? Because she's always sucking up to you?'

'No, because she and my mother are best friends even if we're not and they have been for many years. I'm sure you don't want them to fall out over something as petty as this any more than I do, because I bet that would make your mum even sadder than she is already. She's not had an easy life and I'm sure she would be much happier if we could all live in peace.'

Josie was pleased to see Shelagh looking at her sister eagerly as if hoping for a positive answer, but Hilda's face said she didn't care.

'And whose side are you on, little sister?' Hilda said, her voice mocking.

'It's not a question of sides,' Shelagh said. 'It's a question of doing the right thing and trying to make everyone feel better, especially Mam. If nothing else, will you at least admit to planting that money in Josie's purse, because I saw you, you know. I watched you do it.'

There was a momentary surge of protest on Hilda's face, as if she was about to challenge Shelagh's assertion, before it quickly disappeared. 'What if you did?' she said defiantly, looking from one to the other. 'You can't actually prove I did anything wrong, whereas I've got evidence that she did.' She jabbed her finger in Josie's direction.

Josie gave an exasperated sigh. This was going nowhere and she crossed the shop floor smartly to go back to her room. She stopped in the doorway as one last thought that might offer a glimmer of hope came to mind. 'By the way,' she said, smiling directly at Hilda, 'I've been meaning to tell you that I heard you singing in the bath yesterday and you've got a lovely voice, you sounded just like your mother.' She was gratified when both girls stared in her direction, even though Hilda looked at her as if she was mad, at least it showed she was listening.

'I beg your pardon?' Hilda appeared to be bemused.

'I think that you have a very sweet voice,' Josie said. 'You must have inherited it from your mother.' For a moment Josie thought she saw something approaching a smile cross Hilda's lips.

'Do you think so? Do you know, I always wished I'd been able to sing with her?' she said and her eyes actually sparkled.

'Perhaps you should forget all this nonsense and think of offering to sing with her at the coronation party, then,' Josie said. 'I think she'd like that very much indeed, and it would cheer everyone up. I hear they're looking for entertainers.'

'Are they?' Hilda's face sparked into life if only briefly.

'Yes, better get in quick!' Josie said. Out of the corner of her eye she thought she saw Shelagh's nod of approval and so Josie walked away toward the kitchen satisfied that she might at least have sown a seed that could possibly lead to peace.

Chapter 25

Annie Walker stared gloomily out of the Rovers' window, watching the remaining rivulets of heavier than usual April showers join forces and gather momentum as they trickled down the recently cleaned pane.

This was not what she had wanted, the rain threatening to spoil her big moment after she had planned for the historic event so carefully. She had organized the delivery in such a way that all the street would be able to turn out to watch and possibly applaud while she and Jack took a bow. But the sodden pavements were empty, the front doors of Coronation Street remained firmly shut; and as her attention was drawn to the large Radio Rentals van that was pulling into the kerb outside the pub there was hardly anyone abroad to notice. It was the only vehicle on the street and the few people who had ventured out were hiding under their umbrellas, doing their best to give it a wide berth in order to avoid the backsplash from the overfull roadside gutters. It was infuriating that instead of the delivery men making a grand entrance that could be watched and admired by neighbours and passers-by alike, the driver and his mate pulled their hoods down over their heads and quickly slipped inside the back door of the van. The ramp was lowered and Annie's only concern was that they should be able to get their precious cargo under cover and into the pub before it could be affected by the deluge.

Annie was disappointed. She had really been looking forward to delivery day, hoping to turn it into something quite special, which was why she and Jack had agreed not to tell anyone of their plans once Mrs Sharples, their only other rival in the neighbourhood, had let it be known that she would not be purchasing a television for the coronation and had dropped out of contention. They had hoped to spring a surprise on everyone; they hadn't even told Billy and his sister Joanie until the last possible moment. Jack always preferred a cautious approach rather than having everyone talking about it in advance.

Annie had even pictured herself smiling graciously as she accepted the mantle of 'first in the street' with a minimum of fuss and the many accolades she and Jack would doubtless receive for their forward-thinking after a brief, impromptu unveiling ceremony.

'Where do you want it, love?' The older of the deliverymen asked Annie as he pulled the hastily withdrawn tarpaulin from the trolley and threw it into the back of the van. Jack directed them to the back parlour.

They manoeuvred the trolley into place so that they could slide out the cabinet and plug the lead into the new electric socket on the skirting board. Annie dried off the shiny mahogany cabinet with a soft cloth as if she was protecting glass and slid the folding doors back so that a pinhead of light appeared in the centre of the convex screen. The white light gradually grew bigger until the whole screen was filled with an amazing series of black-and-white patterns that constituted the test card they had been told to expect. The signature tune that was projected into the room at the same time was so loud it made Annie gasp.

'This ain't half a big'un!' The younger deliveryman looked impressed. 'Seventeen-inch screen! And you know you'll get a far sharper picture if you dim the lights and close the curtains?' He made a move towards the windows.

'Yes, yes, I know all that, the man in the shop gave us a demonstration. But they can stay where they are for now, thank you,' Annie said sharply. 'We can see to them later when we have time to sit down and watch; for now we have a pub to open as soon as this is installed.'

Jack looked at his watch. 'Talking of which, can we offer you a pint in the bar?' They both nodded their thanks. 'And if you could just show us what all the knobs and buttons do . . .' he said. Annie threw him an impatient look but didn't contradict.

'There's no need for that. I can show them,' a voice behind Annie said, and she turned in surprise. Billy seemed to be home suspiciously early from school despite the fact that they were both watching him like a hawk, particularly since he had been caught drinking and smoking and had been threatened with being sent off to Accrington, but there seemed no point in spoiling everyone's fun today.

'It's only just arrived. In good time for the big day. Isn't it magnificent?' Annie boasted. She didn't try to hide her own pleasure and was gratified by Billy's reactive 'cor!' She beckoned him forwards to inspect it properly. 'First in the street,' Annie said proudly. 'What do you think about that?'

'It's a corker,' Billy said. 'What's a thing like this cost?'

'Never you mind that,' Jack said, even though it was a rental agreement and they hadn't bought it outright.

Billy shrugged. 'Why didn't you tell me you'd got such a good'un?' He leant over to twiddle a few knobs and watch the picture as it began to change.

'Hey, there'll be less of that!' Jack admonished. 'You can look but don't touch and don't think of coming within a mile of it with one of your fancy screwdrivers. I know you and your "I only want to see how it works".' Jack imitated a child's voice. 'Until we know what's what I'll be the only one allowed to touch it.'

'What happens when you come crying for me to fix it when summat goes wrong,' Billy shot back, and Jack laughed.

'There'll be no need for any of that,' Jack said, pointing to the label stuck on the inside of the cabinet. 'Rental means they take care of repairs and here's the number to ring. We don't have to worry about a thing.' And Jack chuckled.

There was a definite buzz in the Rovers as a selection of favoured customers were taken into the back room to be introduced to Coronation Street's first television set and Annie was gratified to see that by the evening word had spread sufficiently for most of Weatherfield's longest-standing residents to brave the elements and come and gawp at the Rovers' latest acquisition. When they came, they stood in a cluster by the bar, awaiting their turn to go into the back room to see it and once they had seen it they were unable to talk of anything else.

'Well, aren't you the sly ones?' Ena Sharples was one of the first to comment, not willing to concede that she had never before seen one at such close quarters. 'But I'll hand it to you, you got what you wanted. You're the first, and with a whole month to spare before the coronation.'

'Isn't it just what's needed right now to cheer everyone up, something that brings us all together?' said Ida Barlow, arriving on a rare visit with her husband Frank, all agog to see the new acquisition, and she gave a wink in Mrs Walker's direction. 'Weatherfield is now bang up to date and it's going to benefit the whole of Coronation Street.'

'We do our best.' Annie acknowledged Ida's comment with a smug smile.

'I'm excited already, I can't wait to see the coronation, imagine . . .' Martha Longhurst said, clapping her hands together like a little girl.

'I've been really looking forward to the party and now we're going to be able to see the ceremony as well,' Ida said. 'A real treat. I knew someone in the street was bound to get a set in time for us all to watch,'

'And I knew that that someone would be Mrs Annie Walker,' Ena Sharples retorted with a toss of her head.

'There's nowt wrong with that, is there?' Ida said defensively.

'Not if it means she'll leave the rest of us in peace to put the finishing touches to the party plans without her interfering,' Ena said.

'How's everything going on that front?' Annie ignored the jibe, pretending she hadn't heard it and fixed a smile on her face.

'All under control I'd say, wouldn't you, Mrs Caldwell?'

Minnie looked surprised at Mrs Sharples' question but she nodded her agreement. 'They've got me and Martha roped in ready to make up the sandwiches,' she said, unaware that Mrs Sharples had rolled her eyes heavenwards.

'And I shall be organizing the cakes,' Elsie Tanner from number 11 had arrived in time to add. 'Though I'll have to get my skates on if I'm to get hold of any proper sugar in time to make some myself.'

'I'm sure you'll find a way, you usually do,' Ena Sharples muttered, but Mrs Tanner had already downed the last of her gin and tonic and gone to inspect the television.

'Did I hear right that you've given your permission for the men to take the piano outside so long as the weather's improved by then?' Ena Sharples asked Annie Walker, but before she could reply Ida interrupted. 'My Frank has volunteered to be on the lifting team,' she said proudly.

'Does that mean someone's persuaded Mrs Lappin from the corner shop to sing?' Mrs Sharples wanted to know, but Ida shrugged. 'That's not been settled, she hasn't agreed yet,' Ida said.

'What if she says no? If we don't have a proper singer leading, it will just be the usual dirge, won't it? You lot are all tone deaf!' Mrs Sharples brushed her hand down her coat as if she were removing some imaginary fluff while she carefully arranged her facial features into a disapproving frown.

'I don't think you need to worry about that, Mrs Sharples,' Ida said quickly. 'It's a proper party we're having – popular songs, patriotic victory songs, that sort of thing. It would be nice if Mrs Lappin decides to sing some of her own musical repertoire, something with a bright happy tune. But I'm sure you don't need to worry cos there won't be any kind of hymn singing,' she said looking directly at Mrs Sharples.

Ena Sharples looked affronted. She took a deep breath so that her cheeks looked as though they were about to pop. Even Minnie Caldwell and Martha Longhurst had to look away while they smothered their smiles with their hands and Mrs Sharples set her jaw and glowered.

'Talking of Mrs Lappin,' she said stiffly, 'do you know how the decorations are coming along? I heard there was a bit of a glitch – are you sure they're going to be ready in time? She's in charge of that, isn't she?'

'I believe it's Josie, that young lodger of hers who's taken charge of all the sewing,' Minnie Caldwell piped up. 'Apparently she'll be making most of the decorations herself. I understand that she's very reliable so that shouldn't be a problem. And I've heard that she's even offered to do a bit of dressmaking as well, to turn out some new outfits for the coronation for them as wants one. I myself shan't be needing anything new but there's not much time left to put your order in if you want it to be finished in good time.'

'Me neither,' Ida said, 'I don't need owt new, though I wonder if she might be able to do something to brighten up my best frock? How about you, Mrs Walker, are you having anything new?'

Annie hesitated. 'As a matter of fact I have been thinking I might. Something a little more fashionable, you know, with a longer, fuller skirt,' she said. 'Though of course I haven't seen any of her work and I would require some evidence that she can sew well before I would hire her to make anything for me.' She gave a little laugh. 'Does anybody know if she is much of a seamstress?'

'I believe that she is,' Ida Barlow said. 'Several people have tried her out recently.'

'Well, I'd get your order in sharpish if I were you, Mrs Walker,' Ena Sharples said, an innocent look on her face, 'before she gets booked up.'

Chapter 26

Josie's order book was filling rapidly, something she found very gratifying. Not only was she enjoying the sewing she was now being asked to do, making new outfits and restyling old ones, but she was pleased not to be serving in the shop every day where she had been in constant dread of her short-comings being exposed. She felt guilty when the day-to-day running of the shop naturally fell back once more onto Elsie's shoulders, but there was nothing she could do about that and she did offer to help out whenever she could, as she had done that day. It wasn't always easy to predict when the shop would be busy but it had been busy that morning, ever since the first queue had formed before they had opened, and there had been a steady stream of customers throughout the day. It had been a struggle for them to close even for half an hour at dinnertime and at the end of the day there was still much work to be done restocking the half-empty shelves. Josie offered to stay on after closing time and she and Elsie were busy well into the evening, filling in the gaps in preparation for the next morning.

'It seems funny to think that we've been working together all day but have not had a single moment to chat,' Elsie said brightly as Josie dragged in several more boxes of tinned goods to be unpacked and began to build them into a display. 'I've been meaning to tell you how pleased I was to see you and Hilda together yesterday.'

Josie felt herself stiffen but made no comment.

'I gather from Shelagh that you've been trying to patch things up between the three of you,' Elsie said.

Now Josie was aware of the heat in her face as Elsie made eye contact.

'But she didn't say much about it,' Elsie said, 'so I was hoping you would tell me what's been going on?'

'There's nothing to tell,' Josie said quickly.

'Josie!' She felt Elsie's hand on her arm. 'Josie, you can't fool me. Something has been happening and I get the distinct feeling that there's something you're not telling me.'

Josie knew that Elsie was continuing to stare at her but she still said nothing.

'H-have you asked Shelagh?' Josie said.

'No, not yet, I wanted to ask you first because some days you look as if you have the weight of the world on your shoulders and I thought it might help to talk about it.'

Josie wanted to laugh, for that was exactly what she had thought about Elsie sometimes, but she had no wish to come between the sisters and their mother right now so she had decided to say nothing.

'There's nothing to tell. Really,' she said cagily. She had never been one to lay bare her feelings and she had no intention of doing so now. 'You really don't have to worry about me,' she said. 'I can look after myself.'

'But that's just it,' Elsie said. 'Can you?' She stopped what she was doing but Josie refused to look at her.

'Oh, come on!' Josie said with a laugh. 'You know what it's like growing up in the theatre. You learn very quickly to fend for yourself. You have to if you want to survive.'

'I know, I was a youngster on stage too and it was the same for all of us,' Elsie said. 'But you're not in the theatre now.'

Josie shrugged.

'Well, I want to make sure that you know that I don't believe for one minute that you had anything to do with stealing Hilda's money,' Elsie said.

'Thank you for saying that,' Josie said. 'I appreciate you having confidence in me despite all that's happened.' She took Elsie's hand and squeezed it, looking directly into her face now.

'It's not just me that you have to thank,' Elsie said. 'Cos you know that Shelagh and Charlie have also said the same thing.'

Josie nodded.

'But the one thing I am still curious about,' Elsie said, 'is that business about the till. No one has come up with a solution to that mystery. In future I'm going to have to keep a closer eye on it and I thought that maybe you could help me. I've checked it over tonight and I'm satisfied that it's correct. I thought maybe if you wanted to double-check and we did the same each night we might be able to get to the bottom of what's going wrong.'

Without a moment's thought Josie put her hands up defensively. 'No, thanks all the same but I'm sure it's fine. I appreciate what you're trying to do but I'm not going anywhere near it. That's the one thing I do agree with Hilda about,' Josie said, 'and I'm sure there could be a whole load of different explanations as to why it goes wrong sometimes.'

Josie was suddenly on her guard and physically took a few steps back from the cash register. She shut her eyes for a moment and when she opened them again she could see Elsie scrutinizing her face. Josie turned away, not wanting the older woman to be able to read the fear and pain that she knew must be in her eyes.

'There's nothing to be afraid of, Josie,' Elsie said softly, her hand resting on the girl's arm. 'I can assure you that if I'd have thought for one minute that you weren't completely trustworthy I wouldn't have let you within a mile of the shop, never mind the till.'

The image of Elsie chasing her away made Josie want to laugh but as she felt unsure where the conversation may be heading, it felt safer to change the subject.

'Well, I equally want you to know how grateful I am for all your kindness and trust and I've decided I want to give you a little present,' Josie said with a sudden warm rush of feeling.

'Oh no, you don't have to do that,' Elsie protested.

'No, of course I don't have to – but I want to.' Josie smiled, for that was just what her mother would have said and she went behind the counter and produced a large envelope that she had been keeping for just such a moment.

'What is it?' Elsie was curious.

'Why don't you open it and have a look.'

Elsie did so and gasped. 'It's a pattern, for what looks like a very smart and very modern-looking dress.'

'It's what I'm going to make up for you for the party, if you like it,' Josie said.

'Goodness, it's the height of fashion, isn't it?' Elsie said. 'Do you really think I could wear something like that?'

'Of course you could,' Josie assured her. 'That's the whole point, for you to have something more modern and up-to-date. I thought you might like to have it for the coronation party,' Josie said.

Elsie's cheeks flushed. 'Well, if you really think it would suit me . . .' she said hesitantly.

'Not only will it suit you but it will be perfect if you do decide you'd like to take up the invitation to lead the singing.'

The colour drained from Elsie's face as quickly as it had first gathered. 'Oh no, we've discussed that already. I've told you before that I couldn't possibly do that. I don't have what it takes any more to get up on a stage and sing in public. Not in front of the whole neighbourhood. I don't have that kind of confidence any more to sing in front of a large crowd.' She absent-mindedly rubbed her hand over her neck. 'I don't have the same power in the old voice box, you know; my vocal cords let me down many years ago and they've never been the same since. I'm sure you know that was why I had to give up my career when I did, so I shan't be doing any singing.'

'That's a shame,' Josie said. 'But it doesn't have to stop you looking smart. Why don't you look inside the envelope and see what else is in there.'

Elsie pulled out several small swatches of materials and began to examine them. 'Gosh, some of these patterns are lovely and the material feels so soft. What are they for?'

'I thought you might prefer to choose your own material, and I've picked a variety for you to look at and decide which you like best. They're all sunny-looking and bright, and they're the right weight for the style of dress to allow the pleats to fall into place perfectly. They'll definitely show the style of dress off to best advantage.'

Elsie rubbed each in turn between her fingers, savouring the feel of them, her face glowing. 'Are they really silk?'

'No, I'm afraid none of them are real silk but they are the best of the bunch of the latest man-made fibres and the advantage is that they shouldn't crease too much,' she added, amused at the way Elsie was fingering the samples and making admiring noises. 'If you choose which you like best then I can go and see what's still available. If you do it soon then I'll still have plenty of time to make up the dress ready for June the second, the big day.'

Chapter 27

If Annie Walker had dreamt that what she liked to think of as her legendary status as the queen of Coronation Street would be enhanced by the Rovers' acquisition of a television set then she was very much mistaken. It didn't take long for her to find out that there were disadvantages to being the first to have one and people were beginning to appear from all over Weatherfield as if it was their right to be allowed to watch it.

'Thank goodness it's only rented,' she reminded Jack when the problem first arose, 'we can always send it back.'

'Why would we want to do that?' Jack looked puzzled. He didn't seem to find it such a problem.

'Because it's already becoming a nuisance in ways I never would have predicted and it's still four weeks to the coronation. Do you know, only yesterday I caught a young woman from Rosamund Street wandering about back here in our private quarters with her three small children. When I asked her what she thought she was doing a) in our private area and b) in a pub with young children, she said they were looking for the room where she'd heard they could watch *Children's Hour* and she grumbled but made no apology for trespassing when I explained why that wouldn't be possible!' Annie said crossly. 'If anything, she seemed very put out when I told her we were not a public service and although we did have a television, it was for our private use only.' Annie was furious when Jack chuckled. He didn't seem to be too concerned about the incident.

To make matters worse, Annie had thought that she and Jack were alone when she had taken him behind the curtain in order to vent her anger and she was surprised when she heard the sound of someone coughing and clearing his throat in the back room. She swung round. 'Mr Tatlock!' She didn't know whether to sound angry or curious about finding him there and in the end settled for something in between.

'May I ask what you are doing on this side of the

counter? The bar is through there as you well know,' she said somewhat stiffly. 'Unless you have decided to come and serve yourself. Is there anything I can help you with?

'What have you been telling people?' she whispered an aside to her husband and glared at him as Albert shuffled his feet in embarrassment.

'I actually invited Albert to come and see the cup final with me,' Jack said before Albert could reply. 'You may or may not know that the match is on this afternoon but it's certainly one of the reasons I wanted to get the telly ahead of the coronation,' Jack said, making no attempt to whisper. 'Come this way, Albert,' he said, 'and let me buy you a drink. The telly's warming up and the kick off isn't until three.'

Annie felt betrayed that Jack was brushing aside her objections in such a cavalier manner and when Albert went back to the bar she turned on her husband angrily. 'Have you invited *all* your friends in this afternoon?' she asked scathingly.

'Only the ones I really like. I thought that was the whole point of getting a TV, so we could watch it! What else is it for if not for watching the match?' Jack didn't look at all put out but Annie didn't let up.

'Jack, it's in our living quarters, the only place we can get a bit of privacy, so surely we have to monitor who watches? We can't have the world and his brother tramping through our home like this. I simply won't allow it.' Annie could feel her voice begin to crack and took a deep breath. 'I thought we would at least restrict invitations to the right sort,' she said.

'But Albert is my friend.' Jack came and stood beside her, putting his arms round her. 'Now, Annie, love,' he said soothingly, 'it's nothing to get your feathers ruffled about.'

'Oh, isn't it.' Annie brushed his arm away and smoothed down her skirt with a gesture of irritation. She looked up as someone else came into the little vestibule and peered about. 'Can I help you, Mr Barlow?' she said, her voice sharper than usual.

'You've no need to bother, I'll see to him,' Jack said. 'And before you ask, Frank is also here at my invitation to watch the match and there are several others who'll no doubt be arriving shortly. It's going to be a grand game, Blackpool v Bolton Wanderers with Stanley Matthews playing.'

Annie made a tutting sound, signifying her irritation, but Frank Barlow rubbed his hands together and grinned at her.

'He's right, it's going to be a good'n, honestly,' he said. 'Isn't it marvellous to see it without having to go to Wembley? I've never been able to do that before.' Annie didn't respond. 'And I've told our

Kenneth and David they can drop in, David's football mad,' Frank added with a grin and wink. 'Jack said it would be all right.'

'Did he, indeed?' Annie didn't bother to hide her exasperation.

'It's not as though they'll be in the pub area. I'll see to that. But they've never seen Matthews play,' Frank Barlow said by way of explanation. 'It's all very exciting for them.'

'I'm sure it is.' Annie gritted her teeth and looked at Jack. 'I think we may need to have a word before you settle down to watch anything. Jack, if you will . . .?' she said and she pulled the curtain roughly aside and swept into the kitchen, trusting that Jack would follow her.

Once they were alone, she said, 'I am extremely concerned, Jack. It seems that some people are assuming that because they drink here they're entitled to watch whatever they want, whenever they want, on our television.' She spoke sharply but to her annoyance Jack laughed.

'You do like to exaggerate, don't you, Annie? But you're not going to stop us watching what's going to be one of the best cup finals for years. I promised Albert and Frank they could watch with me and they're my mates.'

Annie could see that she needed to tread a bit carefully. Jack was the landlord and the man of the house, after all. 'That's all very well, Jack, and of course I understand about the final, but I'm beginning to worry about all the time you'll be spending entertaining folk. Where it will all end?'

It was only now that it was beginning to dawn on Annie that what had seemed like a good idea at the time now had a serious downside that could possibly turn into a potential nightmare and she honestly didn't how best to handle it.

'You're worrying too much, love, as ever.' To Annie's annoyance Jack was still laughing it off.

'That's all very well, but the big day that we got the set for is almost here and someone has to think ahead and show some common sense or we'll be overrun in our own home. I don't know if you are aware, but the whole street seem to think they are coming here to watch the coronation.'

'Wasn't that what we led them to believe?' Jack said raising his eyebrows.

'No!' Annie was affronted. 'I certainly didn't,' she protested sharply. 'Whatever we might have thought originally we can now see that we may have bitten off more than we can chew. We may have thought we were planning an act of benevolence for the street but I can see now that it may not be possible to seat as many people as we first thought. You can't sit too close to the screen, so how many chairs are we actually going to fit in?'

'I haven't given it much thought yet, but you're right: we will need to talk about it soon.'

'Not only talk about it but take some drastic action,' Annie said, dramatically waving her arms.

'What are you suggesting we do about it, then?' Jack said. 'Have a secret ballot? Draw lots? Or maybe sell tickets on the black market?'

'You can mock,' Annie said crossly, 'but unless we start thinking seriously about this problem soon, we could end up with a riot on our hands come the coronation.' Annie lifted her head and held it high as she always did whenever she was convinced she held the moral high ground. 'I can see now that we will need to control the numbers and I certainly don't want to be the one to have to tell any of our neighbours that there's no room for them.' Annie pouted, frowning. 'But as it was your fault, then I should by rights leave it for you to deal with.'

'Hang on, the TV lark was your idea! Come on, love.' Jack's voice was cajoling now. 'We'll deal with it together, like we always do. But just not at this minute, as it's getting close to kick-off time, you understand.'

Annie looked at him angrily. 'Well, if it becomes too much of a problem I shall simply close off the room and ask Radio Rentals to come and take the television away. And I'm being serious.'

'Not before I've had a chance to watch the

football this afternoon, you won't,' Jack said. 'And *I'm* being serious. But I know you wouldn't want to deprive me of a bit of football, would you, my love,' and he went over to Annie and planted a kiss on her cheek. Then, 'Right, now, I'm off to get my pals together and we're going to enjoy the match,' he said and Annie didn't try to stop him as she fixed on her customer-welcoming smile and went back to the bar.

It was unfortunate that the first person Annie Walker saw was Elsie Tanner, her nemesis from number 11 Coronation Street, who was sitting in her usual corner, nursing a gin and tonic. Mrs Tanner was smiling, no doubt having overheard much of the exchange, and that made Annie clench her teeth as if preparing to do battle while at the same time doing her best to pretend that nothing had happened.

Mrs Tanner got up and came towards the bar, seeming to look at her with a pitying expression on her face and that forced Annie to keep up her smile. She couldn't let anyone see how much she was already regretting acquiring the television.

'And you thought your only headache was going to be whether or not to take the piano outside,' Elsie Tanner said as Annie took up her position by the pumps. 'But now everyone thinks they should be entitled to a front-row seat,' she said. 'Maybe you'll have to think of converting the Snug; you'll fit more in there.'

'I suppose it's a nice problem to have,' said Annie Walker, attempting a benign expression. 'We're very fortunate to be in the position of being able to make a lot of people happy.'

'Yes indeed,' Mrs Tanner said, 'so long as you're not thinking of turning on your most loyal and long-standing customers. They're the ones you really want to keep happy.' She paused but Mrs Walker didn't rush to fill the silence.

'Do you know, I was saying to my daughter Linda only this morning, that this is the first coronation I'm going to see. I was too young to know much about the last one. But of course we've no way of knowing how long I'll live or how long the young queen will be on the throne, so, who knows, it may be my last.' She laughed then gave a chesty cough before she drained her glass. 'In the meantime I think I've earned my place on the front row, don't you? I nailed the Tanner colours to the Rovers' mast a long while since.' She leaned across the counter, causing Annie to take a step back. 'I'm looking forward to watching from my front-row seat.'

'You and all our other regular customers, I'm sure,' Annie said, and she gave Elsie Tanner an enigmatic smile.

Chapter 28

Behind the scenes in the corner shop the Lappin household seemed to be in turmoil, as everyone except Josie was rushing about, in and out of the bathroom, preparing to go out. Josie gave up waiting outside the bathroom door, knowing she'd have a long wait before it would be her turn but as she turned to walk away a strong voice began to belt out old wartime songs. They echoed around the tiled room, making it sound as if they were coming from a diva standing on a remote mountaintop, but then the voice became softer, its tones more gentle, more like a bird warbling a romantic waltz, and Josie didn't know whether to join in or ignore the sounds and pretend she couldn't hear them. It was all her fault, Josie knew, for Hilda had hardly stopped singing since Josie had complimented her on her singing voice. Josie had made the mistake of telling her that she sounded like her mother, Elsie, and she had even suggested that they might make a good singing duo. Since then Hilda seemed intent on entertaining the family, only now her performances were even louder and more enthusiastic than ever, with a new level of exuberance that Shelagh put down to Hilda having a new boyfriend.

'My sincere apologies,' Josie apologized to Shelagh who put her hands over her ears as she joined the bathroom queue. 'I made a mistake complimenting Hilda on her voice and I think I spoke out of turn. I never thought through that there might be such possible consequences.'

'You weren't to know about the man,' Shelagh grinned. 'How could you? Or that she'd take him so seriously. He seems to have convinced her that she's so wonderful that she's capable of doing anything she puts her mind to, including going on the stage, which is all she's been talking about.'

'Goodness, no, I didn't know about him or about the stage idea. But then I've been keeping out of her way lately. Who is he? Where did she find him?'

'According to Mum, who's as shocked as anyone, he's the new man from the Pru,' Shelagh said.

'Why, what happened to the old one?' Josie asked without thinking.

'He dropped down dead on the doorstep, apparently. Not our doorstep, thank goodness. But he was replaced pretty quickly by someone much younger – and better looking. Hilda opened the door to him one night and fell for him over the red book – and that was that. You must have been out that night but I thought she might have told you.'

'Are you kidding? I'm the last person she'd tell.'

'She made quite a fuss at the time, inviting him in like Mum used to do with the old Pru guy, but then we'd known him for years. She insisted on making him a cup of tea, the new one, that is, and then one night he asked if he could take her to the pictures. She seems to have forgotten about Charlie Wright finally.'

'I suppose you don't have to worry if a man from the Pru asks you to go out with him. You can at least trust someone like that if he's already handling all your life insurance and stuff,' Josie said. 'He knows all about your business anyway. Though I do pity this young chap if Hilda pounced on him like that at the door.'

'Poor lad,' Shelagh agreed. 'I just hope he realizes what he'd be taking on. But they've been out together a few times already and he keeps coming back for more. She's so taken with him I'm surprised she didn't mention it.'

Josie looked sceptical. 'Hilda may have melted a little but we're still not really friends,' she said.

'At least Charlie got out in good time. I felt sorry for him at first that he ended up on his own, but I'm sure he'll be better off in the long run – I always thought he deserved better than Hilda.'

Josie was surprised to hear Shelagh talking like that but she didn't want to be drawn into a conversation about Charlie and thought it might be safer to change the subject.

'You know, I always thought "the man from the Pru" was a joke; it never occurred to me he might be a real person,' Josie said.

'Oh, this one's real enough and there are dozens like him, of course, not just one. It's not like Santa Claus.' Shelagh laughed. 'In fact, he's not like Santa at all, he doesn't bring any presents.'

'And she won't be able to play games or to try to fool him about money. She can't pull any financial wool over his eyes,' Josie said. 'He'd know in a flash whether her savings were genuine or not,' she added with a chuckle.

Shelagh turned to look at Josie and frowned. 'You wouldn't tell him what Hilda did to you, would you? Maybe that's why she's never mentioned him to you, because she's afraid.'

'What do you take me for?' Josie said, feeling a little hurt. 'She's got nothing to fear from me. I thought she'd understood that I've no wish to keep up this revenge business. We've all seen what can happen when things get out of hand, and how quickly that can happen.'

Shelagh put her hands up in a gesture of surrender. 'Sorry. I didn't mean to imply . . .'

'Actually, I've always been a bit wary of insurance men,' Josie said. 'My dad, Al, was an insurance broker and though it makes no sense, I always felt let down when he died so young. It was stupid, really; it was hardly his fault that he'd had rheumatic fever as a kid and that it left him weak. But somehow, unconsciously, I've never really trusted insurance blokes since then. No, Hilda's welcome to him. I shall be steering well clear.'

Suddenly a loud screeching noise came from the bathroom and Shelagh put her hands over her ears and giggled. 'I don't know about insurance brokers not being trustworthy, but I can certainly blame you for trying to convince a certain someone they can sing. When she misses the high notes like that, it's actually painful to listen to and you really shouldn't be egging her on.'

'Sorry, but it wasn't so much about praising the quality of Hilda's voice that I was thinking about.'

'What were you thinking about, then?' Shelagh asked.

'What occurred to me was that if Hilda would agree to sing with her it might be possible to persuade your mother to sing again. Who knows? What she lacks is confidence and it might be just what your mother needs is to have someone singing up there with her.' Josie looked at Shelagh thoughtfully. 'Maybe you should think of getting up there with them, then the three of you could sing together,' Josie suggested.

At that moment the bathroom door was flung open and Hilda came out wrapped in a towel.

'At last!' Shelagh said. 'I hope you've left some hot water, never mind all that singing nonsense. Where are you going tonight, you and what's his name?'

'His name is Stuart Hughson,' Hilda said, glaring as though challenging Shelagh to respond.

'That's it, I was trying to tell Josie but I couldn't remember it, though I knew it was something silly sounding. Stu Hu, the man from the Pru!' she said in a mocking tone.

'Oh, no, not you as well! I've had to put up with rubbish like that all week at work,' Hilda moaned. 'You could at least spare me the nonsense.'

'Is his name really Stu?' Josie couldn't help whispering to Shelagh.

'Why would she make up something like that?' Shelagh laughed.

'He's called Stuart but no one calls him that,' Hilda

said as if she was responding to Josie's question.

'I'm sure he's very nice,' Shelagh said placatingly. 'Where's he taking you, then?'

'I don't know where we're going,' Hilda said. 'But he said he knows this lovely pub somewhere on the moors. Not one I've heard of before.'

'What are you wearing?' Shelagh asked.

'The plaid pinafore dress with my favourite navy-blue jumper underneath.'

'The one you lent to me?'

Hilda nodded.

'But you can't wear that! Don't you remember, it's got holes in the elbows. I did tell you at the time but I bet you never mended it.'

Hilda clapped her hand to her mouth. 'Oh God, you're right. I forgot about that,' she moaned. 'And I haven't got time now.'

'I can darn it for you if you like, while you're getting ready,' Josie offered without hesitation and she noticed Shelagh give her a startled look.

'Well, you're the seamstress in the house so I won't argue with that; you'll do a far better job than me. Thanks,' Shelagh said.

'Yeah, thanks,' Hilda echoed softly. 'I'll leave it on your bed,' she said, and wrapping the towel more tightly around her she left Shelagh and Josie to fight for the bathroom.

'You gave me such a funny look – did you think

I was going to sabotage her outfit?' Josie said when Hilda had gone to her room.

'I'm sorry, I didn't mean to suggest anything,' Shelagh said, 'but I did wonder why you offered.'

'Thanks a lot,' Josie said sarcastically. 'Here was silly me thinking we were trying to make peace. If all my friends were like you, I wouldn't need any enemies, would I?' And Josie turned her back, disappointed, wondering if there ever really had been a breakthrough in Shelagh's frostiness.

'I'm sorry,' Shelagh said, 'but sometimes, after dealing over the years with Hilda's nastiness, things rub off and words just pop out. I didn't mean anything . . .'

'It's OK,' Josie sighed.

'I tell you what, let me make it up to you.' Shelagh's hand touched Josie's arm. 'I was going to take Mum down to the Rovers for a drink later, I'm eighteen now so I can have a port and lemon, so why don't you come with us? Mum's never mean like Hilda and maybe some of her magic might rub off on both of us.'

It was crowded in the pub and it took some time before they found a table. Elsie Lappin insisted that the first round was on her.

'Gosh it's noisy,' Elsie said as they waited for Shelagh to come back with the drinks. Josie nodded, thinking there was no point in trying to make her voice heard over the hubbub when there was a sudden raucous shout from the darts room followed by the alternate sounds of catcalls and enthusiastic clapping as several people she recognized came out of the games room, darts in hand, and headed straight for the bar.

Josie noticed Charlie several moments before he saw her and she felt a warm glow as he stopped and then hesitated as if trying to make his mind up before stepping across in her direction. She was surprised how pleased she was to see him; it had been some time and when she beckoned to him to come over to their table she could see that he looked equally pleased to be asked.

'Good evening, ladies,' he said as he shook hands formally with all of them in turn.

'A good game of darts? Did you win?' Josie asked. 'I imagine you did, cos you're looking a bit like the cat who got the cream.'

'I did indeed – or should I say my team won? I really can't take all the credit, but I can certainly get the next round in to celebrate. What are you having, ladies?'

'Congratulations!' Josie said, not sure why she felt a sudden blush wash over her cheeks. 'Thank you, are you going to come and join us then?' She didn't ask permission from Elsie or Shelagh to invite him but felt sure they wouldn't mind. Besides, it felt churlish not to as he had offered to stand them a round.

When he came back, drinks in hand, Josie watched him as he prepared to pass them across the table. She was remembering a time not too long ago when she had considered that Charlie Wright was not good enough for her. She stared down at the table, ashamed, as she realized how differently she felt now, but she suddenly felt tongue-tied and unsure what to say next and felt grateful to Elsie Lappin for saving the day.

'There was no need for you to buy us all drinks, Charlie,' Elsie said. 'It really wasn't necessary, though I shall be pleased to raise a glass to your team's success.' Elsie lowered her voice then and Josie struggled to hear as she went on to say, 'But Shelagh and me shan't be a bit offended if you and Josie would like to go to that small table that's just come free in the corner over there.' She looked up at Josie then and smiled. 'Josie, why don't you and Charlie go and grab it? It will be easier for you to talk over there and I'm sure you've got lots to catch up about.'

Josie wanted to hug Elsie at that moment but she felt overcome with shyness, so she smiled across to her and nodded, trying to acknowledge how grateful she was that Elsie was making it possible for her to have Charlie to herself for the rest of the evening as she suddenly realized how much she had to say to him. She looked over to Charlie, pleased to see that he was smiling too for she had hoped that he might be feeling the same way.

Chapter 29

Josie was impressed when Charlie offered to see the three of them back home safely to the corner shop, even though Shelagh and her mother walked on ahead, and she was grateful when they waved their goodbyes and went inside first for she had the sudden urge to kiss him. They had chatted about so many things that it was no surprise for Josie to realize, by the end of the evening, how much her feelings towards Charlie had changed and she was bursting to let him know how she felt. Charlie looked surprised but not displeased as he smiled down at her when he finally pulled away and she was convinced, from the way he looked at her and the gentleness with which he touched her face, that his feelings for her were still the same.

'May I ask what that was for?' he said with laughter in his voice. 'What have I done to deserve that?'

Josie was glad they weren't standing directly underneath the streetlamp so that he couldn't see the redness in her cheeks for now she felt embarrassed, but she smiled up at him letting her actions match her words. 'I just wanted to say thanks for a lovely evening,' she said, 'I hope I'm not being too forward?'

Charlie said nothing but wrapped his arms around her. 'Not if it means I'm allowed to do this,' he whispered into her ear. He held her close so that she could feel the warmth of his breath on her cheek.

Josie leant her back against the porch, taking a deep breath. She stood in the shadows after Elsie and Shelagh had let themselves in through the shop and waited for the lights to go on in the kitchen.

'Well, wasn't that a bonus?' Charlie said, pressing himself close to her. 'I thought I was just going out for a darts match. I didn't expect to run into you tonight,' and he brushed his lips lightly over hers.

'Me neither,' Josie said, surprised how breathless she felt all of a sudden.

'Feel like doing it again sometime soon?' Charlie asked. 'Only this time we can plan to meet up on purpose and we can go somewhere special.'

'That sounds nice. I'd like that,' Josie said, and was gratified to see his eyes light up.

'We don't have to go to the Rovers, do we?' Charlie said. 'We could take a chance and be more adventurous. I think we should go somewhere completely different. We can take the car if you'd like and go a bit further out.'

'Surprise me,' Josie said. 'But you do know what happens to the best-laid plans?' she added jokingly, as they agreed a time and she felt a warm glow of excitement as he kissed her once more before he strode away.

The weather was cloudy but warm on the May Sunday they had agreed to meet and by the time Charlie arrived and Josie had clambered into the car, full of eager anticipation, a light drizzle had begun to fall. Neither of them said much as he drove onto the moors to what Charlie said was his favourite drinking hole and Josie didn't want to spoil the surprise by asking too many questions. The rain had eased off and they left the car in the pub's car park before going on a walk, returning in good time for lunch.

'Boy! I'm ready for that drink now,' Charlie said as he lifted the latch on the upper half of the stable door that led into the main bar.

'And I could eat a horse to go with it,' Josie said, making them both laugh.

'We might have to settle for fish and chips,' Charlie said. 'I believe horse hide is rather tough to chew.'

'OK, I'll be flexible,' Josie said, thoroughly enjoying their banter as they lined up by the counter leading to the restaurant bar to give their order.

'To eat in the restaurant? Or you can hop on a bar stool in here or in one of the alcoves,' a tall young man behind the counter asked in a heavy Australian accent.

'You choose,' Charlie invited her, and Josie looked around the public bar to see where she would like to sit. She hadn't got very far when she froze abruptly, horrified to see Hilda Foyle. She was sitting by the window at the far end of the room that faced into the garden and she had her back to Josie. She was looking over the shoulder of an earnest-looking, curly-haired young man who had a studious expression behind thick-rimmed glasses. *Stu Hu, the man from the Pru*, was all Josie could think of and she wanted to laugh out loud as the silly rhyming doggerel sprang into her mind. She took a step back and sat down on a bar stool nearest the door.

'Here, we can sit here, that will be fine,' she said, and she shrank back hoping she hadn't been seen.

'What's up?' Charlie said. 'Seen something you shouldn't?' He looked puzzled at her odd behaviour.

'More like some*one*,' she said. 'I bet you'll never guess.'

'Hilda Foyle, or is it Lappin,' Charlie said immediately.

'How did you know?' Josie was astonished.

'I can't think of anyone else who could spark such an extreme reaction,' Charlie said. 'Would you rather we go somewhere else?'

Josie was tempted but she took in a deep breath and said,' No!' before she could change her mind. 'Why should I feel as if I've got to hide?' she said. 'Let her be the one to feel embarrassed.' She spoke with a firmness and belief she didn't actually feel. 'I've no need to run away,' she added, trying to look resolute.

Charlie put his hand over hers and squeezed her fingers. 'That's great. I was hoping you would say that,' he said, 'because you're right. Let her worry about meeting you, not the other way around.'

Josie smiled up at him. 'That reminds me,' she said, 'I've never really had the chance to thank you for supporting me when Hilda accused me. I appreciate you backing me up despite the evidence against me.' She hesitated before adding, 'I really didn't steal that money, you know.'

'Yes, I do know,' Charlie said. 'And I really believe you.'

'The only problem is that I can't prove my story and until I do . . . Or should I say, until Hilda confesses that she set it all up? Because I *know* she did. I keep trying to appeal to her better side and to get her to admit her role in all this. But the trouble is I'm not convinced she's *got* a better side . . .' Josie's voice faded and Charlie whispered, 'You don't need to spell it out. I understand and it's ok. The only thing I still don't understand is regarding the odd happenings with the till. You know more about that than you're saying, don't you?' he probed.

She realized that Charlie was staring directly at her and wondered if now might be the time to speak, but she couldn't hold his gaze for very long and she pursed her lips tightly as she looked away.

'I'm sorry,' he said, 'I've timed it badly. I didn't mean to push you and I can see you're not ready to talk. But when you are, I want you to know that I'll be here to listen.'

Josie felt choked, wondering if now might be the time, but when she suddenly saw Hilda coming towards her, her arm linked with that of her new young man, she knew that she couldn't speak now. It was a secret that she had guarded for many years and she would have to keep it for a bit longer. She knew she wasn't yet ready to tell the truth, even to Charlie.

Josie was surprised when Hilda stopped at their table and tilted her head towards Josie by way of acknowledgement. She ignored Charlie.

'What are you doing here?' Hilda asked. She obviously intended to pause only for a moment and immediately began shifting awkwardly from one foot to the other with an irritated expression on her face.

'Probably the same as you,' Josie said. 'Is the food nice?'

'So-so, but we're more interested in getting into the countryside and having a ride out on the moors,' Hilda said affecting posh vowels. 'Stuart has a Hillman Minx, you know. It's the perfect car for the country – so comfortable.'

Josie chose to ignore Hilda's boast and she turned to the young man on Hilda's arm. 'I don't think we've met, have we?' she said.

He thrust his hand out in Josie's direction though Hilda looked as if she was about to walk away. 'Stuart Hughson,' he said.

Josie solemnly shook it. 'I'm Josie,' she said. 'I lodge at Hilda's house.' She could see Hilda did not like her introduction and she would have said more if Charlie hadn't held his hand out to introduce himself.

But before there could be any further conversation, Hilda cut in, 'Enjoy your meal, I'm afraid we really must be going,' she said. 'We have a lot of ground to cover if we want to complete the run we're following.'

'A run?' Charlie duly obliged by asking.

'Yes. It's in the *Evening News* every week and we find it *so* helpful. We've seen so much of the local country that way.' And without a goodbye or a second glance Hilda all but dragged Stuart out of the pub.

Charlie laughed when she had gone. 'Do you know, I have a lot to thank you for,' he said and Josie raised her eyebrows. 'Seriously, I think I had a narrow escape there, with Hilda. To think she once set her cap at me, and if it wouldn't have been for you I might have fallen for it. Seeing her now with that soppy fellow on her arm? Well, I don't envy him. I think you saved me from a fate worse than death.'

Josie laughed. Then his expression changed and he put his hand on hers. 'I think I've got by far the better deal,' he said, gazing at her. Then he wagged his finger. 'Though you were a tricky enough customer at first. I had a hard time tracking you down, you know; you were never available, rarely there at the shop.'

Josie gave an enigmatic smile. 'You tried hard, I'll give you that, and you never gave up. Are you glad or sorry about that now?'

'What do you think?'

'I hope you're not sorry,' Josie said shyly.

'Not at all,' he said. 'But I do feel a bit sorry for you.'

'Oh! And why is that?'

'Because I've got the prettiest girl in town whereas you're stuck with a poor Weatherfield window cleaner!'

The way he said it made Josie laugh out loud and she shook her head. 'She's welcome to her man from the Pru, is Hilda. From where I'm sitting it looks like they deserve each other.'

'I'm sure you deserve better than me,' Charlie said.

'I don't know what makes you say that.'

'Tell me one thing you like about me.'

Josie thought for a moment. 'Well, I like your choice of pubs,' she said lightheartedly, 'even if they do have some very awkward customers.' And as she spoke she realized that it was time that she stopped apologizing for poaching Charlie away from Hilda. He had never wanted her and now Hilda had made it obvious that she no longer wanted him it was surely time for Josie to accept that he always made her feel very special indeed.

Chapter 30

Christine Hardman was more miserable at home now than she had ever been, for it had begun to look as if her parents' dream was about to come true and the move to Oakhill that her father had been anticipating and saving up towards for so long was finally about to happen. Even her mother seemed to be looking forward to getting out of Weatherfield, for it had always held bad memories for her, memories that she had rarely talked about over the years but which had had a profound effect on her life and the life of the family. It seemed to Christine that, after suffering so many years of a dull marriage, for both of her parents the move was going to mean a fresh start. But not so for her. Starting up a greengrocery business was not something she would have chosen and Christine was feeling very sorry for herself, aware that it was her parents' dream that they were fulfilling, not hers. All it meant for her was that very soon they would be going to the other side of Weatherfield where she had no friends and would know no one and the prospect was nothing short of misery.

What she had been looking forward to by the end of the summer was leaving school even though she was a bit too young at the moment, but lots of kids dropped out early and got jobs, and she felt very mature compared to lots of her classmates. But without certificates in enough subjects she might not be able to fulfil her own dream of going to college and becoming a properly qualified secretary. She might be forced, instead, to work in her father's new shop. It was all he talked about, telling her how excited he was and outlining what he expected of her when they finally made the move. Christine had always been closer to her father than her mother and she wanted to be able to support him in this new venture, but not at the cost of her own hopes and dreams and she was frankly horrified at the thought of having to get up earlier in the mornings than she had ever done in order to accompany her father to the market so that they could buy the freshest fruits and vegetables to bring back to the shop.

No, that life really was not for her; she needed a fresh start too but for her that meant going to London with Billy. So she was more determined than ever as she secretly began to lay out her plans.

Most people in the neighbourhood knew by now about the Hardmans' impending move and they didn't lose any opportunity to tell Christine how lucky she was, going to live in such a smart area of town, but no one apart from Billy knew about her plans to run away to London and she wasn't about to tell them. It seemed to her that being so close to the coronation it would be a good time to go. They would all be busy with their own arrangements and no one would notice until it was too late. She and Billy would be able to sneak away while everyone else was wrapped up in the excitement and the events of the big day.

Billy hadn't said anything since she had last brought the topic up, but as they walked to school together one warm sunny morning Christine was aware that they would soon be sharing their final day at Bessie's Street Seniors and she decided that it was time for them to confirm their plans.

'You know my parents will be moving soon?' she said as the school gates came into view and she could hold back the excitement about her own move no longer. 'I think it's the perfect time for us to finalize our plans, don't you? It would be good if we could get some of the details sorted before they actually make the move to Oakhill, then we can get them out of the way.' She wasn't sure if he was listening so she slowed her pace and waited until he had slowed his, then she said, 'I was thinking that it would probably be a good idea for us to go on coronation day itself, or possibly even the night before. Either way, everyone will be far too busy with their parties and things to even notice that we've gone.'

Billy, who seemed to have been deep into his own thoughts, stopped walking and plunged his hands into his pockets as he idly kicked at a pile of stones. 'Hang on,' he said frowning. '*Our* moving plans? Going where? What the heck are you talking about?'

'I'm talking about us; when we go to London.'

'London? Now you really have lost me. What are you talking about London for? Why would you want to go there?'

Christine stopped too and stared at him, a deep frown furrowing her forehead. 'What do you mean? It's what we've been talking about, you and me, for ages. We've always planned to go there together as soon as we left school.' Christine felt a fluttering sensation in her chest and it didn't signal good news.

'Maybe *you* did, but *I* certainly didn't.' Billy's manner was brusque. 'I might want to go there at some point in my life but I wouldn't dream of going now. I'm playing in a football match on Saturday for starters and I can't let the gang down.'

Christine's mouth dropped open.

'Then there's the coronation. I told you my parents have rented a television specially so I'm not missing that, or the party afterwards. The gang's all geared up and if it's anything like the last street party they had on Coronation Street where we almost started a riot, it'll be a good laugh.'

Christine stared at him, a devastated look on her face. 'But, Billy, it's what we've talked about for ages. You promised!'

'*You* might have promised,' he said, 'but I was most likely only half listening. That's how it is with me sometimes. I thought you knew that.'

Christine's vision blurred. She could feel her lower lip begin to tremble and she was afraid that the tremor in her voice was going to give her away.

'If you ask me again about London in a few years' time, I might fancy it then. But if it's now that you've set your heart on then I'm afraid you're on your own.'

Chapter 31

As the coronation drew closer, Billy avoided Christine. Her notions about London had scared him and he needed time to think. She had obviously got the wrong end of the stick about something he might once have said about London and he thought it would be better to let things cool off. Besides, there was a new gadget in the house for him to play with. He had very much enjoyed watching Blackpool thrash Bolton Wanderers in the cup final four goals to three but he still hadn't been able to get close enough to the television to find out how the thing worked. He'd had to restrain himself that day and let his father lead the way.

He had been fascinated by it from the moment it had arrived and he had been itching for a chance to investigate it thoroughly. This however was not easy as he was being extra careful not to cross his father, so as not to give him any reason to totally deny him access. Indeed, he had been on his best behaviour ever since its arrival. It was the one privilege, he realized, that could very easily be withdrawn. But his chance came on the Saturday afternoon before the coronation when he'd overheard his parents making plans to be out for a while, leaving Dot on her own in sole charge. That would be a great opportunity for him to have a closer look at it, he thought, particularly as there was to be television coverage of the afternoon's cricket match that was being played at Old Trafford.

All was quiet when he stole into the darkened room and flicked the switch of two of the wall lights. Then, rolling back the cabinet doors, he stood thoughtfully while he investigated the row of buttons at the front of the set. He rubbed his eyes and moved in for a closer look.

'Know how to use it, do you?' Billy spun round, surprised to see Mr Tatlock standing in the doorway.

'It can't be that complicated,' Billy said cockily, not willing to admit that he didn't even know how to turn it on.

'Well, go on then. I'm sure your dad won't mind us watching a bit of cricket. He told me I could come to watch it if I liked, and I've checked the *Radio Times* and it's on now. Is he about?'

'Er, no, he and my mum have gone out,' Billy said.

'Then he must have forgot about the cricket or I'm sure he wouldn't have gone out when there's a match on. Go on, switch it on, I'm sure he won't mind.'

'I'm not totally sure which one is for . . .' Billy wavered and scratched his head. He didn't want to mention his father's edict.

'I watched your dad the last time I was here and I think it's this one . . .' Albert Tatlock reached across Billy, knocking him off balance, and as he turned the first knob in a row of unmarked knobs a white dot appeared in the middle of the screen.

'No, that can't be right!' Billy responded sharply. 'You should get a proper picture with lines and shapes and things,' and he roughly knocked Mr Tatlock's hand away. His own hand then hit the vase of flowers that Mrs Walker had so tastefully arranged, knocking it off the top of the cabinet and splashing water everywhere. Billy jumped back out of the way. There was a bang and a loud popping sound followed by a puff of smoke and then the entire screen went blank. Even the white dot disappeared.

'Bloomin' heck,' Mr Tatlock said. 'What's all that about?'

At that moment the door was flung open and the semi-lit room was flooded with light. 'What the . . .!'

Jack Walker stopped abruptly and faced the two culprits while Annie, following close behind, bumped into him. Her hand flew to her face.

'What's happened to my beautiful flowers?' she wailed. 'And I do hope you've not broken my best Doulton vase. And look, there's water everywhere.' She looked first at Billy and then stared accusingly at Albert Tatlock.

'Never mind *your* flowers, what's happened to *our* television?' Jack Walker snapped and for once Billy looked stricken and didn't say anything. He could hardly accuse the older man when they had both been at fault and he didn't know what to say.

'We were only trying to turn it on,' Billy said eventually, not wanting to look at his father. 'It was an accident.'

'It's the truth, Jack, don't blame the lad,' Mr Tatlock said, looking down at his shoes.

'Never mind that it's the truth!' Jack brushed the excuse aside and pointed his finger at his son. 'What did I tell you? What, eh?'

'That I wasn't to touch it,' Billy mumbled miserably. 'I'm sorry. But it really wasn't my fault.' His words trailed off and he dropped his head.

'Well, let's look on the bright side,' Annie said with an air of false gaiety. 'We won't have to worry about not fitting enough people in the room to watch and we won't have to limit the crowd for the coronation on Tuesday. It won't really matter, will it? Unless there is a miracle nobody will be watching anything now, at least not here. And that's a shame,' she said, although she looked as if she wasn't really sorry at all.

'We'll have to try and see if we can get Radio Rentals to take a look at it,' Jack Walker said. 'I wonder how soon they could come? We've only got a couple of days left now.'

'Do you think they might be able to fix it in time for the coronation?' Mr Tatlock sounded relieved.

'I don't know,' Jack said. 'We can but try.'

'And if they can't then all our problems will be solved at once.' Annie smiled, but if anyone had looked closely, they would have seen it didn't quite reach her eyes.

Chapter 32

Christine was not normally one to cry but when she arrived back home late in the afternoon, she couldn't help herself. Billy had been so offhand when she had tried to talk to him about going to London she couldn't believe it, and it seemed as though he had never listened to a word she'd said. A football match indeed! His gang coming before her? She had thought he liked her. Why was he so keen to show her he had never taken her seriously? It didn't help her mood to hear her parents shouting at each other upstairs, just like they always did, only this time she seemed incapable of shutting out their voices or avoiding hearing what they were arguing about. Was this how it was always going to be? she wondered.

No, she told herself firmly, there had to be more to her life than this. Surely things would change and it would be different if they moved to a new shop? But what if they weren't? How could they change when the characters remained the same? Would a change of location be enough? She wiped her eyes. Well, *her* life was going to be different, she was determined about that, and if Billy didn't wish to be a part of it, then so be it. She crept upstairs, thankful that her parents' bedroom door was shut and she quietly closed her own door as she began to systematically root through her small wardrobe and chest of drawers, pulling out all her favourite items. Fortunately, she had had the forethought to ask for a suitcase for her last birthday and she was glad of it now as she tossed the items carefully inside and jammed the lid down. She didn't need much, just enough to tide her over until she was able to find a job. Though she had no idea how long that might take, once she got to London.

She glanced again at the advertisement for the secretarial college that she had safely stowed in her purse. She had looked at it so many times it was barely readable any longer and she smoothed out the creases before she put it back in her wallet. To her relief, all seemed quiet in her parents' room now and she crept back down the stairs and hid the suitcase behind the coats that hung over the umbrella stand in the hall where she knew no one would ever look or even notice it. She would pick it up later when she was ready to steal away from the house for the final time. She would catch the first train to London then and she would leave Weatherfield, as far as she was concerned, for ever.

Chapter 33

Josie was glad she had offered to make Elsie Lappin a new dress as a sort of peace offering and thank you gesture for all that she had done for her. Elsie had certainly done all she could to ensure that life at the corner shop became more tolerable for her lodger. Shelagh had also been amenable to accepting the olive branch Josie had offered, although the same could not be said of Hilda, who seemed determined to continue her personal vendetta for as long as possible. Coronation day was almost upon them and the Lappins were all in the kitchen as Josie was putting the final touches to Elsie's dress. Josie took a step back to admire her own handiwork and announced that she was pleased with the result.

'She does look rather good in it,' Shelagh agreed. 'It really suits you, Mum, I think Josie's done an amazing job. Don't you agree, Hilda?'

Josie didn't expect Hilda to reply. She had almost given up hope of Hilda ever admitting that any of Josie's work might be right, let alone good. But that didn't stop Josie continuing to try to mend fences and she was shocked to hear Hilda say, 'She's right, Mum, it looks nice. I like the material, it looks really fresh and bright.'

To Josie's surprise Hilda ran her hand over the crisp cotton sunflowers that settled flatteringly over Elsie's hips, draping down to her slim ankles and outlining her trim figure. 'You've chosen well there, Mam,' Hilda said.

'It's Josie you should be complimenting, not me,' Elsie suggested, and predictably Hilda wrinkled her nose slightly and she pulled her hand away from where she had been stroking the material.

'What dress do you intend to wear, Hilda?' Josie asked politely.

'You've got to wear the brown one, you look lovely in that,' Shelagh replied and Elsie agreed.

'If you'd like, and if you don't mind Mrs L, I've got some of this material left over. There's still enough time for me to make you a little bolero jacket, Hilda. It would go with that brown dress perfectly, if it's the one I'm thinking of.'

Hilda's cheeks reddened as all eyes turned on her and for a moment she looked as if she couldn't bring herself to accept Josie's offer. It was Elsie who spoke up first and her voice was unusually sharp. 'Oh, come on, Hilda,' she snapped, 'how much longer is this nonsense going to go on?'

Hilda looked too stunned to respond immediately but Elsie hadn't finished. 'You know it's high time you two shook hands and made up,' she said indicating Josie. 'We're getting a new queen in a couple of days' time and we should grab the opportunity to start our own new regimes. We can look on the beginning of her reign as a chance for each of us to make a fresh start.'

'I think you're right, Mum.' It was Shelagh who replied and she spoke directly to Hilda. 'Life's too short to be spending so much time bearing grudges and taking the hump. It's a total waste of everyone's time and energy.'

'You know there have been lots of feuds and goings on with the royal family themselves, what with the abdication and things,' Elsie said, 'and even they've had to find a way of making some sort of peace, at least in public. So why can't you? You only have one life and it seems like such a pity to waste it being filled with anger and hatred.' Elsie's voice quivered and changed timbre. 'You should be thinking of your father at a time like this, you know, I bet the new Queen is thinking of hers. They were both taken before their time and that should make you want to make the most of life and stop wasting whatever time you have ahead of you on petty squabbles. You're very lucky to have the chance to make a fresh start while you're still young enough to enjoy it.' She paused, allowing her words to sink in. 'So please, Hilda, when Josie's making a genuine offer to do something nice for you, why can't you just say thank you and accept?'

Before Hilda could respond Shelagh stepped forward. 'Mum's right,' she said. 'And I agree with her. I can't bear this stupid bickering any longer. We all need to take stock and think about what things like jealousy and bad-will are doing to us all, not just to Josie and Hilda.'

Josie looked surprised at that. She had known for some time that Shelagh was on her side but she had never heard her air her opinions so strongly.

'It's time for us to stop this shilly-shallying and face the truth,' Shelagh said. 'I'm sorry I didn't actually summon up the courage to say this before but I'd like to say now that I'm ready to stand up for Josie publicly so that we can close off that episode – because I know for a fact that it was Hilda who planted that marked money in Josie's purse.'

Elsie frowned. 'How can you know that with such certainty,' she asked, 'when Hilda herself won't own up?'

'Because as I told Josie ages ago, I saw her do it,' Shelagh said. 'And it's high time Hilda admitted it.'

Josie took a deep breath but exhaled quickly as Shelagh went on, 'And as Josie knows to her cost, that means nothing unless Hilda is willing to confess.' She turned to Hilda who stood with her hand covering her mouth. 'You know how I feel, Hilda,' Shelagh said. 'It's up to you now to confess and apologize. If there is to be a real peace pact then you need to admit that you engineered the whole sorry business and that Josie was wrongly accused.'

There was a few moments' silence during which nobody moved. It was Josie who spoke up first. 'Well, thank you, Shelagh,' she said. 'I hope you know how much your kind words mean to me. I may be many things but the one thing I am definitely not is a thief.'

'You must admit that's what I've been saying right from the start of all this nonsense.' It was a man's voice that suddenly spoke and they all looked up in surprise to see Charlie Wright standing in the doorway between the shop and the kitchen. He was nodding his head in agreement; amid the tension that had filled the room, no one had heard the shop-door bell.

Charlie stopped, looking from one to the other in embarrassment when he realized what he was interrupting and Josie took a deep breath, delighted to see him and surprised. She felt as if her blood was pounding in her veins with each heartbeat and she felt like she wanted to announce it to the world. Was it just a chance drop in, she wondered? Or had he come to speak up for her as he had promised to do?

'I'm sorry for butting in like that,' Charlie said, 'but no one answered when I shouted, "shop!" I didn't mean to interfere. Have I come at an awkward moment?'

'A very good moment I'd say.' It was Elsie who spoke up first. 'I would imagine that you know what we're discussing and I'm hoping that we are about to hear the truth at last. You do seem to have been in on this from the beginning, so why don't you take a seat and join in? Can I get you a cup of coffee?'

Charlie sat down but said no to the drink while Hilda turned to face Josie. 'If you're not a thief, then what are you?' Hilda said, a cross look on her face, 'because it was amazing how often the till balance was wrong whenever you were in charge.' It was a comment that was greeted by an audible sigh from both Elsie and Shelagh.

'Josie's not on trial here,' Shelagh said. 'If anyone

is, you are, Hilda. You're the one who's got to apologize so why don't you say the magic words and have done with it?'

'We're still waiting.' Elsie drummed her fingers on the arm of the chair but she stopped when Hilda all but exploded.

'Oh, all right! I admit that I did mark the money and planted it in Josie's purse but it was nothing more than she deserved, waltzing in here thinking she could take over our shop, our house!'

'I never did,' Josie protested. 'I was invited and even then I was reluctant to come, as your mother will tell you.'

But Hilda ignored her, making a pretence of thinking while she turned her attention to Charlie before she added, 'Oh yes, how could I forget that she also wanted to take over my boyfriend.'

Josie went from hot to cold and she closed her eyes; she couldn't bear to look at Charlie, Hilda had made it sound so cheap.

'Girls! Girls!' Elsie called them to order. 'Enough! Thank you, Hilda. That was all we needed to hear, a straight apology without embellishments and we can consider the matter done. And calling Charlie your boyfriend is a bit of stretch, Hilda!'

'I'll readily apologize for trying to flirt with Charlie,' Josie said. 'I know what I did was wrong.' She had to look away as she said this, for she was aware of Charlie's scrutiny. 'I really shouldn't have tried to come between you and Hilda like that, and I'm sorry.'

'Hilda?' Elsie said, but Josie hadn't finished.

'However, there is something else I want to say while we are all here together.' She took a deep breath, not sure if she could continue, but she felt that she owed it to Charlie. 'It's something that I have been hiding for a long time.' Josie looked down at her hands. 'It's not just you I've been hiding it from – I've actually been keeping it secret from the whole world. But I think now it's time to come clean.'

Josie was aware that they were all looking at her keenly, and she knew that once she started she wouldn't be able to stop, but it was time.

She saw Charlie shift his position at the kitchen table and wondered if he could reach out his hand to touch hers should such a gesture be required. For a second Josie caught his gaze and as she glanced around the room was aware that she had everyone's attention.

'It's something I've not been able to admit to before to anybody,' Josie began, 'and it isn't going to be easy to talk about it now but I have to. I realize that I can't hide behind it any longer. I've told you I'm not a thief, and I'm not. The truth is . . .' her voice was starting to break, but she pushed on ' . . . I can hardly read or write. What I am is all but illiterate, and what's the other word? In-innumerate. I can't add up either.'

There were several sharp intakes of breath followed by an awed silence as they absorbed the news and they all swivelled to look at Josie full face. She had to lower her eyelids so that she didn't meet anyone's gaze full on.

'I've always had difficulties with my letters,' she went on unbidden, 'ever since I was a little girl because unfortunately, soon after I started to learn the letters and numbers and how to read and do simple sums, we began travelling all over the north, my mum and me. Every few weeks I was going to a different school and no one got to know me well enough to notice that I was struggling to read or that I had trouble with numbers. Sometimes I didn't go to school at all and even if they had noticed, I wasn't anywhere long enough for anyone to do anything about it and in the end no one cared that I couldn't tell an A from an H or a two-bob bit from a half-crown.

'I did my best and I suppose it was amazing that I got by at all, but how badly I was getting by went unnoticed, with everyone assuming that someone else was dealing with it. But of course I came a cropper when I tried working in that big shop. I suppose really I was stupid to try and I couldn't ever be sure I'd got the change right, or that I'd read the labels correctly. So many things looked the same that I mixed things up and I got easily confused. I still do, but I've always felt too ashamed to tell anyone or to ask for help so problems arise like me giving the wrong change at the till. I did try asking for help once but the teacher didn't listen; perhaps they already thought it was too late.'

There was no other sound in the room as Josie told her story and even as she talked she thought again about how easy it had been to hide her difficulties and to be constantly overlooked. 'I couldn't ask other kids for help,' she said looking directly at Charlie now. 'It was too embarrassing to explain. The others in the class made fun of me and bullied me anyway and I was too old to admit that I didn't know my basic letters and numbers.' She realized she was still addressing Charlie directly and that he hadn't taken his eyes off her.

But it was Elsie who said, 'It's no wonder then that you took so easily to the practical stuff like dressmaking where what's most important for success is a touch of creative inspiration, good sewing skills and a bit of common sense.'

'And it does explain the till discrepancies,' Shelagh said.

'Yes. I could never be sure exactly how much change I should give out nor how much was in the till,' Josie admitted.

'Then I really do owe you an apology,' Hilda said, to Josie's astonishment. 'I had no idea.'

'Can I just add something?' Elsie said although she didn't wait for permission. 'Josie, I think that what you've just done was brave, very brave indeed. It takes guts to admit to something like that, don't you agree, girls?' And she made sure she included Hilda in her sweep of the room.

'Not many of us here could have done what you just did,' Josie was shocked to hear Hilda say while everyone else nodded. 'I'm really glad you did. Thank you.'

'I'm proud of you, well done,' Charlie said, and to Josie's delight he picked up her hand and kissed the tips of her fingers.

Chapter 34

When Tuesday, 2 June, the day of the coronation of Queen Elizabeth the Second, finally dawned, Annie Walker wasn't the only one to be fussing and flapping and complaining about the weather; although it did seem to her that she was the only one in Coronation Street who was doing anything practical towards making appropriate changes. She was rushing about putting the finishing touches to the decorations and supervising the laying of the tables, determined to do everything possible to make the day a success. Naturally, she was disappointed with the weather, everyone was, but there was nothing they could do about that and they were doing their best not to let it spoil the party atmosphere that had already begun to build as the food was produced and then laid out on the decorated tables.

May had been such a warm month that everyone had been banking on the sunny spell continuing into June. But it didn't. Annie woke up to a dull breezy day with some drizzle and the threat of further rain and a temperature that was actually colder than it had been back in November. When she tuned into the Home Service on the radio for an update she found the forecast for the remainder of the day was equally depressing.

'A mostly grey day with rain or showers, some possibly heavy,' was what the forecaster promised, and so far the morning skies had been cloudy just as they'd said and there had been the odd spot or two of rain which could become heavier and more persistent.

The day had been declared a public holiday and, according to the radio reporters, hundreds if not thousands of people were already gathering in London, lining the procession route, and there was an amazingly festive mood among the crowd as they waved their flags and sang some rousing songs. Annie felt sorry for them when she looked out of the window at the dull dampness that seemed to have shrouded Weatherfield, for according to the radio the weather in London was no better. But people had come from far and wide, from all parts of Britain as well as from the outreaches of the commonwealth, the US and countries all over the world, all wanting to join in the celebrations, all determined not to let the weather dampen their spirits and spoil their fun.

According to John Snagge and the team of BBC radio reporters, some people had started lining the route between Buckingham Palace and Westminster Abbey the previous day in order to ensure their place, and they had camped out in the streets overnight to be sure of securing a good position. Even those that had arrived that morning were in position well before the procession was due to start, determined to be among the first to see the new queen. She was to set off from Buckingham Palace and to finish at Westminster Abbey in time for the special ceremony and service. Marching alongside the fairy-tale golden coach, the stately procession included liveried footmen as well as special guards dressed in full military regalia, complete with high busby hats. The cheering crowds were in high spirits and were mostly bedecked in red, white and blue, waving flags and banners, eager to be among the first to see the new queen's Norman Hartnell-designed dress. And they were extraordinarily cheerful, strangers chatting to strangers, small groups spontaneously bursting into song, all determined to let nothing dampen their enthusiasm.

Meanwhile, in Weatherfield Annie was still feeling anxious, worrying about what might or might not happen regarding the television. She still didn't know if there was definitely going to be a television as the technician had promised to come first thing in the morning, but had not yet appeared, and nothing had been settled about how many people might be able to squeeze into the small specially designated room to watch it should it be fixed. Jack insisted on telling Annie to relax.

'Don't get so worked up about it all,' Jack kept saying, 'what will be will be but it will all work out, you'll see.' Annie, on the other hand, wasn't so sure. She had hoped that everything would have been in place by now and was a little surprised at Jack's relaxed attitude. She secretly thought that before the water accident her husband had been more partial to watching the television than he was prepared to admit and she wondered if he had made some deal with Radio Rentals. Ignoring Jack's promise to sort out the details regarding the piano, Annie took it on herself to get a team of men together to move it outside in readiness for the singsong that the party organizers had promised. With that in place, Annie hoped she might be able to relax sufficiently to go and change into her lovely new frock.

As she came back indoors, satisfied at last that everything was on track, she thought she would look into the television room to see if anything had happened yet and she was surprised to see Billy hovering by the door. He gave her a beaming smile but that only served to put her on her guard. 'Has the man come to fix the television yet?' she asked him, frowning.

'No, not yet, but I've come to tell you that it doesn't matter, I can fix it; all I need is a decent screwdriver.'

Annie raised her eyebrows in alarm.

'I've been on to this mate of mine,' Billy went on without looking at her, 'and he told me the same thing happened to their tele and he fixed it in no time.' He laughed. 'Another minute and I'd have done this one already. You'd never have known there'd been a problem.' He jerked his thumb in the direction of the small room where the television sat, unplugged. 'I thought I'd surprise you and Dad. I was going to nip in before he came back. In fact, I can still do it now. What do you think?'

'Oh, it would be a surprise all right!' Annie said sarcastically. 'I do hope you're not serious, Billy. Don't you remember what your father said? Right now it would be better if you kept well clear of this room and got away immediately while you still can.

If I were you I wouldn't let your father see you anywhere near here.'

Billy looked disappointed but for once Annie didn't care. 'I have every faith that the Radio Rentals' man will come as he has promised,' she said brightly, 'so you really don't need to worry about it.'

'But it's the first time something as big as this has been televised! I bet loads of things have gone wrong with lots of television sets and they've most likely made lots of promises to lots of people. They won't be able to get to them all in time to see the coronation.'

'Well then, we'll have to tell people that there will be nothing to see at the Rovers,' she said with a false heartiness. 'It's not as if any of them were paying for the privilege, so we won't have to give them their money back.'

'Aw, Mum! Let me have a go. I can fix it, I'm sure I can. Or I can at least try,' Billy cajoled, but for once Annie wasn't susceptible even to his most persuasive voice. Billy hesitated but Annie looked as if she really meant business and he jammed his hands deep into his trouser pockets and wandered away, trying to think of a different approach. Annie was relieved to have averted at least one potential crisis but she couldn't help wondering how long it would be before Billy's gang of mates turned up the way they had at the VE celebration parties and what other high jinks they might have dreamt up to brighten their day.

Annie had originally told those who wanted to watch the television broadcast to make sure they were in place by eleven o'clock, when, according to the *Radio Times,* the BBC cameras would be rolling not only on the procession route but inside Westminster Abbey as well. What she hadn't been prepared for was Elsie Tanner arriving at ten thirty, claiming to have forgotten what time Annie had said she should come. But that was before the television had broken down and Annie had had to warn everyone that they were awaiting an engineer. Even Mrs Sharples hadn't arrived that early, although Annie was surprised when shortly afterwards she saw the two women sitting together in front of the mahogany cabinet. It was an unusual sight, seeing them side by side and occasionally talking together but they made no apology for prematurely commandeering the best seats in the house, in the centre of the front row of chairs.

'I'm afraid the TV man hasn't arrived yet,' Annie said, trying not to show her irritation. 'So it's still in the balance whether we will have anything to watch.'

'Don't worry about us,' Elsie Tanner waved her hand. 'We'll just keep hoping, won't we, Mrs S?' And Annie felt as if she had been dismissed.

'I didn't know what to say,' Annie confided to Jack when to her relief he appeared in the vestibule. 'Neither of them made any attempt to budge.'

'Well, I came to tell you that there's still no sign of the man, so they may as well stay there for now.'

'What if he doesn't get here on time?' Annie ventured to share her nagging anxiety, and as she said it she was surprised at how sorry she felt that she might not be able to see the pictures for herself. She hadn't realized how much she had been looking forward to actually seeing Richard Dimbleby and Sylvia Peters making history as they reported live from the abbey. To Annie's annoyance, Jack merely shrugged.

'I suppose it's one way to solve the accommodation problem,' he said and he chuckled while Annie, furious that he could make light of something so serious, flounced off to the kitchen.

The men were preparing to unlock the wheels on the piano and to half carry it, half drag it outside when there was a shout that the Radio Rentals man had arrived and several people rushed to the window to see his van pulling up outside as if it was their own television that he had come to repair. Annie heaved a sigh of relief and took no notice that his first words were, 'I'll warn you now that I might not be able to fix it.' She stood back and she watched as Jack ushered him inside with his impressively hefty toolbox. He took one look at the wiring, the damaged carpet and the socket in the wall and he sucked in his breath and shook his head.

'Own up,' he said. 'Who put the flowers on the top of the cabinet?'

'How did you know that?' Jack asked.

'Because I suspected that's what had happened and I only had to glance at the water damage to confirm. Don't worry, you're not the first and you won't be the last. It's happened to over half my call-outs this morning alone,' the engineer said, looking disgruntled, probably because he was working on a public holiday, 'though I somehow doubt you'll be doing it again.'

'Is it something you can fix?' Annie asked tentatively, although she didn't wait to hear the reply before turning to Jack. 'I didn't want to upset you this morning,' she said, 'but our Billy was hanging around the television room earlier and the cheeky monkey was only dying to fix it himself.'

'Good heavens, I hope you didn't let him touch anything?'

'No, of course not. I didn't even let him inside the room, though I was worried what might happen if the man didn't get here soon. Another few minutes and I think he would have had a go, no matter what I said, but fortunately he didn't have a screwdriver.'

'I thought I'd told him to keep well clear of this room!' Jack looked incredulous and Annie was relieved that Billy had made himself scarce.

'Where is he now?' Jack snapped.

'Bothering someone else, no doubt.' Annie was trying to make light of it and she didn't know what to say when she saw Ida Barlow emerging from the kitchen, shouting, 'Come back here with that cake! And don't you dare touch those sandwiches,' as she tried to push past Annie on her way out to the street, balancing a plate in each hand.

Word seemed to spread quickly up and down Coronation Street and the Radio Rentals' van was no sooner pulling away from the kerb, the driver grinning and waving, than the people from the street began to crowd into the Rovers. Some went straight into the bar while others took their places at the trestle tables where they started into the food before they had even sat down.

Annie went to stand outside for a few moments and kept looking up to the skies, praying the rain would hold off, then she hurried back inside where those who wanted to watch the ceremony now that the television had been pronounced to be in full working order, were hurrying to take their places as they crowded into the small room. Annie could see that Ena Sharples and Elsie Tanner, who'd been joined by Albert Tatlock, had managed to hold on to their seats and were still in pride of place in the front row – and from the fierceness of their looks they looked entrenched, with no intentions of moving.

Annie was surprised to see how many people were already crammed into the room, some happy to stand at the back, others pulling out, muttering that they would come back later, and she decided Jack was right, people were sorting themselves out without any interference from her or Jack, and when Billy and his friends appeared and tried to muscle their way into the room, Annie had no compunction about shooing them off sharply to make way for the older residents. She no longer felt quite so anxious about the numbers building up because the atmosphere was congenial and friendly, not to say jingoistic, with people waving their flags and banners even indoors, and there was a palpable ripple of excitement as a cheer went up when the first pictures of the young queen setting off from the palace in her fairy-tale coach were flashed onto the screen.

That was when she saw George Hardman hovering near the door, a panic-stricken look on his face and she beckoned him to join her.

'Mrs Hardman not with you?' Annie asked, concerned that May Hardman might be ill. 'I think there's still a couple of chairs free over there if you'd like to sit down, but if you don't claim them now I'm afraid it may be too late. It's getting very crowded as you can see.'

'It doesn't matter,' George said. 'I shan't be stopping. We're not ready to come to the party just yet.'

'Oh, that's a pity,' Annie said, ' because the procession is just beginning, so don't leave it too long.'

'I'm actually looking for your Billy – do you happen to know where he is?' George said.

Annie's smile wavered momentarily and a dark fear flashed across her eyes. 'You've just missed him, as a matter of fact, he was here a moment ago. He's not in any trouble I hope?' And she gave what she hoped was a girlish laugh.

'No, nothing like that.' George was holding his brown felt trilby in both hands, nervously sliding the petersham headband through his fingers as he passed the hat from one hand to another. 'It's about our Christine.'

'Oh?' Annie was taken aback and from the look on George's face she didn't know whether she should be reassured or concerned.

'Actually, Mrs Walker, I'm worried sick,' George blurted out, 'and I hope your Billy might be able to help. I know that him and our Christine are friends.'

Now Annie stared at him, dreading what he might say next.

'I'm afraid she seems to have gone missing,' George said, and Annie shivered as her blood felt as if it had turned to ice.

Chapter 35

George had been well aware of the celebration preparations in the build-up to the coronation although he had trudged back and forth to work each day doing his best to ignore them. But for some time now it had been impossible not to be involved on some level with so many reminders in the streets, in the newspapers and on the radio. Even among the residents of Weatherfield there had been little else talked about for weeks, so that by the day of the ceremony itself the atmosphere had almost reached fever pitch. Everyone was wishing the young queen well and they all wanted to celebrate the crowning in their own way. For the residents of Coronation Street that meant laying on a big blowout of a party with the bonus for some of being able to watch the actual ceremony at the Rovers on their newly installed television and they were all set to enjoy themselves. But there had been no joy among the Hardman family at number thirteen; there hardly ever was these days. George knew that poor Christine hadn't been happy for some time, though he had chosen to ignore the signs and refused to discuss the situation with her. But now he feared that by not listening to her he had pushed her to the edge until she had simply decided to disappear.

Was it all his fault? Or was May partly to blame for not being a good enough mother? George had certainly woken up to a different coronation day than the other residents of Coronation Street and he didn't know who to blame.

'What do you mean, she's not slept in her bed? Where *did* she sleep then?' George had wasted no time in attacking May when she had confessed tearfully that she couldn't find their daughter, and she had to admit when she had gone to waken her and had found her missing that she didn't know where she might be.

'You're not making any sense, woman. What kind of a mother are you not knowing where your daughter is?' George was aware of being even more belligerent than usual and he knew it was because of his own feelings of guilt, but he couldn't let go, even though he was shocked to see how quickly May had crumpled in the light of his accusations. All he achieved was to spark off an even more acrimonious row than usual, harking back to events as long ago as the war.

'How dare you accuse me of being a bad mother! If that's true it's because I've never had a proper husband – it works both ways you know!' May screamed at him.

'Yes, of course it cuts both ways,' George retorted. 'But a proper husband needs a real wife, which is something you've never been.' He paused for a moment while he glared at her before lowering his voice to an almost sinister sounding level. 'What kind of a wife keeps her husband at bay for months – no, years?' he asked spitefully. 'You've not let me near your bed since Christine was born.'

May looked down at her feet but then she lifted her head and blushed as she said haughtily, 'Why should I let you come anywhere near me? What makes you think I would want second-hand goods?'

George gasped.

'An adulterer is a betrayer, no matter how you try to dress it up,' May said.

He opened his mouth to object but then thought better of it for in his heart he knew that whatever she was accusing him of – it was true. He deserved her name-calling, for he *had* betrayed her, though he didn't know how she had found out. It wasn't something they had ever talked about and he didn't want to talk about it now, but he knew he couldn't deny it and he didn't try.

'My husband and my sister!' May spat out the words. 'It was nothing short of disgusting,' she said contemptuously, 'not to say humiliating.'

'Why humiliating?' George did his best to defend himself. 'No one knew.'

But then he stopped. Was that really true? He liked to think he and his sister-in-law, Madge, had kept their brief affair a total secret and fooled everybody but he hadn't been sure, even then.

He had come home on pre-embarkation leave to find an almost empty house because his wife and daughter had been evacuated to Blackpool. Only May's sister Madge was there, having been asked by May to look after the house so it wouldn't be taken over by the authorities. Before he'd left for the war, there had been a spark between them and when he had returned to Weatherfield for 48-hour leave, finding only Madge at home, the attraction on both sides had been irresistible.

George felt a sudden chill and as he thought back he shivered. Their romance had been short-lived; he wasn't on leave for long, but it had been so easy the way they had slipped into a brief affair. So easy and it had felt so good, *too* good. Madge was very different from May; she had been warm and loving, understanding of his needs, and she was far more accommodating than her sister had ever been.

George very rarely cried but he found himself tearing up just thinking about her even after all this time and he thought guiltily back to the few glorious days they had shared. He remembered then the letters he had written after he had returned to his unit, gushing, overindulgent, eloquent even, and the down-to-earth but loving ones he had received in return. Madge was killed after an air raid on neighbouring Mawdsley Street caused a wall to collapse and killed her, also killing his dreams of a different life. Could his wife have seen those letters? When Ena Sharples had secretly returned them to him after he had been home on leave a week after Madge was killed, with May and his daughter still in Blackpool, she had sworn that May couldn't possibly have known about them.

'I found them among poor Madge's effects, and I thought it safer to give them straight to you,' Mrs Sharples said. She had come to the house while he was still on leave and she handed them over triumphantly to an astonished George. 'I swear I was the first person to go down to the site where the bomb fell. They were found hidden in the pocket of her slip, close to her heart,' she explained. 'When I realized what they were I thought I'd best remove them and save them for you, though as God is my witness I swear I read no more than I had to in order to establish who they belonged to. It's your business and nowt to do with me,' she'd said haughtily, and when she was sure there was no one else about she produced them from her own handbag and gave them to George. 'Since Madge has gone, no one else but me has set eyes on them, I can promise you that,' she said. 'Though I can't speak for who Madge might have shown them to.'

'No one, if I knew Madge as well as I think I did,' George said, more to himself than to Ena Sharples. 'They were private when they were written and as far as I'm concerned, they'll remain that way now she's gone.'

'Just what I thought,' Ena said, 'and that's why I kept them safe and why I'm giving them directly to you now. And if May ever does find out, I promise you it won't be from me. Rest assured that's the last time I'll mention them.'

'Thank you. I appreciate your thoughtfulness.' George had been genuinely touched by her unexpected kindness and he believed her, even though he still wondered if May knew. The thought that his wife might have discovered his secret made him feel even more guilty, but there seemed to be no other explanation for her having withdrawn her favours so effectively for so long, even though that withdrawal had begun before his affair. That, for him, had meant that his entire marriage had been one of frustration and guilt and it had left him feeling as though he had lost the ability to love. After Madge he felt that he no longer had the ability to express any depth of emotion because his ability to feel anything deeply had died with her. He had once hoped he might be able to channel the love that he had buried through his daughter, but it seemed now that he had even failed in that, for Christine abandoned her home, abandoned him, and had run away. He had let her down but he had no time to wallow in self-pity. There was only one way he might begin to make amends. It was imperative that he should find her before she could come to any harm.

George's first port of call had been the Rovers, for he felt sure that if anyone knew of Christine's whereabouts it would be Billy Walker, the only local lad that she had ever spoken of or seemed to have anything in common with, and as he stepped over the threshold of the Rovers' double-door entrance he had crossed his fingers and taken a deep breath. He was disappointed not to find Billy in the pub but when he came out again he spotted him in the middle of a group of boys of a similar age, standing huddled together outside the Rovers. The party seemed to have started for them for they all had their eyes on one of the long trestle tables, reaching out to help themselves every now and then to the sandwiches and glasses of pop. When he thought that no one was looking, Billy went round the group topping up the liquid in their paper cups from a hip flask that he then slid into his back pocket.

'I hear you've been looking for me, Mr Hardman,' Billy called out as soon as he saw George. 'What can I do you for? Have a sandwich,' he said, grinning as he thrust a plateful under George's nose.

'It's our Christine, she's gone missing.' George wasted no time. 'I was hoping you might have some idea where she's gone.' George came over so as not to have to shout across the table.

'She was talking about going to London if that helps,' Billy said after a few moments' thought, 'though I never took her seriously. She did have something she'd cut out of the *Evening News*, though. It was an ad for a college of some kind that she wanted to apply to.'

'A college in London? Oh no!' George groaned. 'What kind of college? A secretarial one by any chance?'

Billy shrugged his shoulders. 'I didn't take much notice, sorry,' he said off-handedly.

'If she has gone to London then I suppose she'd have to have gone by train,' George reasoned. 'And if that were the case, what's the chances of her still being at the station?'

Billy frowned. 'One of my mates has got wheels; for a few bob I bet he'd give you a ride down there.'

He paused before adding, 'That is if you don't mind hopping on the back as there's only two wheels!' And Billy and the gang burst into uproarious laughter as though he had delivered the funniest punchline ever.

Even George's mouth twitched at the thought of him in his best brown suit clinging on to some young lad's leathers, but he was pleased when another, older voice, piped up, 'I couldn't help overhearing, and if you need a ride into Manchester I've got a car outside – with four wheels,' he added as the gang gave an ironic cheer. 'I could give you a lift to the station if it would help.' The young man extended his hand. 'I'm Charlie Wright. Most folk know me round here, I'm the local window cleaner.'

George shook his hand eagerly. 'That's really a very kind offer, Mr Wright,' he said. 'I'll happily pay you for your trouble only I need to get after my young lass as fast as I can, before she does something foolish.'

'Call me Charlie, please,' he said.

'I'm George from number thirteen,' George said and Charlie nodded. 'Let's not waste time, then. Let's get going,' he said. Then he laughed. 'No charge but you can stand me a pint when we get back once we've found her safe. I bet we'll be back in time to see the royal procession.'

'Where are you going?' At that moment Josie came out of the kitchen where she had been helping with the food. She was carrying a cup of tea and waving to Charlie with her free hand.

'I've no time for that now, thanks all the same. Sorry, but something's come up and I'm going to help George here. I'd better be off,' Charlie said as he dangled his car keys in front of an astonished-looking Josie. 'Don't worry, we'll be back soon,' he said and he ran off to the car with George in his wake.

George didn't know much about cars but he was surprised how fast the old jalopy could go when Charlie really put his foot down, despite the bumpy cobbles, and he silently urged it along, too mithered to strike up any meaningful conversation. They had a smooth run into town as there were notice-ably fewer cars about and even fewer pedestrians on the streets than was usual for a Tuesday morning, everyone no doubt already glued either to their radios or their televisions as the coronation unfolded. Nevertheless, George was glad when they finally pulled up in the car park at the foot of the approach to London Road Station and for once he didn't notice the bad eggs smell that was belching out of the steam engines as they idled on the platforms, nor did he wait for Charlie to straighten the wheels before he jumped out and ran onto the station concourse where there seemed to be hundreds of people milling about, rushing back and forth, several visibly panicking that they might miss their train. A porter offered to carry George's bags, until he pointed out that he had no bags and asked instead for guidance to the platform for the next London train. George didn't get as far as the platform, for there in the Ladies' Waiting Room he saw Christine stretched out on a bench, fast asleep, and it was all he could do not to rush inside to gather her up into his arms and carry her to safety.

'I don't know how anyone can sleep through this racket,' he called over his shoulder to Charlie as he paused to listen to the shrieks and squeals of the young children who were dashing about the con-course. In the background the drone and noisy hubbub of the crowds seemed to be competing with the strings of messages that were constantly being put out over the loud but crackling speaker system. Christine showed no signs of stirring until George ventured into the wating room despite the large Ladies Only sign. He gently shook her shoulder. 'Christine,' he said softly. It took a moment then she sat bolt upright, looking startled.

'Dad? What are you doing here?' she asked, looking puzzled.

'No, that's what I should be asking you,' George said.

Christine tried to shake off the sleep that still

enveloped her and she rubbed her eyes until they were red-rimmed.

'How long have you been here?' George asked.

'I'm not sure. I came sometime during the night. I was looking for a train to London,' she said as if it wasn't obvious.

'That's what Billy thought,' George said.

'Billy? Where is he? Is he here with you?' She tried to stand up and brushed down her crumpled skirt while she looked around eagerly.

'No, he's back at the Rovers,' George said, and Christine sat down again, disappointed. 'Though when we said we were looking for you he was the one who suggested we try here first.'

'That's because I mentioned something about coming to London last week,' Christine said miserably. 'I'm surprised he was listening.' She looked crestfallen. 'When I told him months ago what I intended to do, I thought he was going to come with me. But it turned out I misunderstood.' She shrugged. 'I do wish he'd changed his mind. I might have been brave enough to go through with it then.'

'What do you mean, brave enough?' George wanted to know. 'What happened?' Now he sounded anxious.

'I'm sure I could have done it if he'd stuck with me,' Christine said tearfully. 'But the train was late and there were so many people trying to get on when it finally came, that it got overcrowded very quickly and I got scared. That's why came into the Ladies' Waiting Room –it just felt safer.'

'Of course,' Charlie said. 'I imagine everybody was wanting to get to London in time for the coronation.'

'It would have been nice,' Christine said, a dreamy look passing over her face. 'I've been dying to go to London for ages anyway, and to be there for the coronation would have been really special.' She pulled her lips into an expression of resignation and her eyes filled. 'But when it came to it and I was on my own, I must admit I didn't have the courage to get onto the train.'

By the time the car reached Coronation Street Christine was curled up on the back seat and didn't even wake up when Charlie carried her into number thirteen and her anxious mother undressed her and put her to bed.

'I can't thank you enough,' George said to Charlie when he'd briefly explained to May what had happened. 'You've earned that pint, and some.'

'Yes, thank you for chasing after her so promptly.' May angled her head almost coyly.' Sorry if it cut into your day, but I don't think the ceremony has started yet, though the partying might.'

'Without your help, Charlie, it might not have resulted in a happy ending,' George said warmly, and the two men shook hands before Charlie left, promising to meet up in the Rovers later when the coronation excitement had begun to settle down.

May and George stood beside Christine's bed gazing down at their daughter, each wrapped in their own thoughts. George shuddered. 'I can't bear to think of what could have happened to her,' he said, covering his face with his hands.

'I only hope when she wakes up and we tell her what happened that she fully appreciates the significance of what you did,' May said.

'I hope so too,' George said as his face set into a grim smile.

'Why don't we go downstairs and have a stiff drink?' May suggested. 'I know I could certainly do with one. And I think there are a few things you and me need to sort out. No more secrets for a start. Why don't we start our coronation celebrations early?'

'I agree. And once she's had time to sleep it off, what the three of us need to do is sit down and have a serious talk.' George stared directly at May, though she refused to meet his gaze. 'We all need to deal with things that should have been dealt with a long time ago,' he said and May reluctantly nodded agreement.

'Will you tell her about . . .?' May began tentatively, when they were seated at the kitchen table, though she wasn't able to finish.

George looked at her sharply then he said, 'If she asks, I'll tell her – and you – anything you want to know,' he said. 'No more secrets, like you say.'

May agreed. 'She'll be delighted when she hears that we won't be moving into the new shop yet. The thought of the move has been bothering her a lot recently.'

'Hmm, you could be right. I don't think I've been paying sufficient attention to what's been going on and how we've all been affected,' George admitted.

'She might even be able to do her secretarial course in Manchester once she leaves school in July if she still wants to, and we can leave off discussing the notion of her working in the shop. I think we should leave that over until nearer to the time when we might actually move,' May said.

'Yes, I still want to.' George and May both looked up, startled, at the sound of their daughter's voice, and they were shocked to see her wraithlike figure framed in the doorway. Her hair was tousled and she looked as if she were sleepwalking but her words had been strong and clear.

'What are you doing up already? You've hardly had time for any more than forty winks,' George said.

'I'm all right,' Christine said, 'but I thought I heard you say something about no more secrets and I didn't want you talking about me behind my back. I can sleep later.'

'Yes, we did say that,' May said. 'Is there something special you want to say?'

'I want to go to secretarial college,' Christine said. 'Preferably in London.'

George and May looked at each other and then they both nodded.

'I made a big mistake when I planned for this time and I don't think Billy is ready for such a move so I shall have to go on my own.' She came into the kitchen and sat down with them at the table. She reached across and put her hand on her mother's arm. 'And you're quite right, Mum. I don't want to talk about the shop, not yet, anyway. But what I *really* want is to be able to choose for myself what I do in the future. I don't want either of you to decide for me.' She raised her head and looked steadily at both her parents in turn. Despite the weariness that was etched onto her face she stood her ground firmly, as if challenging them to disagree.

'OK. I understand,' George said, 'but right now you look more like a ghost from a coronation past and you're not too old for me to tell you that you must get back into bed right now, before you keel over.' And firm though his voice was, he said it with a smile.

'Then tomorrow we can all have a fresh start,' May said. 'It will be like a new reign beginning,' she said and Christine nodded her approval.

Chapter 36

Josie was surprised to see that Charlie had returned so quickly and she was relieved to hear that Christine was safe and well, though she was sorry that he had missed so much of the procession. She had thought it would be fun to watch the coronation on the television at the Rovers and when she heard that Hilda and Shelagh planned to be there with their new beaux she decided to invite Charlie to join her. They had begun to seriously step out together and she was surprised how much they enjoyed each other's company at the pub, or in the cinema, even listening to music on the Lappins' radio, and since they were getting on so much better she'd imagined it might be fun for them to watch the coronation together. He had readily accepted her invitation, but what she hadn't reckoned on was him missing most of the ceremony by being a good Samaritan.

'I'm sorry I wasn't able to save a chair for you,' Josie said when Charlie eventually appeared in the doorway of the television room, 'but as you can see, the room is rather packed. And I'm afraid they had to start without you,' she added with a grin. The room was filled to capacity, mostly with women and a few children waving flags and 'ooing' and 'awing' over the magnificent pageantry.

'That's OK, you sit down and make sure you don't lose your place,' Charlie shouted across to her. 'Maybe they'll repeat some of it later, but right now George is waiting for me at the bar and I think we could both do with a drink. I'm just amazed at how many people are packed in here anyway,' Charlie said, 'standing room only at the back.'

'I know,' Josie said. 'And people have been swapping places so that everyone can see something.'

'Well, you sit down and enjoy, Josie,' Charlie said. 'I'd hate for you to miss any of it on my account. I can see that it looks rather splendid even from here.'

'That's exactly what it is, splendid,' a voice shouted, 'so leave us in peace to enjoy it!' Josie thought that the voice seemed to be coming from Elsie Tanner who had remained firmly seated in the centre of the front row and her comments were greeted by much laughter. 'You don't want to miss one minute of it, really it's wonderful,' Mrs Tanner called out and she turned round and waved two miniature Union Jacks in Charlie's direction. 'Makes me proud to be British,' she then said to no one in particular and a general shout of 'Here, here!' went up. Charlie added several rounds of 'Hip! Hip' before he left the TV room and, as he headed for the bar, he heard the others in the room supplying the 'hurrahs!' at the appropriate moments.

'It's only a shame it isn't in colour.'

When Josie turned her attention back to the screen she recognized Ena Sharples' voice, managing as usual to find something to grumble about.

'That doesn't matter,' Elsie Tanner said, 'I've got pictures of the real thing here so you can see what colour things are.' And she waved a magazine in the air as did several others in the crowd.

'You don't need much of an imagination to picture how well those horses have been groomed or to catch the sparkles of the old gold coach. I can see from here that someone's had a good go with their Brasso and a spot of elbow grease there,' someone else said.

'Never mind the coaches and horses, it's the soldiers *I'm* more interested in,' Elsie Tanner shouted and several people giggled. 'What colour are they dressed in, I wonder.' She flicked through her magazine.

'Bright red tunics mostly, with black furry hats and white gloves, according to *Woman's Own*.' Ida Barlow waved a copy above her head. 'And quite a lot of them have got gold-coloured sashes and shiny brass buttons,' she said.

'Right dapper,' Elsie Tanner said, then she turned her back on the television and winked at the audience while Josie could imagine Mrs Sharples rolling her eyes to heaven.

'That's just typical of her,' Ena Sharples said, pointing to Mrs Tanner, while Ida Barlow called back, 'You take no notice of her, Elsie, I'm with you on this one. Some of them uniforms are right grand and the way they balance those great big hats is nothing short of amazing. Can you see, that one looks like it's hanging on by its chin strap.'

'I can't wait to see the Queen's dress,' young Joanie Walker said, when there was a momentary lull in the room and silence for once from the commentators.

'All in good time,' Annie Walker said. 'Once they get to the Abbey we should be seeing lots of the queen and her attendants, I imagine, and we should be able to see some of the details of her dress and train.'

'Don't wish the time away too quickly, Mrs Caldwell,' Josie laughed. 'I want it to slow down not speed up. I feel like I want to savour every minute. For my money, this is really a very special day already and we are only part way through. But it's one I'll certainly never forget.'

There was a pause in the proceedings in the Abbey while the Archbishop of Canterbury did what they called the anointing of the new monarch, a private ritual that neither the congregation nor the television audience were allowed to see, and Josie took the opportunity to leave the television room and stretch her legs. She made up a plate for her and Charlie with what was left of the sandwiches and cakes before they all disappeared and she went to find him in the bar.

'Ooh, they look good,' he said, not put off by the edges of bread that were beginning to curl. 'You can pile them as high as you like cos I'm starving! And I've found us a space in the main bar where we could sit for a few minutes if you're ready for a short break.'

'That's good,' Josie said, as he led the way to one of the few quiet corners in the room, 'because I'm afraid it's begun to rain and everyone's trying to come indoors.'

'That's why I grabbed this table. I didn't want you to get wet,' Charlie said with a grin.

'Well, you've turned out to be quite the rescuer today, haven't you?' Josie joked when they finally sat down.

'I like to think I do my bit when and where I can,' Charlie said affably, although the expression on his face said he wasn't sure how to take her remark.

'George Hardman seemed to be extremely grateful,' Josie said.

'I'm sure he was. I wouldn't have wanted to find that a daughter of mine had spent the night in a railway station, exposed to the elements.'

'I suppose you might feel differently if you were the one being rescued,' Josie said cautiously. 'There's always the chance that you didn't want to be found, although that might depend on who was doing the rescuing.'

'What if the rescuer was me rescuing you?' Charlie dropped his voice and leaned in closer to her.

'You?' Josie looked at him sharply. 'But what would you want to rescue me from?' She laughed and too late realized he was blushing.

'Oh, I don't know. There's rescuing and rescuing. I wasn't thinking about knights on dashing white chargers, that's a bit extreme these days. I was thinking more along the lines of reaching out with a helping hand,' he said sounding surprisingly serious.

Josie wasn't sure where this conversation was going. 'Could you be more specific?'

Charlie cleared his throat. He was looking uncomfortable now, as if he had said more than he had intended, and he looked down into his lap. 'I was remembering the incidents when you worked in Mrs Lappin's shop and some of the problems that arose concerning the till,' he said hesitantly. 'You know, the stuff that you were brave enough to talk about eventually, though it took a while.'

Josie felt her cheeks flare. That was an episode she had hoped was behind her.

'We've never talked about it since but maybe we should,' Charlie said. 'Though I don't know if now is the time . . .'

Josie didn't know what to say so she didn't interrupt when he went on, 'The thing is, I've been thinking about it again recently and wondering if there was any way I could help you. Like with arithmetic and reading.' Now he looked at her directly. 'No one need ever know, if that would bother you, but I'm sure if we could do some work on it and you could improve your skills, it could make a huge difference to y-your confidence, like.'

Josie stared at him. She could see that he was struggling with the words and that it had required a great effort of will for him to say what he had, but she made no attempt to help him. Instead she said, 'I'd rather not think about that right now, thank you very much. And if you don't mind, I'd better get back to the coronation now; I'm sure they will have finished the private bit of the anointing by now. Enjoy the sandwiches, I'll see you later.' And she stood up, ready to leave.

'I'm sorry if I've offended you . . .' Charlie stood up too. 'I was only trying to help by suggesting that I might be able to give you assistance, that you don't have to go through it all on your own, but I can see that it was bad timing and I'm sorry. I didn't mean to spoil your day.'

'Seriously, how could *you* help me?' After a short pause Josie sat down again, aware that the sharpness of her manner might have appeared rude. 'What do you think you could do that all the teachers I had over the years couldn't do?'

'I'm not sure.' Charlie was honest. 'But I could try. You aren't the only one, you know, who has problems like this and I believe there are different ways of approaching it. I just thought it might be worth a try.' He leaned forward, obviously interested, and Josie realized she had been wrong to fob him off.

'I took the liberty of going down to the local library,' Charlie said.

Josie was astonished. 'Really? And what did you find out?'

'Just that there are various night classes available for adults with your difficulties. I didn't get into the details but I could give you some names if you want to follow it up. I wasn't sure if you'd be interested.'

'I don't know if I am or not,' Josie said tentatively. 'To be honest, you've caught me on the hop. It was the last thing on my mind today.'

'I realize that and I apologize. I also know it will be hard coming to it as an adult. But I could find out more if you'd like me to, and let you know. Or better still, why don't you go to the library yourself? They've always been extremely helpful.'

'Charlie, I appreciate that you've gone to an awful lot of trouble on my behalf, but what I don't understand is why it should be so important to you?'

Now Charlie seemed to be embarrassed and he refused to look at her. Then he said quietly, 'Because I've some mad notion in my head about us one day opening a business together.'

Josie's jaw dropped. 'You and me together? Business partners?'

'Maybe more than that, Josie.'

Josie didn't know whether to laugh or cry. 'Really?' She tried to gather her thoughts. 'I know we've both talked about our dreams before, but I've never seriously thought any of them could come true,' Josie said, her eyes wide.

'Why not?'

'Because in my experience life's not like that. That's not what happens to dreams. They either die or just fade away.'

'It doesn't have to be like that,' Charlie said, then he set his mouth in a hard line. 'There's no reason why we shouldn't be able to open our own business together if we want it badly enough.'

Josie frowned. 'What kind of a business had you in mind that would accommodate both of us?' she asked, looking sceptical.

'I told you I was thinking quite seriously about starting up a cleaning business that I'd be able to run and you could have some kind of a dressmaking and alterations business that you would be in charge of. I do believe there is money to be made in both of those areas.' Charlie sat back and smiled. 'Is that sufficient enticement for you to work on improving your basic skills?'

'Oh, I should say so! That would be quite wonderful. I wonder how long it would take for us to actually get going on them and get them established.'

'Well, that would depend on you.'

'On how quickly I could learn?' Josie asked, and she was surprised when Charlie didn't answer immediately.

Then he said slowly, 'I was going to say it would depend on whether you would like to become Mrs

Charles Wright before or after you complete the classes.'

For a moment Josie stared at him, not taking in the meaning and implications of his proposal at first. Then she gasped out loud. 'Do you mean . . .? Are you serious?'

'Yes, on both counts,' Charlie said. 'I know that we need to get to know each other a bit more . . . and I hope you'll agree that we both need to know what we're doing if any kind of business is to be successful, and being able to read and write and work out numbers properly would set us up right.'

'Oh Charlie, I would do anything—' she began.

'In order to marry me?' Charlie interrupted eagerly, sitting forward in his chair.

Josie laughed. 'Yes!' The word came out louder than she had expected and she had to look away as several sets of eyes swivelled in their direction. She reduced her voice to a whisper, 'Yes, Charlie I *will* marry you, and I promise I will find myself a class and I'll work really hard – with your help.'

'I know you will, and that's why I've always believed in you.' He picked up her hand in both of his and traced his finger up and down her ring finger, smiling as he did so. Then he put her hand to his lips and kissed the tip of each finger.

'Do you think we should get a ring before we get a television set?' he asked, his voice jocular. 'I mean, we have to get our priorities right from the beginning, don't we?'

Josie felt as though 'engaged' had been written in large letters on her forehead and she wanted to shout out the news from the rooftops, for in the weeks before Charlie proposed she had slowly been realizing that she was falling in love with him, although she could hardly believe it herself. She was surprised that no one had overheard their conversation and congratulated them already. But somehow she managed to keep calm although she knew she couldn't keep the smile from her lips or a sparkle from her eyes. She wondered, now that the ceremony was over and the golden carriage was on its way back from the Abbey to Buckingham Palace, if the new queen was feeling much the same way right now.

Fortunately there had been a break in the rain while everyone had been filing out of the television room, and people went straight to the party tables outside where the empty plates had been piled with replacements that the ladies in the kitchen had worked so hard to provide. Josie would have liked to see Elsie Lappin as she felt she deserved to be the first to know about Charlie's proposal, but she hadn't seen her or the girls since first thing in the morning. She was making her way over to where Charlie had secured two seats for them at one of the long tables when someone struck up several cords on the piano, trying to gain everyone's attention. Annie Walker was standing by the piano and she held her arms up for silence.

'I hope you all enjoyed the morning as much as I did,' the Rovers landlady said when everyone had quietened down. 'And now we need to celebrate our new queen in the best way we know how. How better to have fun than to have a good old-fashioned singsong? So while there is a break in the weather, let us make the most of it. I'm sure you don't want to listen to my voice—' There was much good-natured booing and catcalling at that, the sound of feet stamping and hands pounding on the tables. Annie held her arms up again. 'I won't keep you any longer, but I shall pass you on immediately to our entertainer for the day, our very own Miss Melody Mae.'

Elsie Lappin stepped forward and, without any further to-do, began to sing. Josie hadn't even had time to process what was happening and she had to stop herself cheering too loudly and drowning Elsie out. But then, to Josie's amazement, Hilda stepped up beside her mother and the two of them harmonized together without effort. Josie felt her

345

eyes moisten. Elsie Lappin was singing again and this time with her own daughter. They went through a short repertoire with the whole street cheering loudly at the end of each song, and when they announced their last-but-one song, everyone joined in with gusto to sing 'How Much Is That Doggie in the Window', laughing and obviously enjoying themselves.

Finally Hilda put up her arms and thanked everyone for their support. 'We are going to end this afternoon's entertainment with a rousing song that has kept us all going through both of the wars,' she announced, 'please join us for a rendition of "Pack Up Your Troubles".'

A huge cheer went up and then everyone began to sing. As they reached the chorus, Hilda took hold of her mother's hand and with her free hand beckoned to Shelagh and Josie to come to the end of the table to the makeshift platform and join her. Josie hesitated at first but Charlie pushed her forwards so that she stood between the mother and her daughters, holding their hands. There was silence for a moment as the crowd took note of what was happening and then Josie looked at Charlie and when he waved and blew kisses to her she began to sing and, one by one, people joined in until soon the whole street was full of singing and laughter. Josie broke the chain of hands when she saw Charlie reaching out to her and as he wrapped his arms around her she found herself looking straight into his eyes. Was this what he meant by being her rescuer? she wondered. And in that moment she felt as if the residents of Coronation Street and the whole neighbourhood of Weatherfield were singing for her.

Epilogue

Annie Walker bent down awkwardly to pick up the newspapers and magazines that had been piled on the floor next to one of the more comfortable armchairs so that she could use the new vacuum cleaner to pick up the crumbs and the dust. As she did so, dozens of images of the new queen fluttered onto the floor and she only narrowly avoided sucking them into the vacuum bag. She instantly switched the machine off and studied the cuttings. They were mostly pictures of the golden carriage drawn by horses, and the beautiful young queen and her handsome husband that Annie's daughter, Joanie, had cut out ready to go into her scrapbook. Annie smiled at the thought of Queen Elizabeth the Second already taking her place in history. What will the future hold in store for her, she wondered.

Most of the extra chairs had already been removed from the television room to the bar and the remainder had been stacked as if in anticipation of the next event. But everything that had been a part of the celebrations had now been confined to history and filed away under the heading of a day to remember. She stopped in front of the television and switched off the cleaner then she stood looking at the mahogany cabinet. It had served its purpose. It had been the first in the street and the Rovers had been the first pub to have one, but its purpose was now complete. The coronation was over and no one knew how long it would be before the next one. It was strange to think that if the young queen stayed healthy the four-year-old prince and heir would probably be grown up by the time it was his turn.

Annie looked at the television set and sighed. She had already decided to call Radio Rentals in the morning and ask them to take it back. Jack had tried to argue with her that they had some kind of contract, but she was sure she could use her powers of persuasion.

She placed the loose cuttings in Joanie's scrapbook, ready to be glued in, and looked again at the stately young woman who was now a crowned queen. The coronation was well and truly over after months and years of preparation. What would the years to come have in store for Queen Elizabeth? Annie couldn't say why, but she thought the young queen was just what the country needed, and that her subjects would love her every bit as much as the King she had succeeded, perhaps even more.

'Congratulations, Your Majesty,' she whispered. 'Long may you reign.'

But now it was time for her to get back to the bar. No time for excuses because she knew what the residents of Coronation Street were like – the Rovers customers wouldn't wait!

Coronation Street –
The Corner Shop
Remembered

The corner shop in any local neighbourhood provides an important service for its residents, and the shop on the corner where Coronation Street meets Viaduct Street in Weatherfield is no exception. For Elsie Lappin it provided a happy haven and a secure home and business not only for her, but also for her daughters Hilda and Shelagh, and their lodger, Josie. Elsie's life there was tinged with sadness, too, as she inherited the shop only after her first husband Tommy Foyle had died. The same was true for several of the owners of that iconic corner shop over the years, whose time there was often fraught with difficulties.

The official address of the corner shop in Weatherfield, where Elsie eventually lived and worked, was

No.15 Coronation Street. It was what is nowadays called a convenience store, selling a wide range of groceries, tinned goods, dairy products, fruit and veg and even cigarettes during its history. All the while it has been owned and run by several different proprietors and their assistants.

Cedric Thwaite was the first owner after he bought the premises in 1902, for the princely sum of £35, only a few months after his immediate neighbours had moved into their new houses in the surrounding streets. It was similar in size and shape to the other houses in the terrace and behind the shop area, there was a living room, kitchen/scullery and a staircase leading up to the bedrooms. Downstairs was a spare room which was used by the various owners either for storage or as part of their private living quarters. The back door led out to a small yard with a private outside lavatory.

At first Cedric ran the shop himself but he found that to be a lonely experience when he realized, too late, that customers had no wish to linger and gossip with a man who was not only a part time local lay preacher but also a heavy drinker. Unfortunately, things didn't improve for him even after he married. Not only did his new wife, Lottie Hofner, speak little English but she was shunned when their neighbours found out she was German. Anti-German sentiments increased, and the crunch came in 1914 when Cedric and his wife were violently assaulted by an angry mob. Unhappily, Lottie spent the remainder of the war interned as an Alien in a camp on the Isle of Man, while Cedric went to live with his brother in Newcastle and sold the shop on to Tommy Foyle.

Tommy had been wounded while on army service in India and was unfit to fight again. After he married his first wife, Lil, the two of them ran the shop together, but he was pushed to the point of bankruptcy by Lil's family with their credit demands, forever wanting goods 'on tick'. When Lil died suddenly from bronchitis, Tommy married local singer Elsie Castleway, and when her career ended abruptly the new Mrs Foyle was happy to become her husband's assistant. With the two of them working side by side the shop's fortunes improved greatly and although, like everyone, they endured wartime rationing and reduced supplies, they kept the shop going by careful management and the occasional brush with black market goods, for which Elsie was rumbled and fined.

Tommy suffered ill health, suffering a stroke which confined him to bed during the war years, and on VE Day Tommy died suddenly from a heart attack. Elsie became the new owner, eventually remarrying salesman Les Lappin, who joined his wife behind the counter. Unlucky Elsie was left a widow again when Les had a heart seizure in the shop, but she carried on valiantly, eventually selling up in 1960 to Florrie Lindley.

Over the years, the humble corner shop on Coronation Street has seen many dramas and countless iconic characters have popped by for their groceries, as well as finding themselves in charge of restocking those shelves — David Barlow, Blanche Hunt, through to the blighted Clegg family, Alf Roberts and his wife Audrey, Reg Holdsworth and Dev Alahan. The shop has seen it all, much of it accompanied by the gossip of Ena Sharples or Hilda Ogden, but always providing a listening ear and a pint of milk when needed.

The corner shop is a British institution and there has never been any quite like the one on Coronation Street.

Acknowledgments

As the intensity of Covid and its effects on our daily lives thankfully fade into the distance, the importance of those who have continued to offer their support and assistance comes to the fore in sharp relief. I would like to thank my helpful and ever supportive editor, HarperFiction Publishing Director Kate Bradley, and agent Kate Nash, and their respective teams, for without them there would be no books. I would also like to thank my own personal team; friends, family and colleagues who have helped to make even the most daunting aspects of the creative process seem surmountable and fun. I am particularly indebted to award winning writers and fellow Romantic Novelists' Association supporters

Sue Moorcroft and Pia Fenton (Christina Courtney); life coach Ann Parker, and my non-fiction co-author Jannet Wright. Special thanks also go to Helen Centre and Vivienne Canter, for their invaluable research contributions, and Hanna Klein and Kathryn Finlay for their continuing support.

Discover more of Maggie Sullivan's
Coronation Street series

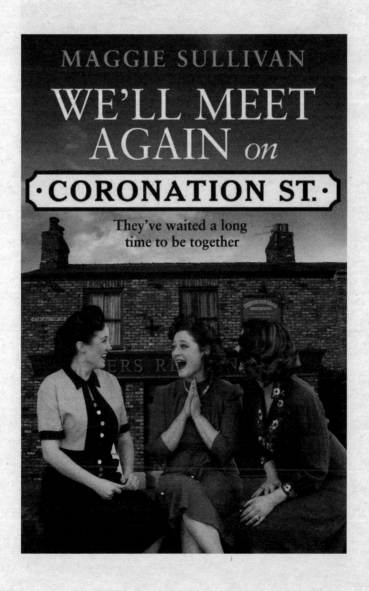

MAGGIE SULLIVAN

WE'LL MEET
AGAIN *on*

·CORONATION ST.·

They've waited a long
time to be together

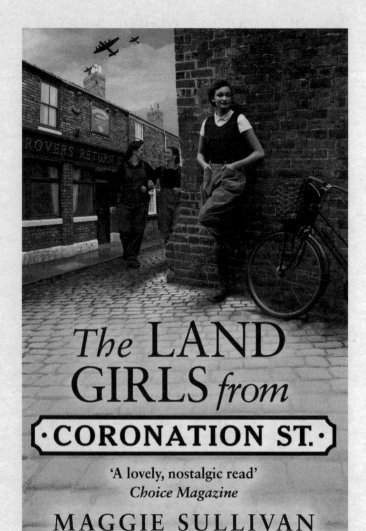

The LAND
GIRLS *from*
·CORONATION ST.·

'A lovely, nostalgic read'
Choice Magazine

MAGGIE SULLIVAN

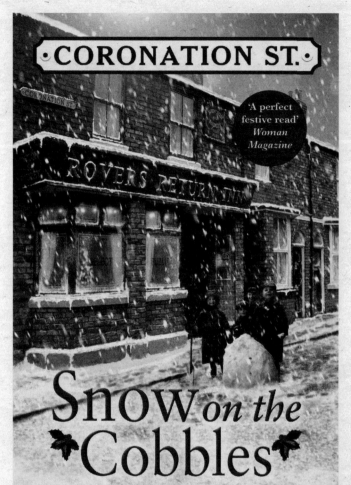

Mother's Day on

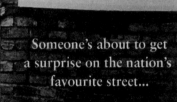

·CORONATION ST.·

Someone's about to get
a surprise on the nation's
favourite street...

MAGGIE SULLIVAN